Hollywood

Hulk
Hogan™

World Wrestling Entertainment™

Hollywood Hulk Hogan™

Hollywood
Hulk Hogan with Michael Jan Friedman

POCKET BOOKS

New York London Toronto Sydney Singapore

Pocket Books, a division of Simon & Schuster UK Ltd
Africa House, 64–78 Kingsway, London, WC2B 6AH

Copyright © 2003 by World Wrestling Entertainment, Inc. All Rights Reserved.

World Wrestling Entertainment, the names of all World Wrestling Entertainment televised and live programming, talent names, likenesses, slogans and wrestling moves, and all World Wrestling Entertainment logos and trademarks are the exclusive property of World Wrestling Entertainment, Inc. Nothing in this book may be reproduced in any manner without the express written consent of World Wrestling Entertainment, Inc.

This book is a publication of Pocket Books, a division of Simon & Schuster, Inc., under exclusive license from World Wrestling Entertainment, Inc.

Originally published in hardcover in 2002 by Pocket Books

All rights reserved, including the right to reproduce this book or portions thereof in any form whatsoever.

Pages 9, 17, 26 Courtesy of the Bollea family.

Pages 80, 82, 90, 96, 120, 123 ,125, 127, 130, 144–45, 218, 222, 232, 316, 326, 331, 334, 344, 356, 361, 363, 372, 376, 378, 382, 406 Courtesy Pro Wrestling Illustrated Photographs. Pages 64, 68, 86 Courtesy Jim Cornette. Page 117 NBC Publicity Photo. Page 180 © Jacques M. Chenet/CORBIS. Page 215 © BETTMAN/CORBIS. Page 235 © David Cumming; Eye Ubiquitous/CORBIS. Page 341 Henry Holmes.

All other photos Copyright © 2003 World Wrestling Entertainment, Inc.
All Rights Reserved.

ISBN: 0-7434-5769-2

First Pocket Books paperback printing June 2003

10   9   8   7   6   5   4   3   2   1

POCKET and colophon are registered trademarks of Simon & Schuster, Inc.

Front cover photo by Rich Freeda, 2002 World Wrestling Entertainment

Visit us on the World Wide Web
http://www.simonsays.co.uk
http://www.wwe.com

To my mother and father,

who put up with my irrational decision

to be a wrestler twenty-five years ago;

to my beautiful wife, Linda,

who has put up with two decades'

worth of emotional highs and lows;

and to my kids Brooke and Nicholas,

for treating me like a normal dad

when I've been anything but normal.

A Rock and a Hard Place

You can be the Babe Ruth of wrestling and still have something to prove.

That's the way I felt on March 17, 2002, at *WrestleMania X8* in the Toronto SkyDome. I had something to prove to myself and a lot of other people, and there was only one place I could do it—in the ring. Against a guy called The Rock. In front of nearly 70,000 screaming fans.

It was already preordained that The Rock would win this clash of titans. We both knew he was going to come out on top that night.

But that didn't make my job easier. If anything, it made it harder. It would have been simple if all I had to do was put a boot in his face and lay a legdrop on him and strut around afterward like I owned the place.

Yeah, that would have been a piece of cake.

Unfortunately, that wasn't the way it was supposed to go down. I was supposed to lose the match, but I was supposed to do it in a way that made even bigger stars of both of us. And that was going to take some doing, brother. Losing this match the way I needed to lose it was going to be a lot harder for me, a lot more complicated, a lot more demanding of my skills as a wrestler and as an entertainer than anything I had done before.

Because this wasn't just a wrestling match. It wasn't just two guys tossing each other around in a ring for a piece of leather with a buckle on it. This was our shot at immortality. This was our chance to create something that people would talk about for a long time to come. Nobody had ever had an opportunity exactly like this one in the whole, long history of wrestling, and maybe no one ever would again.

It wasn't like all the movies I'd done where you could roll the cameras over and over again until you got it right. This was one time, one chance, don't screw it up or else.

And for me, there was something even bigger at stake in that arena. Immortality is great, but before you can even think about that you've got to get respect—and the person I've always found it hardest to get respect from is myself.

I'm always asking myself, "What've you done for me lately?" And before that *WrestleMania,* as I paced the long,

Hollywood Hulk Hogan

curving corridor backstage like a lion in a cage, my answer had to be, "Not much."

Two years earlier, I'd left another wrestling organization under a black cloud. Basically, I was kicked out on my ass and told I'd never wrestle for them again—that I was a has-been who could never be the attraction I used to be.

They had got me doubting myself. I was forty-eight years old. I'd had three knee surgeries over the past year and a half and I would eventually need to replace the knee joint altogether. And what they had said about me in public was dragging me down like a boulder hanging from my damn neck.

But I hadn't gone under the knife three times just to accept the verdict they'd laid on me. I did it to have an opportunity to make things right again, to end my career on my own terms and not someone else's.

I didn't want people to remember me as the guy who wrestled until he was washed up. I wanted them to remember me as the guy who wrestled longer than anybody and went out on top. I wanted that to be the ending of the movie.

That whole time I was sitting at home and recuperating from my surgeries, all I ever wanted was one more chance. Just one shot at making things right again. And here I had gotten one.

Of course, it wasn't just my knee that was giving me trouble. I'd just gotten over a hundred-and-three-degree fever that damn near killed me and eventually landed me in a Florida emergency room, so I wasn't as strong as I wanted to be. Plus I had cracked a couple of ribs a few weeks earlier and I hadn't given them a chance to heal, so it hurt like hell just to breathe.

But I wasn't going to let that weak crap keep me from wrestling. I told myself, "Save the drama for your momma. There's seventy thousand people out there waiting to see you face The Rock. A fever doesn't mean a thing. Cracked ribs don't mean a thing. You've got a job to do, go out there and do it."

I was wearing black and white, the colors of the New World Order—a gang of street-cool, renegade wrestlers— with a matching feather boa and sunglasses. I had been wearing the same thing since I came back to the World Wrestling Federation as a bad guy in the beginning of the year.

But people had been cheering me anyway. It didn't seem to matter what I said or did, or how badly I treated them. They still cheered for me and booed my opponent. And that was the problem I had to face in the ring that night in Toronto.

Not just to lose. Not just to lose in a way that didn't diminish me. But to get people cheering for The Rock again too, so when the match was over we would both come out smelling like roses.

I knew a bunch of the other wrestlers thought I was going to fall flat on my face out there. I hadn't had to prove anything since I came back. This was my first chance to show them I could still hack it.

To show them . . . and to show *myself*.

Vince McMahon, the guy who runs the company, came over to join me as I waited for my music to start. I was so nervous and pumped up at the same time, I looked at him and I told him, "Everybody screws with me, brother. My wife makes me work hard, my kids make me crazy, the government screws with me, the IRS screws with me . . . and sometimes even you screw with me, Vince. But out there, that's my damn house and nobody can mess with me. Now I'm going out there to collect my money. I'll see you when I'm done."

He looked at me like "Huh?"

As soon as I said it, I regretted it and I wanted to take it back. It sounded cocky and arrogant, and I hadn't meant it to sound that way. I was just trying to tell Vince that I was focused, that I was as ready as I could be.

5

A Rock and a Hard Place

And instead I sounded like an ass.

All of a sudden, my music started and I walked through the curtain and down the ramp, an ocean of people waving signs and cheering for me at the top of their lungs, and millions more watching on Pay-Per-View at home. And I was thinking, "Way to go, brother. If you had a ton of pressure on you before, you've got *two* tons now."

It was bad enough all these people in the wrestling business were waiting for me to slip on a banana peel so they could say, "We told you so. He's too old, he's too crippled, he's too bald-headed, he doesn't have it anymore."

Now I had Vince wondering about me.

So as I made my way down to the ring with the music thundering and all the lights on me, all I could think was, "God, I'm such an idiot. Now I'd *really* better not screw up."

Growing Up

Hollywood

2

My mom and dad met about as far away from the Toronto SkyDome as you can get, down in Central America, in the Panama Canal Zone. My dad, Pete Bollea, had gone down to Panama to work as a pipe fitter. My mom, whose name is Ruth, was a secretary working for the Navy.

She had been married before and had a son named Kenneth Wheeler. He's thirteen or fourteen years older than I am and wound up going to military school, so I didn't see much of him when I was growing up. I was closer with my brother Allan, who was my full brother and only seven or eight years older than I was.

For a while, our family lived in Augusta, Georgia. I was born there on August 11, 1953. But about nine months later we all moved to Tampa, which wasn't nearly as built up as it is now. It was more like a small town in those days. Kids would roam around all day on their bikes and not come home until the streetlights came on, and their parents wouldn't ever have to worry about them.

We lived in a little two-bedroom, wooden frame house that my dad bought for five thousand dollars. Our neighborhood was what you might call lower middle class. Every ethnic group was represented—Italian-Americans, Puerto Rican-Americans, Irish-Americans, all across the board.

My dad worked for Cone Brothers, a construction company that was laying in storm drains for all the major malls around Tampa. He wasn't especially big, five feet eleven and maybe two hundred and ten, two hundred and twenty pounds, but he was tough in his way.

He grew up in a place called Hanover, New Hampshire. His parents had six or seven girls and he was the only boy. His mother was real heavy-handed, a strict disciplinarian. You didn't want to cross her. But on those occasions when I went up to visit them, it was my grandfather who really fascinated me.

He was a farmer, a big guy with real big hands, and he had a picture of this rock he once picked up. The thing had to weigh six hundred pounds, maybe more. It was just a superhuman feat.

I remember watching him cut wheat and corn and tend to the cattle. He had a lot of cattle. And a lot of milking machines in his barn, I remember that. I don't think his life was anything glorious, but he worked hard to give his family some security.

I'm not sure why my dad left New Hampshire. I never asked him. But I know he was a hard worker too, a guy who took pride in what he did.

I went on the job with him a few times when I was a kid. He was a foreman at that point and he had a couple of key guys who he relied on. There was one guy in the crane who would dig the ditches and another one in the hole who he trusted to bend the pipe and make everything fit.

But sometimes the guys in the hole were assholes who were lazy or didn't know what they were doing. Then my dad would get impatient and he would jump into the hole and do the work himself. And that was dangerous sometimes, because we had a lot of soft sand in Florida and holes had been known to cave in. I remember my mom worrying about my dad being way down in a twenty- or thirty-foot ditch with all that soft sand around him.

And it wasn't just the danger that I remember. Sometimes guys would laugh at my dad for working so hard. The guys he had kicked out of the hole because they weren't doing the job right, they would be looking down at the old bald-headed man working his butt off and cracking up because he was doing their work for them. I'll never forget that.

But my dad was good at what he did. I used to watch him working with trigonometry tables, bending the pipe to just the right angle because sometimes he was the only one who knew how to do that, and make the water flow x number of miles in y amount of time.

He worked until the sun baked his brains out and he put up with a lot of stuff on the job, but he never said a bad word about anyone. He might have had a nip of cream sherry or a couple of beers now and then, but you never heard him say, "That guy's no good," or "That guy's an ass-hole." To this day, he's the only person I ever met who never said a bad word about anyone.

Unfortunately, as hard as my dad worked and as good as he was at his job, construction workers didn't make a lot of money. Since there were only two bedrooms in the house, my brother Allan and I had to share one of them growing up. But Allan was a big guy, as big as I am now by the time he was grown. After a while, we got too big for the bed and ended up sleeping on the floor.

It wasn't exactly luxurious, but somehow my mom made us feel like we weren't deprived of anything. I remember every Friday, she would make minute steaks for us. That was a big deal, brother, getting a skinny little steak on Friday. That was a main event kind of deal.

My mom is a tall woman, about five feet, eight inches in her prime. Before she met my dad, as a teenager and into her early twenties, she was a real good dancer. She even taught it at some point. I remember seeing pictures of her when she was a kid with a little dance uniform on.

My mom always used to tell me that she thrived on stress, that stress was her energy. She was always trying to figure out how she was going to pay the bills or take care of some family crisis.

And before long, there were plenty of them.

You see, when my brother Allan became a teenager it was cool to be a redneck, and if you were a redneck you drank a bunch of beer and you went out and got into fights every weekend. Allan got real good at street fighting. He had this reputation around the Port Tampa area that if he fought you he would kick your ass.

This was back in the old days, where if you got into a fight and got arrested, you'd spend the night in jail and get out the next day for a twenty-five-dollar fine. That was the pattern with Allan. Hardly a weekend went by when he wasn't either fighting or hurting someone or getting hurt himself, so he was constantly getting thrown into jail and getting bailed out. It was an ongoing saga with him.

I remember how upset my mother and father used to get when they found out my brother had gotten into another fight. They were always trying to figure out why he was getting into trouble, always trying to piece it together. They would always say they weren't going to help him anymore, but of course they helped him anyway. So there was a lot of turmoil in my house, a lot of talking to and about Allan.

Being a lot younger than he was, I had other things on my mind. I was too busy playing corkball and stickball and running around with my friends to really think about the trouble my brother was getting into. But on some level, it made me uncomfortable. I didn't like the turmoil. I just wanted things to be normal.

One of the things I liked to do most was play with this black Tonka truck I'd gotten for Christmas. I would take it out and play construction in the dirt all day long, from the time I woke up until the time I had to go in for dinner. I made believe the truck was the big red one my dad drove when he was laying pipe. I would use Popsicle sticks for people and dig holes in the ground and make a whole construction site with that one Tonka truck.

The funny thing was as I sat there in the dirt I'd look for rocks of a certain size, bigger than a BB but not as big as a dime, and when I found them I'd stuff them up my nose. I don't know why that type of thing appealed to me. I just knew I could be happy stuffing rocks up my nose all day long. It was like my hobby or something.

Then one night as I was lying in bed I couldn't breathe all of a sudden. My parents panicked and stuck a flashlight up my nose and saw I'd stuffed a rock way up into my sinuses. They had to take me to the hospital and have it pulled out. That was the first inkling they got that their son was a rock stuffer.

Another thing I liked to do was pick these little orange spotted caterpillars off the oleander trees and collect them in glass jars. I remember having a fight with one of the kids in the neighborhood over them. His name was Roger and he was a red-haired, freckle-faced kid who was usually one of my good friends. But that one day he decided to steal my caterpillars, so I picked up a rock and as he was running home I plunked him in the back of the head. The rock split his head open and he bled like a stuck pig.

But then, I'd always had a strong throwing arm. When I was eight, I started putting it to good use in Little League. I was pretty good at baseball. When I turned nine, I became one of the few kids my age ever been allowed to play in what they called the majors.

I was a hard-throwing pitcher and a pretty good third

baseman. The problem was that I was fat and really slow, so if I didn't hit the ball over the fence I couldn't get an extra base hit. The other team would always throw me out at second.

And let me tell you, brother, it didn't take a genius to figure out why I was fat. Even when I was really young, I was a serious candyholic. My favorite vice was Baby Ruth candy bars. They used to make them real big, like about six or nine inches long. I just remember I'd buy two or three of them at a shot and shove them down my throat one after the other.

By the time I got to first grade, I was pretty chubby. I couldn't do as many push-ups as the other kids, I had a problem when it came time to climb a rope, and I ran like I was pulling a piano.

At Ballast Point Elementary School, we had a football field. One of the phys ed teachers, who was real strong but had a short leg and would walk funny, used to make the kids run across the field and back again. But not me. I was so fat he put me at the far goalpost and had me run just one way. And even with my head start, the other fifty kids would still beat me.

Whatever games we played at school, I was the last one to be picked. Nobody wanted a kid on their team who looked like the Goodyear blimp. And it wasn't just in sports that kids didn't want to pick me.

Every other Friday, this teacher would roll out an amplifier and a record player and make us dance with the girls. Of course, the girls got to choose who they danced with, and they never wanted to dance with *me*. They'd dance with just about anybody but me.

Out of all thirty boys in phys ed class, I would be one of the two or three that got snubbed. Our reward, which we thought was great at the time, was that the coach told us to go and play soccer. So we'd get a ball and go kick it around and laugh at all the boys who had to dance with the girls. I thought I was lucky. It didn't sink in that I hadn't been picked because I was a fat kid.

And it wasn't just my weight that made me different. I remember in first grade, a girl named Sarah with glasses and curly blond hair shared a desk with me. On the first day of school, she sat down and stared at me for a minute like I was some kind of freak. Then she said, "Has your head always been that big?"

My head was huge all right, probably the same size that it is now. But I didn't need her to point it out to me. Before I got to first grade, a neighborhood bully named Butch had teased me about the size of my head every chance he got.

In school, I figured I was finally safe from that stuff. Then along came Sarah.

But she didn't get the last laugh. See, she had a sweater tied around her waist that she was really proud of. By the end of that first day of school, Sarah ended up peeing in her pants and peed all over her sweater. I figured it was her punishment for being mean to me.

It's weird the things you remember as a kid.

Fortunately, there were ways I could excel even if I was a fat kid with a big head. One of those ways was bowling.

Growing Up

From the time I was eight years old until I was twelve, I teamed up with a kid named Vic Pettit, who later became a professional bowler. We were the Florida state doubles champions five years in a row and one of us—Vic more often than me—was always the singles champion too.

When I turned nine I started using a sixteen-pound ball, which was a little crazy. Adults use sixteen-pounders. The damn thing should've torn my arm out of its socket, but I was a big kid and somehow I was able to handle it.

One of the reasons we became such good bowlers was there was a bowling alley just five blocks from my house. It was called Pin-A-Rama and Vic and I would go there every week without fail. I never thought about it at the time, but we must have spent quite a bit of money in that place.

Vic's parents must have thought so too because they eventually bought the bowling alley. Unfortunately, that was about the time I lost interest in bowling and got caught up in other things. Good timing, huh?

The other sport I continued to play for a long time was baseball. I remember one day they installed a brand-new electric scoreboard. In our town, where kids didn't have much in the way of toys or bikes because their parents didn't have much money, it was a real big deal to hit a home run. Then you got to take the whole team to Burger King for a Whopper or something.

Sure enough, the first night they had the scoreboard, I hit a ball right over it for a home run. That was a good day. A real good feeling.

When I was twelve, my last year in the Interbay Little League, I was named to my town's All-Star team. We were playing a real good team from West Tampa and I was batting fourth in the lineup.

The first three guys on my team all got up and hit home runs. Bam, bam, bam! You want to talk about pressure? I was the cleanup hitter, brother. I wanted to hit a home run so bad my stomach was tied in knots.

The first pitch to me was high and inside. I didn't care. I just stepped back out of the box and jacked it over the left-field fence. It was a rocket. I just blind drove it out of the park. I was two hundred pounds by that time so all I could do was wallow around the bases, but I'll always

Growing Up

remember hitting that home run in that inning with my boys.

I stayed with baseball after Little League through Pony ball and then Babe Ruth ball. And I probably would have kept at it, maybe even tried to make a career of it, if I hadn't gotten hurt.

One day when I was sixteen, I was playing third and a batter on the other team hit a slow grounder down the line. I picked the ball up with my right hand and threw it on the run, fired it sidearm as hard as I could to the first baseman. Big mistake. As soon as I released it, I knew I had messed up my arm. It turned out I had broken something. After that I was never the same as a baseball player.

Of course, there was one sport I loved to death but never in my wildest dreams thought I'd participate in. That was wrestling.

From the very first time I saw it on TV, as a very little kid, I was hooked. By the age of six or seven I was looking for it every week. My hero was Dusty Rhodes, the American Dream. I'd sit home on Sundays to watch the local wrestling show and if they didn't have Dusty Rhodes on I'd be really pissed. I'd start stomping around the house and cussing under my breath.

Pretty soon, I talked my father into taking me to see the matches at the Armory on Tuesday nights. It was better than TV, that's for damn sure. The wrestlers were like Greek gods to me. They were giants, larger than life, and the combination of entertainment and physicality that I saw in the wrestling ring was something I had never seen in other sports.

And that, I guess you'd say, was where it all started for me.

Of course, I had other heroes. If you were a baseball player when I was a kid, you had to worship the New York Yankees. There was Mickey Mantle, Roger Maris, Yogi Berra, Joe Pepitone . . . and because the Cincinnati Reds had their spring training camp in Tampa, I liked Pete Rose and Johnny Bench a lot too.

But Dusty Rhodes . . . he was it, brother. He was the real deal. Dusty Rhodes was the first guy in Florida to do the show business thing in the ring. He had a Muhammad Ali–type rap—"Dusty Rhodes, the tower of power, the man of the hour, too sweet to be sour." He was a white guy but he talked like a black guy, and it worked for him.

And then there was the promoter Eddie Graham. I didn't know he was the promoter at the time, of course—I thought he was just a wrestler like everybody else. But Eddie Graham was one of my heroes too.

The bad guys came through the Armory like a revolving door: Ox Baker, Pak Song. The Giant Korean. The Missouri Mauler. The Assassins. Jos LeDuc. Crusher Verdu. Every bad-guy monster wrestler showed up at one time or another. And they were all big men, three hundred pounds, and hairy as hell. What I know now is that a lot of the good guys lived in Florida and the bad guys' job was to come in from time to time and make the good guys look like bigger stars than they really were.

I saw Andre the Giant wrestle at the Armory. I saw Haystacks Calhoun. The parade of talent was awesome. It was unbelievable.

By the time I got to high school, I was watching wrestling in person twice a week. On Tuesday nights I'd go to the Armory and on Wednesday afternoons I'd see the same guys at a place called the Sportatorium, on Albany Avenue just north of Kennedy Boulevard in downtown Tampa. That's where they taped the weekly Sunday wrestling shows in front of what was basically a studio audience before the wrestlers moved on to Miami, which was always the next town on their itinerary.

The Sportatorium was an old, dimly lit wooden building with a tin roof on it. It was a couple of stories high, probably five thousand square feet of space altogether. As you walked in the front door, there was a little box office window manned by an old-timer named Charlie Lay. Charlie would give all the wrestlers their schedules and their instructions.

Over to the side was a double set of doors with a hot dog stand and a popcorn stand alongside them. That's where the "marks" (what the wrestlers called the spectators) would walk into the arena—if you could *call* it an arena. It looked more like a garage with a ring set up in the middle of it.

The bleachers, which ran maybe seven rows deep, held about fifty people—but even that was too many for comfort because there wasn't any air-conditioning and it was no big deal for the temperature to get up to a hundred degrees in Florida. If I said it was hot as hell, it would be an understatement.

Still, the people would ignore the heat and yell and scream for their heroes to beat the bad guys, who I learned early on were known as "heels." And when you body-slammed somebody in that ring it was really loud because of the size of the Sportatorium and the way it was built.

When you were done with your match, you could roll out of the ring and take about ten steps and walk over to the announcer's table where you'd find Gordon Solie, the commentator for Florida Championship Wrestling. You could walk over there and pop off at Gordon or sit down and talk about what was happening in the ring. Or if you wanted, you could have a confrontation there with one of the other wrestlers. You could jump the guy or scream in his face or whatever you had to do. Gordon's table was the hot spot where all that took place.

I was always running down to the Sportatorium, every chance I got. Hell, I purposely set up my schedule so after lunch I would have phys ed, a shop class, and then a study hall—nothing classes I could blow off to go see the wrestlers. Then, at about two o'clock when the matches were over, I'd haul my ass back to Robinson High School and park my car without anybody noticing. The last thing we had to do is go back to our home room and I always managed to make it back there in time.

Watching those matches at the Sportatorium, seeing the wrestlers up close . . . it was as attractive to me as getting that glimpse of the girl you're in love with or waking up in the morning to see the present Santa brought you. It was like somebody who had never been to Disney World seeing the fireworks or the Magic Kingdom for the first time.

But make no mistake, I never *ever* imagined I'd become

a wrestler. I knew my physical limitations. If I was so fat I couldn't outrun anybody or climb a rope, how could I ever get into a ring and wrestle? So I put that possibility out of my mind—even though at the same time, I was drawn to it like a hunk of iron to a giant magnet.

The Hollywood Ranch

3

If you cruise around the Internet and check out what's been written about me, you'll read that I was arrested for street fighting at the age of fourteen and sent to a reform school called the Florida Sheriffs Boys Ranch.

I'm here to tell you it's not true. It's *absolutely* not true. I was never arrested for fighting and I never wound up at that type of place.

The idea may have been concocted by a promoter as part of a wrestling story line and got picked up by the press, or it might have come from somebody confusing bits and pieces of my life. Who knows? But I'm going on the record and saying I never got sent to the Florida Sheriffs Boys Ranch.

Where I *did* end up was a place called the Christian Youth Ranch, and what happened to me there became a turning point in my life.

When I was a kid, my family belonged to Ballast Point Baptist Church, but we didn't attend on a consistent basis. Maybe we'd show up every other week or so. All I remember about those Sundays was getting dressed in my clean clothes and trying my hardest to stay awake, which wasn't easy.

Then, when I got to Monroe Junior High School, I began playing football with these twin brothers—Ronald and Donald Saterwhite. Both of them are preachers now. Every day after practice they tried to talk me into coming to some kind of ranch for Christian kids. Finally, I gave in and went with them.

The ranch was about two and a half miles from my parents' place, in the direction of downtown. It didn't look like much—just a house that had been built out bigger than the other houses in the area. But there was a bunch of friendly-looking kids there, all of them sitting around and singing, and talking about the Bible. I was curious so I sat down and joined them, and afterward we went out to play basketball and mess around.

It turned out they needed someone to play guitar at the Youth Ranch so they could sing the gospel songs. I was taking guitar lessons at the time and I could play the simple type of chords and progressions that you find in religious songs, so the next time I showed up I brought my guitar. That became my incentive to keep coming back—that I would get to play the guitar while everybody sang.

The guy who ran the ranch was a minister named Hank Lindstrom. He's the one who explained the lesson of John 3:16 to me. He told me that life isn't a once-around-the-block type of deal. He said if I accepted the fact that Christ died on the cross to pay for my sins, I'd be cleansed of them. And even better, I wouldn't perish but would have everlasting life.

That sounded like a hell of a deal to *me*.

So when I was fourteen, after hanging out at the Youth Ranch for a couple of years, I accepted Christ as my savior. And from that point on, I felt like I had a better understanding of life and why you should treat people the way you want to be treated. I just seemed more aware of everything.

Maybe it was because I was fourteen. Maybe it was because I was getting older. But whatever it was, I saw things differently than I had before.

I'm not sure I would have learned all that if I had ended up at the Florida Sheriffs Boys Ranch.

Music,
Money, and
Matsuda

4 **Music's always been one of the**
great passions of my life, almost as big
as wrestling. If you love something, you
usually get good at it, so I guess it was
inevitable that I'd turn into a pretty
decent musician.

By the time I got to ninth grade, I
was known for my guitar playing, and I
got my first little band together. We
called it Infinity's End. At first, we were
just screwing around. Then we started
getting dates to play at parties on the
weekends, and we were booked up

almost all the time. Our keyboard player was a guy named Gary, whose father was our manager. He would drive us around in his station wagon with a U-Haul trailer hooked up to it.

I remember we had to wear socks when we played, and Gary's mom painted our blue jeans with black-light paint—so when the black lights came on in front of us, all of the paint would light up. It seemed like a pretty cool idea at the time.

For a bunch of kids, we did all right for ourselves. We played "Ina Gadda Da Vida" and all the old Steppenwolf songs. We knew everything that was on the radio. And we had two guitar players, a drummer, a bass player, and a keyboard player, which was pretty intense for a ninth-grade band.

The music remained an underlying theme for me. When I got to high school, I started playing in even better bands and that became my job, my income. I didn't go out after school and work at McDonald's or the hobby shop or something like that. I made money by playing music, and by the time I was in eleventh or twelfth grade—we're talking 1970 or so, remember—I was making like four hundred dollars a week. That was a lot of bread back then. Nowadays, it would be like a couple of grand.

After a while, I became the only person in Robinson High School who had gotten a brand new car on his own. And before my senior year was over, I had a second new car to add to the first one. Both of them were '69 Roadrunners, one an automatic with a 383 engine and the other a four-speed.

But I couldn't have gotten them without the help of Lila Silverwood. Lila was the president of Atlantic Bank on Dale Mabry Street in Tampa, but she had also been my babysitter when I was younger. When I went to her for a car loan I was too young to get it on my own, but Lila cosigned it because she trusted me. So because of her, I ended up with not only two cars but a hell of a credit rating.

Even with the car payments, I was pocketing a ton of money. When I started playing regularly with a really good local band at a place called the Islands Club on Davis Island, I moved out of my parents' house. That was partway through my senior year of high school and I never moved back—though there were times when I had a lot less money than I did in high school, and at those times free room and board sounded pretty damn good to me.

The Islands Club attracted a lot of good-looking women who were too old for me. It also attracted a lot of athletes from the University of Tampa. I remember John Matuszak, who wound up playing for the Oakland Raiders, would come by a lot. The same with Paul Orndorff, another tremendous athlete at the university.

And then something weird happened. *Wrestlers* started showing up.

These guys I had watched and idolized all my life started coming to the Islands Club. Instead of them entertaining *me,* I was the one entertaining *them.* Like I say, it was weird.

It was right about the time the wrestlers started showing up that my friend Scott Thornton's car broke down and he asked me if I would give him a ride to his gym. It was

Music, Money, and Matsuda

Hector's Gym on Platt Street in a really tough area of Tampa, but he was a good friend of mine so after school I gave him a ride down there.

He asked me to come inside with him but I told him, "No way, I don't want to go inside." Hell, I was a fat kid with long hair playing in a band. I was embarrassed to walk into a place like Hector's Gym.

Anyway, he convinced me to go in with him. I saw right away that there were four or five guys in the gym and they all looked up at me like they wanted to kill me. They were like mountain men, each one bigger than the other, with wide, muscular backs and hair all over their bodies. I was scared to death when I saw them look up at me that way.

But it turned out they were nice to me. They told me to come on in and hang out. It was because of how comfortable they made me feel there, that I agreed to stay and keep my friend Scott Thornton company while he worked out. And the next day, I came back to the gym and signed up.

I was tired of being fat. I went to the beach a lot but I couldn't take my shirt off because my pecs looked like a woman's tits. And I was even more tired of not having a girlfriend. Even with my two new cars, I couldn't get a girl interested in me. If you're in high school and you've got two brand new cars and you don't have a girlfriend, you've got to face the fact that there's something wrong with you.

Up to that point, I'd tried to lose weight by drinking Diet Pepsi and Diet Coke and eating crackers instead of food. But it didn't help much. I was still a tub of lard.

I never pictured myself going to a gym. But when I

started working out at Hector's, I found I enjoyed it. And I kept at it, thinking that someday I might get in respectable enough shape for a girl to give me a chance. So the motivation there was definitely the opposite sex.

Then, right after I started working out at Hector's, another weird thing happened. Some of the wrestlers started showing up there. So now I was bumping into them at the Islands Club and also at Hector's Gym.

At first, it was very intimidating working out alongside these guys. Whenever one of them would walk in I would immediately break into a cold sweat. It wasn't just that they were physically imposing. It was that, in my wrestling fan's mind, these guys had such a powerful mystique to them.

Still, you eventually get used to any environment, and after a while I started to get accustomed to the one in Hector's Gym. I became a regular there. And little by little, I got in shape.

I even got up the courage to talk to some of the wrestlers. And the more I talked to them, the more I glimpsed of that world, the more my interest in wrestling grew. Then you couldn't even call it an interest anymore, because it was starting to turn into an obsession.

I was possessed by it, brother. I ate and slept and dreamed about wrestling twenty-four hours a day. And I got this idea in my head, this crazy, far-fetched idea, that if I lifted enough weights and stuck to my diet and trained hard enough . . . maybe, just maybe, I could do a little wrestling myself.

It wasn't that I thought I'd be as good as any of the guys

in the gym. *Hell,* no. But I'd talked to them enough that the fear of them killing me was pretty much gone. I figured the worst thing that could happen is I'd get beat up real bad, and maybe it wouldn't be *too* bad because the wrestlers seemed to have taken a liking to me.

So it got to the point where I got enough confidence to start nosing around. What would it take, I asked, to become a professional wrestler?

Meanwhile, in addition to playing music and training at the gym, I attended a couple of institutions of "higher learning." I went to St. Petersburg Junior College for a couple of years, changed my major about fifty times, and finally graduated with a degree in liberal arts, then went on to the University of South Florida.

Going all the way back to elementary school, the only thing I had ever really been good at was math. Anything with numbers, anything that had a pattern, made sense to me. So I did well in subjects like economics and trigonometry.

The other stuff had always seemed useless. I didn't see the point of knowing "In fourteen hundred and ninety-two Columbus sailed the ocean blue" or "The first hot air balloon was launched in Munich, Germany in 1902."

If college had been all math and music courses, it wouldn't have been too bad. It was all the other stuff that made me think twice about staying in school.

So I was looking into doing some wrestling, I was playing music in clubs, and I was going to school. And at the same time, I was pursuing this one other possibility—banking, of all things.

Lila Silverwood, the lady who had been my baby-sitter, worked at Atlantic Bank in Tampa. She knew I was scrambling, trying to find some direction in life, so she gave me a job at the bank.

Of course, in my heart, I didn't want to work a real job because I'd been spoiled by making more money than any of my peers at a very early age. But Lila told me I was going to be "swiftly promoted" to the top position in the bank's loan department, so I figured it was worth checking out.

I went through the training program and everything, making three dollars and seventy-five cents an hour. But there would be a better salary in store for me down the road, and I was thinking this would be a nice, secure way to make a living.

As part of my training at the bank, I had to look up a bunch of files. Some of them were about wrestlers, guys that I knew. And when I looked into their files, I saw that even back in 1971 there were guys making twelve thousand, fifteen thousand dollars a week.

Here I was excited about a job where I'm making three dollars and seventy-five cents an hour and these guys were making that much money every couple of seconds. That pushed me over the edge. When I saw what these guys were making, it pushed me to go hard after this wrestling thing. I said, that's it, there's nothing else to talk about.

So I never did become a loan officer. I went through the training for a few days and got to know too much.

Soon after that, I hit on a hard lead with the wrestling. I'd been talking to the wrestlers and made friends with a few of them, and found out there was a bar where they would go after they wrestled on Tuesday nights. It was called the Imperial Room.

So I made it my business to go to the Imperial Room after the matches on Tuesday nights. I would have a drink there with the wrestlers—the ones who were friendly enough to talk to me. Some of them were still playing games with me, saying, "Get out of here, kid," that type of thing.

But I made enough contacts where I felt comfortable approaching a guy named Mike Graham. He was the son of Eddie Graham, the promoter, and he had been a couple of years ahead of me in school as I was growing up.

One night, Mike Graham came up to me in the Imperial Room and said, "Come on out to the parking lot. I want to talk to you."

This was back in 1976, the middle of the summer in Florida. Mike Graham took me out to the parking lot, where he had an Econoline van. It must have been one hundred twenty degrees in that sucker, but Mike Graham didn't start the car or turn on the air-conditioning. He just sat down on the engine cover, which was in between the front seats, and looked back at me.

"So," he said, "you want to be a wrestler."

I told Mike that I did and how serious I was about it. Of course, he was used to hearing that type of thing a million times a week. He was always getting approached by guys wanting to be wrestlers.

"Well," he said, "if you really want to be a wrestler I could set you up with Hiro Matsuda, this Japanese guy. He'll make sure you're in shape, make sure you're tough enough. If you can pass his tests, you might have a chance."

Hell, I knew who Hiro Matsuda was. I'd watched him for many years as a kid, and for some of those years he was the Southern Heavyweight Champion. He didn't just use the established wrestling moves in the ring. He also used karate moves, which was a pretty unusual approach in those days.

Let me tell you, brother, I was pumped to work out with Hiro Matsuda. I was ready for anything. Little did I know what he had in mind for me.

Anyway, I figured I didn't need to go to college anymore because I was going to become a wrestler—and not just any wrestler, but the biggest star ever. So I dropped out of all my classes and sold all my books, and quit school.

Then I told the people in my band that I wasn't going to play with them anymore. By then, I was with one of the best groups in the state of Florida, playing Uriah Heep and the Allman Brothers, all the old Southern rock. We were good buddies with the Blues Image and Iron Butterfly. I even did some studio work with Century Artists out of Atlanta, Georgia.

But I was putting all that behind me. Who needed music? I was going to make money in the ring.

So Mike Graham, out of the "goodness" of his heart, made an appointment for me to go and work out with Hiro Matsuda. When the time came, I met Matsuda down at his gym. I was actually going to get a shot at becoming a professional wrestler. How cool was that?

Man, was I naïve.

I didn't know that the *last* thing Eddie Graham wanted was to let local boys into his wrestling promotion. There was a mystique about these wrestlers that they were the biggest, strongest, toughest guys in the world, handpicked from all over the globe. If they let Terry Bollea join this close-knit fraternity, it would mean that they weren't so special after all. It would mean that just anybody could become a wrestler.

That was the word on the street before I went down to Matsuda's gym. Unfortunately for me, nobody told me that. So I walked into the place thinking I had a genuine chance of breaking into the wrestling business.

Another thing I didn't know was that Matsuda was pissed off just having to be there that day. He was wrestling six days a week and this was the one day he wasn't sched-uled to wrestle, so I was basically taking him away from his day off. Hell, I'd have been pissed too.

The first thing he did was get me outside the ring and exercise me. I thought I was in good shape going in, but I quickly found out otherwise. Weight-lifting shape is one thing, wrestling shape is another.

So it didn't take long for Matsuda to get me to the point where I thought I was going to faint. Everything was turn-ing white and my knees felt like rubber. I told Matsuda I was liable to go down at any second.

"All right," he said, "now it's time to wrestle."

So he threw me into the ring.

Before I knew it, Matsuda was sitting down between my legs and putting his elbow in the middle of my shin. Then he grabbed the end of my toe and twisted my foot until—crack!—my shinbone broke in half. The whole thing took about two seconds.

I had barely gotten into the ring and my damn leg was broken.

I couldn't even get myself home. I had an Econoline van at the time with a clutch in it and there was no way I could drive it with a broken leg. I had to wait until my dad came home from work and I could call to tell him what happened.

He showed up a little while later and drove me and my van home. He was pissed, brother, and it wasn't just because I had gone and broken my leg. I had to tell him I'd quit college and given notice to all my professors because I was going to be the next superstar of wrestling—but instead of becoming a superstar, I had let Hiro Matsuda break my leg.

I was hurt and confused. I didn't know why Matsuda had done that to me. I had a lot to learn.

In those days, more than twenty-five years ago, wrestling was a very barbaric and protective business. The attitude was "Why would we let a nobody like you into this elite club of ours just because you lifted weights for a couple of years? What gives you the right to be part of this?"

Today, you get a pair of wrestling boots for Christmas and you can call yourself a wrestler. Back then, you had to give up everything to even have a shot. If you had a family, a wife and kids, you had to leave all that behind.

So what Matsuda did to me was the correct protocol for

a longhaired weight lifter who played in a rock-and-roll band and wore his mother's jewelry. If I had been an amateur wrestler who hadn't made it to the Olympics but was a great Florida state champion, the proper protocol would have been to beat me down and wear me out. But since I had never paid any dues at all, they wanted to see how bad I really wanted it.

Now I understand that he did the right thing by breaking my leg. But at the time, I felt betrayed. I had to regroup and think this through. And without school or music, I had plenty of time to do that.

I wound up living in a hotel room down the street from my parents' house—a place called the Crossway Inn. It was cheap, only about ten dollars a day to live there. I remember when my dad would go to work I would go limp over to their house and my mom would feed me. And when the time came for my dad to come home I would get the hell out of there on my crutches and go back to the hotel.

All in all, I had my leg in a cast for about ten weeks. By the time the cast came off and my leg felt better, I knew what I was going to do. Maybe I should have run as far away from Matsuda's gym as I could, but I didn't. I went right back down there.

Having been a musician, I had a mane of blond hair that went halfway down my back. (Back then I still had a full head of hair, not this big, bald head I've got now.) I cut that off and made my hair short. And it wasn't just my hair that had changed. I went back there with a completely different attitude.

They beat me again, of course. But when my opponent tried to break my leg this time I blocked it and stopped him. And all of a sudden they began looking at me a little differently, like I was something more to them than a damn wishbone.

They had me come down to the Sportatorium after that, and every day Matsuda and the other guys beat me up. They chipped my teeth and tore a bunch of muscles and twisted my knee and screwed up my neck and stretched every ligament in my body. They did about everything you can do to a person.

After three months, they figured out that I wasn't going to quit and their attitudes changed a little. It wasn't that they lightened up on me. I mean, they were still beating the living crap out of me. I was still their whipping boy and their punching bag. But at least I didn't see that animosity and hatred in their eyes every time they got ahold of me.

Even Matsuda started to warm up to me a little.

When I first met him, he was very intimidating. He always seemed to have a scowl etched into his face, like he hated you and looked down on you. But really, he was just being protective of the wrestling business. In his view, you weren't worthy to be in that business until you proved yourself. And to prove yourself to Hiro Matsuda, you really had to go a ways.

His training camp was probably the toughest one to survive. It wasn't like *Tough Enough,* the WWE's reality program where guys compete on TV for a wrestling contract with the company. That's a baby-sitting service compared to what Matsuda put you through. Matsuda's camp was the real deal, the *real* boot camp.

And Matsuda held it against me that I used to go out and chase the wrestlers around every night. He knew if I could get a wrestler to talk to me, I would drink a beer or two with them. Then they would say, "Terry was at the Imperial Room last night having a few beers. That's why he's tired today."

When that happened, Matsuda would glare at me and say, "No alcohol." And he would proceed to punish my body for drinking those beers.

The funny thing was that Matsuda himself always smelled of alcohol. When I would wrestle him, I could smell it coming out of his pores.

Finally, Matsuda and I got to be on friendlier terms, and he told me he drank two six packs of beer every night before he went to bed. "Well," I said, "Jesus Christ, how can you be in this type of shape if you drink like that?"

And he said, "That's why I have to train every day—because I drink like this."

Brother, I might not have adopted all of Matsuda's philosophy, but I was happy to adopt *that* part.

Unfortunately, as time went on, I ran low on money. I was spending almost all my time learning to wrestle, so I had to start selling things to pay for my hotel room. First I sold my van. Then I sold all my musical equipment, all the stuff I had acquired over the past ten years. It was like a yard sale except it went out a piece at a time.

Charlie Lay, the old-timer there, watched me get tortured day in and day out and he had sympathy for me. He kept saying, "Hang in there, kid. I never seen anybody go through what you're going through. Just hang in there."

He told me he thought they were getting me ready for something big. All I knew was I was getting killed little by little. There were days when I wanted to cry because I didn't know what new torture Matsuda was going to devise for me.

But at least two guys got some enjoyment out of it. They were Jack and Gerry Brisco, the tag team champions of Florida Championship Wrestling. They owned a body shop nearby and they would stop in to see Matsuda work me over.

I had originally met Jack Brisco at the Imperial Room. He was a real good-looking guy in a Tom Jones type of way. It turned out he was into rock and roll so he came to some of the clubs I played at and I got to know him pretty well.

I just remember being in excruciating pain and hearing the Briscos laugh at me. I was their favorite form of entertainment. I'm glad I was able to brighten their day because they sure weren't brightening mine.

But I hung in there, just like Charlie said. And a whole year went by, and I still wasn't any closer to becoming a professional wrestler than the day Matsuda posted my leg and broke it. Finally, I didn't think I could take it any longer.

I was out of money and thinking about quitting when Eddie Graham called me up at home. "Terry," he said, "I'm going to be there tomorrow and I'm going to work out with you. I want to show you a few things."

Eddie Graham was a former Southern Heavyweight Champion. I said to myself, "Oh God, what are they going to do to me now?"

So, with all my misgivings, I went down there and I trained with Eddie Graham—but it wasn't at all what I expected.

Hiro Matsuda had taught me a bunch of submission holds, holds that make your opponent give up because he can't stand the pain. If I locked up with a guy, I was supposed to try to take his arm off. That's what I'd been told to do for the last year. I was supposed to take my opponent's arm and post it behind him or try to wrench it out of its socket.

If I got a guy in a headlock, I was supposed to rub my arm bone against his ear to give him a cauliflower ear. If I got a chance to hook a guy—a hook being a hold that was meant to break bones—I was supposed to do that too.

That's what I thought wrestling was about. I thought you were supposed to be as brutal as possible because that was what it took to win.

All of a sudden Eddie Graham told me I wasn't going to need any of that stuff anymore. "When you grab a guy's arm," he said, "don't twist it off. Instead of really hurting him, just slide your grip around his wrist a little. It's up to him to make faces and yell and scream like you're killing him."

I looked at him like he was from Mars or something.

"And when you put somebody in a headlock," Eddie Graham said, "don't try to give him a cauliflower ear. Grab him with the soft part of your arm against his ear so you won't hurt him."

"Why am I trying not to hurt him?" I asked.

That's when he told me the truth—that you weren't fighting somebody in the ring. You were cooperating, working together to put on a show. And instead of the tougher guy winning, the outcome was determined in advance.

In wrestling terms, it was a "work" and not a "shoot." A shoot means you're really trying to hurt somebody. A work means you're working with a guy, dancing with him. Eddie Graham told me wrestling was a work.

I was in shock, brother, total shock. I felt like I'd been betrayed. For the last year, I'd been getting the crap beat out of me learning how to hurt people and keep from getting hurt myself.

What I didn't know was that Eddie Graham and the others thought I was going to be someone special in this business. I had an attitude they had never seen before. I wouldn't quit. So they wanted to make sure I knew what I was doing.

They wanted to be certain that nobody could pin my shoulders to the mat unless I wanted them to. Or if I got into a confrontation in a bar, I could take care of myself. Or if I was in Japan wrestling somebody, I could survive whatever I would encounter over there.

I see now that they were doing the right thing for me. But at the time, I was devastated.

Eddie Graham showed me how to hit the ropes and run, how to take a backdrop, stuff like that. At another time, I might have welcomed it. But my mind was on how badly I'd been deceived.

Then Eddie Graham told me something I *did* want to hear. Finally, I had paid my dues. I was going to start wrestling for real.

My Career as a Bouncer

5 Another thing you may have read about me someplace is that I used to work as a bouncer. Brother, that rumor's not true either . . . unless you count one night at the Proud Lion, which was a bar near my parents' house where some of my high-school friends would hang out.

The guys who watched the door there were all weight-lifting buddies of mine. They were really into the job because the bouncers at the Proud Lion would get all the good-looking girls. I guess there was a certain mystique involved.

I would sit at the door too, but I wouldn't check ID cards. I would just drink and talk and keep my pals company while they were working.

Anyway, a friend of mine was at the door one night and he said, "Hey man, I've got to go. I'll be gone five or six minutes. Would you watch the door for me?"

I said, "Sure, go ahead."

So I became the official deputy sheriff for a moment. But before my friend came back, I saw the lights come on in the bar, which meant it was two o'clock in the morning and the bar was about to close.

All of a sudden, some guy came stumbling out of the place with a Heineken in his hand. I said, "Sorry, brother, but you can't take that beer outside. You're going to have to leave it behind or finish it here."

I could tell he was already drunk because I'd been watching him during the night. But he didn't put up a fight. He said, "No problem."

And I didn't think there would be.

The guy took the Heineken and just chugged it right in front of me. No trouble at all, right? He put the bottle down and I figured he was leaving.

I turned around for a second to say good night to someone. When I turned back, the guy had the bottle in his hand again and he broke it right in my face.

It didn't even hurt. I was just surprised, like I was in shock or something. I went to touch my face and there was blood everywhere.

I might have gone after the guy, but before I could even

think about it two other guys had already jumped him. It turned out I only had some real teeny glass cuts but it could have been a lot worse. Hell, it could have wound up in my eyes and blinded me for life.

Fortunately, it only hit me on the hard part of my head, so there wasn't any real damage. And that was my one experience as a bouncer.

My First Hollywood Detour

6

I had worked my ass off and waited a long time to start wrestling, but I figured I had finally made it.

It wasn't that I thought I'd make as much money as the guys whose files I saw in the bank. I didn't think anymore that I was going to become a star or get rich. My highest goal was just to be able to make a living at it. I thought if I could pay my bills by wrestling, that would be one hell of a goal to attain.

For my first pro match, at the end of 1977, Eddie Graham put a mask on me and called me the Super Destroyer.

Looking back, I see he had developed some respect for me and thought I might be something someday, so he kept me covered up. That way, if I wasn't any good, nobody would know it was me.

Eddie Graham had surprised me when he said I'd finally get a chance to wrestle, so I didn't have any wrestling boots. But Jack Brisco, who had been watching me get my brains beat in for the last year, had gone out and bought me a pair of new white boots. Of course, I had to dye them black because I was supposed to be a bad guy, but I'll never forget that Jack Brisco bought me my first pair of boots.

That first pro match was against an accomplished amateur wrestler named Brian Blair. Eddie Graham didn't think I could beat this guy, so he decided the match was going to be a twenty-minute Broadway. That meant it was supposed to end in a draw.

He told Brian Blair that. All the other wrestlers knew it too. But no one had told *me*. What they told me was I had twenty minutes to go out there and try to beat Brian Blair any way I could.

So that's what I did.

All the other wrestlers gathered outside their dressing room doors for this little preliminary match like it was the biggest wrestling match in the world, which puzzled me at the time. Now I see that they were having a laugh at my expense.

Anyway, I tried like hell to pin Brian Blair and he tried like hell to stop me. By the time the match was over, we had

My First Detour

beaten the crap out of each other. I hadn't pinned him, but I had come closer than some people thought I would.

I'm sure it was quite humorous for the wrestlers who were watching. But I had accomplished something. I had shown the promoter Eddie Graham that I could handle myself in the ring.

I figured that was a good start and I would be appearing on the card on a regular basis. But now that I'd gotten into the wrestling business, they wouldn't book me. They would give me just one night a week, Monday at the Sportatorium, and I'd get paid just twenty-five dollars.

I kept asking, "Why won't you guys let me wrestle?" There was no reason for it—at least none that I could see.

Now I understand the reason. Mike Graham, the promoter's son, had gotten into the wrestling business a few years before me. He was a star already. And in high school, we hadn't been the best of friends. So it was that old high-school rivalry that kept me from wrestling more for Mike's father, Eddie Graham.

Of course, Mike and I are great friends now. But at the time, he didn't want to give me a chance to outshine him.

Charlie Lay kept on encouraging me. He kept saying, "Hang in there, kid." But after four months, I had only wrestled ten matches—even *less* than one a week.

And when I did wrestle, I didn't like it. I would be out there fighting for twenty or thirty minutes in the opening match, punching, kicking, punching, kicking. It wasn't like the exciting wrestling that I had witnessed with the main-event guys who knew what they were doing.

Hollywood Hulk Hogan

In the end, I couldn't make a living at it. Twenty-five dollars a week didn't pay for much, and I couldn't see a time when I'd be making any more than that. Finally, I did the one thing I never thought I would do, the one thing no one on the Tampa wrestling scene expected of me.

I *quit*.

I told Eddie Graham I didn't want to wrestle anymore and I sat down in my hotel room and tried to figure out what I was going to do with the rest of my life. That's when I remembered a guy named Whitey Bridges.

Whitey was a big, blond-haired bodybuilder about forty years old and he owned a bar called the Anchor Club in Cocoa Beach. I'd played there several times with rock-and-roll bands and Whitey and I had become pretty good friends. One time, he said, "Terry, if you ever need a job, give me a call."

So I called him from my hotel room. Before I knew it, I was in Cocoa Beach running Whitey's club for him, doing everything from managing the staff to serving drinks to taking money at the door. It worked out just fine as far as I was concerned.

Then after a while, I said to Whitey, "Listen, brother, we're both into working out. We should open a gym together." He thought it was a good idea and we opened a place called Whitey's and Terry's Olympic Gym in Cape Canaveral.

So now I was running the club and the gym at the same time and I had my hands full. I needed a little help and I had a friend from back in Tampa named Ed Leslie, whose sister graduated from Robinson High School with me.

51

Ed was a couple of years behind us. After I got out of high school he was always tagging along and we would try to ditch him because he was younger than we were. We would always tell him we were going to the beach at ten o'clock in the morning and we'd leave at eight instead.

But eventually I became good friends with Ed Leslie and when I said, "Hey man, I need somebody to help me run the bar and run the gym," he was right on it. The very next day he quit his job and threw everything he owned into his Camaro and drove to Cocoa Beach without a second thought.

We worked together in Cocoa Beach for about a year and we never wanted to leave that place. It was rock and roll and weight lifting and going to the beach and girls and partying and raising hell. I told Ed Leslie that we would never see another year like that as long as we lived.

But in the back of my mind, I knew we should have something to fall back on, so I told Ed I would teach him how to wrestle. Then we could go back to Tampa and wrestle if things didn't work out for some reason.

We didn't have a ring in the gym, but I could still show him wrestling holds and how to move. So Ed and I spent that whole year messing around, never thinking we would ever really have to leave Cocoa Beach.

Then out of nowhere, things started to go sour. Whitey had a girlfriend and he married her, and as soon as they got married she started to resent the idea of Whitey's hanging out with us. "Why are those guys your pals?" she asked him. "They're half your age." Then she took a look at the gym and saw that it wasn't making any money.

The *reason* it wasn't making any money was that we were too hardheaded to let girls train there. No women, period. Whitey's and Terry's was a hard-core, bodybuilding, deadlifting, sweat-your-ass-off-type gym, and we were of the mind that if you let girls into a place you can't cuss and sweat and drop a weight on the floor.

Of course, that was before the era when every strip mall had a Bally's Health Spa or European Health Spa. If we had seen those kinds of gyms, we might have changed our minds and still been in business.

With his wife talking in his ear all the time, Whitey finally gave in. He told me he was going to close Whitey's and Terry's and get out of the gym business. Oh and by the way, he was going to sell the Anchor Club too.

So all of a sudden, Ed Leslie and I were out of work. But looking back, I thank God that it happened that way . . . because if Whitey hadn't closed the Anchor Club and the gym, I might never have gone back to wrestling.

My First Detour

Hulk Hogan

7 Wrestlers speak a different language, a kind of carny talk that lets them communicate without tipping anybody else to what they're saying.

Like if I wanted to tell you that you have an ugly face but I didn't want anybody else to know, I'd say, "Yizou hizave an ugizly fizace." Or if I wanted to say, "That girl over there, she's got big boobs," I'd say, "Thizat gizirl, she's got some bizig bizoobs."

It comes in handy when we wrestle. Instead of going "Duck!" and giving away what we're doing, I'll yell "Dizuck!"

Or I might be standing in the middle of the ring, pointing at you and saying, "How are your wife and kids? I can't wait to see them." But I'll be yelling and sounding angry and speaking carny talk, so it sounds like I'm going to kick your ass.

The other word we use a lot is "Kayfabe."

If I'm telling you about the affair your wife is having and your wife walks up, I'll say, "Kayfabe, here comes your wife." Or if my opponent and I are talking about a match we're going to have and someone outside the wrestling business walks by, I'll say "Kayfabe" and we'll switch to another topic.

It means shut up, talk about something else, close ranks.

In the old days, we used to be a lot more secretive about wrestling. It was always "Kayfabe this" or "Kayfabe that." In fact, a book like this would never have come out in those days.

But even now, there's still plenty of kayfabing going on.

Pensacola, Alabama, Atlanta, and Tennessee

8

When Whitey closed down the gym and the Anchor Club and left Ed Leslie and me out of work, I called a wrestler who I had become friends with—"Superstar" Billy Graham.

I said, "Hey man, I've been training for a year and now I think I'm bigger than you are." By then my arms were twenty-four inches around. They were *huge*.

Billy Graham didn't believe me. He said he had the largest arms in the world.

But I said, "No, I think I'm bigger than you."

"Well," he said, "if you're that big, I'm going to make a phone call." And he called a guy named Louie Tillet in Pensacola, Florida.

In those days, the whole country was divided up into very distinct, very closely guarded territories. The World Wide Wrestling Federation, which was run by Vince McMahon Sr., stretched from Maine to Maryland. The Crockett promotion had the Carolinas. Jerry Lawler and Jerry Jarrett had Tennessee. Georgia was a territory, Florida was a territory, Kansas City was a territory, and San Francisco and Los Angeles each represented a territory. Texas was actually a few territories. And one of the biggest ones was the American Wrestling Association—AWA—which a guy named Verne Gagne ran out of Minneapolis.

Louie Tillet ran the Pensacola-Alabama territory, which included Pensacola and Panama City in northern Florida and Dothan, New Brunswick, and Mobile in Alabama. With the help of my buddy "Superstar" Billy Graham, I got Ed Leslie and myself booked on that circuit.

Louie Tillet was an interesting character. He had these dentures that he would take out after we ate at McDonald's so he could suck the cheese out of his teeth.

In the Pensacola-Alabama territory, I wasn't the Super Destroyer anymore. I was slated to wrestle as a good guy named Terry Boulder, which was a play on my real name. And Ed Leslie was going to wrestle as my "brother," Ed Boulder.

The first place we went was Panama City. We were there on a Thursday night, all excited to be doing this. But I didn't have much experience and Ed Leslie had even less, so I didn't know there were separate dressing rooms for good guys and bad guys.

I just walked into the first dressing room I saw—and it turned out to be the bad guys' dressing room. This guy named David Shultz, who wrestled as Dr. D., saw me in there and yelled, "Who the hell are you? What are you doing here? Kayfabe, get that mark the fuck out of here!"

He wanted to beat my ass. And there were a bunch of other wrestlers there, Roy Wayne Ferris—the Honky Tonk Man—and some others, who could have backed him up. But I was so big, they didn't really jump.

So I just walked across the arena floor to the good guys' dressing room and met all the guys I was *supposed* to be with. But that was my introduction to Dr. D.

Pretty soon, we would raise some hell together and become good friends, and we would stay that way for a long time. And after that, he would end up hating my guts and calling me a steroid abuser. But at the time, all I knew about him was that he had given me a hard time for walking into the wrong dressing room.

There were all kinds of wacko wrestlers on the Pensacola-Alabama circuit. One of them was a guy named Don Fargo, who had a reputation as a real wild man. His gimmick was that he was a Hell's Angel. He had the tattoos and everything.

But Don Fargo *wasn't* a Hell's Angel. He was just saying that. Unfortunately for him, the real Hell's Angels resented his claiming he was one of them. First chance they got, they beat him within an inch of his life.

Needless to say, Don Fargo changed his gimmick in a hurry.

At the time, piercings weren't in style the way they are today. But the girls who liked to follow the wrestlers around after the matches—the wrestling groupies—said that Don Fargo had piercings in unusual places.

When he got a girl in his room, he would strip naked and show his piercings. Just to freak the girl out.

The guy acted like a total nutcase.

Two other wrestlers I met my first week working the Pensacola-Alabama territory were exactly the opposite of Don Fargo. Their names were Afa and Sika and they wrestled as the Wild Samoans.

I was in Dothan, Alabama at my first TV taping and these two guys walked in, both of them over three hundred pounds with their hair sticking up ten feet high in the air. They scared me. I had never seen anything like them.

But right away, Louie Tillet ran over and hugged them like they were his brothers. Scary as they looked, Afa and Sika turned out to be the nicest guys around. And even though they really were Samoan, they spoke perfect English.

I got to be real good friends with them because Ed Leslie and I would sleep in my van on the beach at Pensacola, and the Samoans slept in a van there too. We were all sleeping on the beach because we didn't have the money to pay for a hotel room.

We would get up every morning and use the public showers to shower and shave, and hang out on the beach until three or four o'clock. Then we would drive to New

Hollywood Hulk Hogan

Brunswick or Mobile or Montgomery or wherever we were wrestling that night. It was a small territory, just a couple of hundred miles each way, so it didn't take more than a few hours to get to the venue.

The only place on the Pensacola-Alabama circuit that weirded me out a little bit was Dothan, Alabama. We would wrestle there on Friday nights at the Farm Center, then stay over at the hotel because Saturday morning we'd tape some TV to promote the next week's round of events.

The first night I wrestled there, the wrestlers got some beer after we left the Farm Center and went back to the hotel to relax. Or so I thought. When I got to the hotel, the parking lot was packed.

I didn't get it. When I was there earlier in the day, the lot was almost empty. All of a sudden it was worth your life to get a spot. Then I went inside the hotel, which had a swimming pool right in the center of it, and I finally saw why there were so many people there.

One of the Fuller brothers, the guys who owned the territory, was on the diving board wearing the Southern Heavyweight title belt—and nothing else. Outside of that belt wrapped around his middle, he was stark naked.

There was a huge crowd around the pool, cheering and raising hell. It looked to me like the whole town was there. As I would find out later, it wasn't the whole town—just everybody who had been at the Farm Center watching us wrestle, from the people in the front row to the guys in the nosebleed section.

Before I knew it, this crazy son of a bitch on the diving

board took a dive into the pool, belt and all. That's when I realized he wasn't the only one without any clothes on. As soon as he hit the water, everyone else in the pool—girls and guys—came climbing out, and they were naked too.

I just walked away shaking my head, saying to myself, "This is insane."

Even back then, I knew it wasn't right to run around naked like that with families and kids around who had followed us from the arena back to the hotel. It was like a circus was in town. It was mind-boggling.

But even if Terry Boulder wasn't comfortable at times in Dothan, Dothan was real comfortable with Terry Boulder. In fact, the reaction of everyone in the Pensacola-Alabama territory was very positive.

The wrestling audience was used to the big two-hundred-fifty to four-hundred-pound guys with big beer bellies and hair all over their bodies who didn't work out with weights the way I did. So to the wrestling world, I was Charles Atlas and Hercules rolled into one. And the fans were told that I came from Venice Beach, California, which made me a god to the people in Dothan and Mobile. It made them think I was something I wasn't.

But that didn't mean it was always easy for me. In fact, I can remember one night when the fans almost cost me my life.

I was in Dothan and Louie Tillet told me, "When you get into the ring, tell the fans you're going to give them five hundred dollars if you lose."

I knew I was going to lose because we had already decided that. "Okay," I said, "fine. Where's the money?"

"Oh," he told me, "you don't need any money."

I said, "Are you kidding me?"

Louie Tillet said, "Trust me, man, you don't need the money."

I lost the match one-two-three. Boom! All of a sudden, the ring was overrun by these Dothan, Alabama rednecks. The first twenty rows just swarmed me because they thought I was gonna throw five hundred dollars away.

So there I was all by myself with a full-fledged riot in gear, and these rednecks were kicking me into the ropes because they didn't want me to get away. I was lucky to escape with my life.

Later on, while I was still wrestling for Louie Tillet, I showed up at a morning talk show in Mobile, Alabama to promote a wrestling event. The other guest was a guy named Lou Ferrigno, who was starring with Bill Bixby on a TV show called *The Incredible Hulk*.

Ferrigno was traveling around the country to plug his series, which wasn't doing so well in the ratings. So in between shooting schedules, they kept him on the road, working all the local markets.

When I got on the show, the host looked at Ferrigno and he looked at me and he said, "Oh my God, you're bigger than Lou Ferrigno! You're bigger than the Hulk!"

And I said, "That's because I'm the *real* Hulk."

Now, I had the gift of gab and Lou had a bit of a speech impediment at the time as a result of a hearing loss, and I didn't want to run him down. But I did have the upper hand and I ran with it a little.

Pensacola, Alabama . . .

It was good to have Jerry Lawler in my corner.

Plus the host did my job for me. "Gosh," he said, "your arms are so much bigger than his. It looks like if you arm-wrestled him you'd break his arm."

Actually, Lou Ferrigno was an unbelievable specimen, a real dedicated bodybuilder, and his arms were in much better shape than mine. But I had more bulk on me and my clothes were probably tighter so I looked larger.

That night when I got to the arena and went back to the locker room, all the boys started calling me Hulk. They said they saw me on television and I was bigger than Lou Ferrigno, and the name just stuck.

I wasn't exclusive to Louie Tillet, so I wrestled for a couple of other outfits in between runs in the Pensacola-Alabama territory. One of them was the partnership of Jerry Lawler and Jerry Jarrett, which operated out of Memphis, Tennessee.

Jerry Lawler was like a god in Memphis. At times, he was as popular as Elvis. He even ran for mayor there for a joke. He didn't lift a finger to promote his campaign and he came in third in a fifteen-candidate race.

It was in Tennessee that I became known as Terry "The Hulk" Boulder and won my first heavyweight championship belt. I wasn't "Hulk Hogan" quite yet, but I was getting there.

It was also in Tennessee that I started using a boot in the face and a legdrop as a finish. Nobody else was using the legdrop at the time, so it set me apart a little from the other guys. It also protected my left knee, which had been a nagging problem for me ever since junior high school and would get a lot worse as time went on.

One night in Memphis, I saw Jerry Lawler put a piledriver on a comedian named Andy Kaufman, who had gotten involved in wrestling. Then Lawler and Andy Kaufman showed up on the David Letterman show. Lawler slapped Kaufman and Kaufman threw coffee in Lawler's face, and all of a sudden Andy Kaufman began showing up on wrestling cards on a constant basis.

I didn't understand why they let a guy like Andy Kaufman get into the ring to wrestle, especially after I had worked so hard to pay my dues. But I was young and green in those days. I thought wrestling was about having a good match, getting a six pack of beer and picking up a girl. It didn't occur to me that we were trying to draw money.

I remember a time in the old Chicago Amphitheater, when I was working for Jerry Lawler and Jerry Jarrett, when I happened to walk in on a meeting in the dressing room. Lawler was there, Jarrett was there, and Andy Kaufman was there. It was like walking into a Pentagon meeting. I knew I needed to back right out because I wasn't welcome.

Later on, I passed Andy Kaufman in the hallway. I didn't know him but I didn't think it would hurt to be friendly, so I said hello to him.

His eyes opened real wide and he looked at me like he was scared to death, like he thought I was going to kill him on the spot. He was out of his element, I guess, and he didn't know what to expect.

I never really liked his act. That poo-poo pee-pee stuff he dialed up, the weird alien mouse voice . . . it was out there. It never did anything for me. If you ask me, it was just boring.

There was also a short period of time in 1978 when I worked for a promoter named Jim Barnett, who worked out of Atlanta for the National Wrestling Alliance, the biggest wrestling organization in the world at the time. Jim Barnett was openly and flamboyantly gay. He took one look at me with my tan and my muscles and my long blond hair and said, "Oh my God, I'm going to call you Sterling, my boy. Sterling Golden."

So when I wrestled for Jim Barnett, I was Sterling Golden. When I wrestled for Lawler and Jarrett, I was Terry "The Hulk" Boulder. But no matter what name I used, one thing stayed the same—I wasn't making very much money.

I was wrestling seven days a week, which translated into ten or eleven matches—two on Wednesday, two on Saturday, and two on Sunday—and the biggest check I ever got for a whole week was one hundred twenty-five dollars. That got tired in a hurry, brother.

After every one of my little runs, I had gone home to Tampa to wait for one of the promoters to call me. Finally, one time, I went home and stayed home. As far as I was concerned, I was done with professional wrestling.

The Docks

9

When I came back to Tampa in 1979, I headed for the one place I knew I could make money—the docks of Port Tampa.

A few years earlier, when I was training with Hiro Matsuda and selling off my musical equipment to try to make ends meet, I had a friend named Anthony Barcello, who had been the lead singer in some of the rock-and-roll bands I'd played with. Anthony had a wife and child to support, so if his band wasn't working for a week he would go down to the laborers' union and earn some money that way.

Anthony told me his father had strong ties with the union, so he could get me in if I wanted. I didn't have any brighter prospects at the time so I said, "Hell, yes."

So Anthony Barcello got me into the laborers' union. And the way that worked is I would go to the union hall and they would have a bunch of metal folding chairs, about fifty of them, and everyone would sit down on those chairs and wait for their number to be called.

Then they would say, "Here's a job, one day's work pouring cement at the mall." And you'd work at the mall that day, then you'd come back and sit in the union hall again. But maybe the next time your number was called they would say, "Okay, Terry Bollea, six months' work at a government cleanup of a phosphate factory." Boy, you'd be happy to get *that* job because it meant steady work.

So I did the laborer thing for about six months, splitting my time between that and getting beaten up by Hiro Matsuda. Then one day they needed guys to go down and work on the 22nd Street causeway in Port Tampa. It turned out the job was loading and unloading ships—toting meat, fruit, and vegetables, and once in a while they would have cars come off. I never got to unload the cars. I just basically hauled produce and stuff.

The job only lasted a week. But after that I came nosing around the docks again, and the steward of the longshoremen's union spotted me and saw how big I was. So he said, "How'd you like to be a longshoreman? I'll start you at ten bucks an hour."

That was good money in those days. So my first day I

helped unload a ship for twelve or fourteen hours, and all of a sudden I was a longshoreman. They got me into the union and everything.

Funny thing, I was the only white guy in that union. Every day I'd be hauling stuff alongside forty or fifty monster black guys. But the question of color never came up, not for me and not for them. I just figured I was in a hole with a bunch of guys sweating and cussing and talking trash, and that was okay because I felt right at home.

So I was unloading these ships and working as many hours as I could. They couldn't wear me down back then. I'd sit there and drink coffee all day long. I was so into making the money, if I could make a few hundred bucks every two days, I would stay there and work my ass off. Where most guys would want to quit after eight hours, I had a different work ethic. I was hungrier.

And with all the lifting that I was doing, my arms were getting bigger and bigger. But as much money as I was making, after about six months I figured something out—that the stevedore, the guy up on the deck of the ship supervising the loading, was making even more.

I started asking a bunch of questions—you know, just doing my homework. I found out that when ships leave the Port of Tampa for Singapore, Bangkok, Hong Kong, and Tokyo, and there's fifty million billion pounds of meat on them, you have to load the ship correctly and unload it correctly—because if you don't, you'll sink the ship.

Once I was confident that I knew what I was doing, I talked my way into the stevedores' union. As a stevedore, I

The Docks

directed the loading and unloading of these big, ocean-going ships. I checked boxes and stamped them so everyone knew where they were going.

And I was really excited to be doing this, because I was making six or seven hundred dollars a week, which was huge at the time. I figured I'd do this for a long time because I still hadn't been given a professional wrestling match.

Then came my little professional run with Eddie Graham, my time in Cocoa Beach with Whitey Bridges and Ed Leslie, and my short-lived career as Terry Boulder and Sterling Golden. But all along, whenever I had some time on my hands, I would head back to the docks. So with my wrestling career behind me—or so I thought—I returned to the docks one more time.

And I got real comfortable down there working the ships. It was a predictable existence, unlike the wrestling business. There wasn't an uncertainty factor. I did my work and I got paid. I got out of it exactly what I put in.

Then all of a sudden, I got a call from my old friend Terry Funk.

Terry was a big name in the wrestling business, a second-generation wrestler who had already been a National Wrestling Alliance World Champion. When I was a mark, before I got into the business, I used to chase him around and ask questions all the time.

Most of the wrestlers were mean to me in those days. They would try to scare me off. But Terry Funk was always nice to me.

So this one day, he came down to the docks where I was working and said, "What the hell's wrong with you?"

"What do you mean?" I asked him.

"You could be the biggest star in the wrestling business."

I said, "What are you, crazy? I'm not interested in wrestling anymore. I tried it two or three times now and I can't make any money at it. I don't jump off the top rope, I don't dropkick, and I'm not the most athletic guy in the world. I may look great, I may have a physical presence, but I'm not this technical wrestler from the Olympics."

On top of that, I told him, I didn't like the wrestling lifestyle. "I don't like all the drinking, the hell-raising, the atmosphere. I just want to stay home."

Terry Funk said, "Well, there's this guy in New York, this promoter, who heard about you when you were in the Pensacola-Alabama territory and when you were in Memphis. He heard that wherever you would wrestle the arenas would be sold out, and that the crowd really responded to you. And he wants to see you."

Then Terry Funk told me that this guy in New York was a good friend of his father, who was also a promoter, and that this guy literally ran Madison Square Garden.

"And his name," he said, "is Vince McMahon."

Not the Vince McMahon who runs World Wrestling Entertainment today. This was Vince's father, Vince McMahon Sr.

I didn't know the name and I told Terry Funk I still wasn't interested. And I figured that was the end of it.

But the next day, Terry called me at home and asked me

to come down to the Florida Wrestling Office. I didn't want to go, but I couldn't say no to him. When I got there, it wasn't just Terry Funk waiting for me. Jack and Gerry Brisco were there too, and so was Eddie Graham and his son Mike.

They all sat in this room and talked to me. All along, I had thought that these wrestlers really didn't like me. They said that wasn't true. They were just testing me to see if I could stick it out, if I could make it.

I was almost there, they said. But just as I was about to turn the corner, I had caved in. I had given up. They gave me all this confidence that I could be a big star in the world of wrestling if I came back, if I just stayed with it and kept working hard.

And they said I needed to talk with Vince McMahon.

I still wasn't completely convinced, but they got me to say I'd talk to him. So they called Vince McMahon Sr. and put him on the speakerphone.

Vince said, "I want you to come up north next week."

I was a real horse's ass. I said, "I'll come up but I'm not bringing my wrestling stuff. I'll come up and talk to you but I don't want to wrestle."

Looking back, it didn't make any sense for me to say that. Hell, I was making the trip anyway. But those were the conditions I made and Vince McMahon Sr. accepted them.

So I flew up north. But as it turned out, they didn't bring me to New York. They brought me to Allentown, Pennsylvania.

And for the first time, I came face-to-face with the McMahons.

New York: "You won't regret it."

10

The reason I went to Allentown is that the McMahon promotion used to tape its TV shows up there. When I arrived, Vince McMahon Sr. had his son Vince Jr. and all the wrestlers and their managers in one dressing room, and they were talking about what they were going to do in front of the cameras.

I remember Vince Sr. had these little teeny glasses, bifocals that he would slide down onto the end of his nose, and he would look over the top of them at you. Another thing I remember is he always had four quarters in his hand

that he would click together. And if he wanted to, he could just stare a hole through you.

After I got to know him, I realized he was one of the best guys in the world. If you ever had a problem, you could go to him. And he was the first person I'd ever met who would always make good on his promises. If he told you something it would happen, every single time.

But that time in Allentown, I didn't know him very well. All I knew was that he was holding court in the dressing room and everybody was paying close attention to him.

I was really big at the time and I had a tie-dye shirt on. Because I wasn't really part of the wrestlers' discussion, I peeked my head out of the curtain of the dressing room to get a look at the crowd.

I must have opened the curtain too far because all of a sudden the whole arena went nuts. "Oh my God," they were saying, "there's 'Superstar' Billy Graham!"

Billy Graham was known for having long hair and big arms and a tie-dye shirt and he had just finished a big run in New York as the champion. And with my hair and my arms, I must have looked a lot like him.

The fans just loved Billy Graham. They loved his style. But for some reason he didn't get along very well with the promoters. I guess Vince Sr. wasn't too happy with him at the time, because as soon as the people started screaming, "Superstar, Superstar," Vince Sr. looked at me and said, "Take that tie-dye crap off." He didn't want me to be associated with Billy Graham.

Later on, Vince Sr. took me aside and talked to me one

on one. I told him I really wasn't into wrestling anymore. I told him I got homesick and I didn't like being on the road all the time. I just didn't like the lifestyle.

But Vince McMahon said, "If you'll come up here and give this a try, I guarantee you won't regret it."

I still wasn't sure about the whole thing. I had never been to New York before. I didn't know what it would be like. But Vince had an answer for that.

He had a guy named Tony Altamore, a guy who used to tag team with Lou Albano as the Sicilians. Vince Sr. said he would give this guy the job of riding around with me and being my baby-sitter.

Actually, making Tony Altamore my baby-sitter was probably the worst mistake Vince Sr. ever made. Tony was in his fifties, so he was certainly old enough to be the voice of reason. But most of the time he was like a devil on my shoulder, egging me on to drink another beer or to stay up late raising hell, or to show up at the wrestling venue at the last possible minute.

Also, even though Tony Altamore had a wife at home, he knew the girls who would come to the arenas when we were on the road. So when we pulled into a new town, he already knew all the girls' names and faces and how many times they'd been to the wrestling matches and where they went afterward and which girl had been with which wrestler.

He knew all that stuff. And hell, I was single at the time. So Tony Altamore would turn out to be great company for me on the road, but not in the way Vince meant him to be.

Anyway, it wasn't just Tony Altamore that Vince

McMahon was offering me. He said he would find me a place in West Haven, Connecticut, not far from where he lived. Vince was making it real easy for me. All I had to do was go home and get my stuff.

I guess he saw some potential in me. I mean, I looked different from other wrestlers. If they were blond they weren't as tall as I was. If they were as tall they weren't built like I was, or if they were built like I was they didn't have the type of arms I did.

Plus I was a fan of Muhammad Ali, so I used to talk like he did. Having played with rock and roll bands I had perfected this rap, this knack for talking to the crowd in between songs. I knew how to keep things going and I wasn't afraid to step out front and say something, whereas most guys would hem and haw about it.

The other promoters I'd worked for—some of whom were wrestlers themselves—might have seen that package, but they didn't have the vision to see where I could take it. They saw me as a guy they could bring in for six months, a guy they would make a star so they could beat me and make themselves even bigger stars.

But Vince McMahon didn't wrestle, so I think he looked at me in a different light. He saw me as a guy who could carry the load of being a star in his organization for the long haul, and that's what he was betting on when he hired me.

Of course, I didn't know any of that at the time. I just figured I was moving to a bigger stage, not that it was a long-term engagement.

The Wild Samoans

Anyway, I flew back to Tampa, packed up my car, and headed for New York. But before I left Florida, I picked up the Wild Samoans, Afa and Sika. They were going to wrestle for Vince McMahon, too.

The Samoans were close friends of mine because of all the time we had spent together in Florida and Alabama, so we had a good time on the trip north. Then we got to a point on the road in New Jersey where the signs were kind of confusing, especially for somebody who had never been up that way before.

I pulled my car over to figure it out. And when I did that, a New Jersey state trooper came by and saw me with my car all full of boxes and stuff. It must have looked suspicious or something because he pulled onto the shoulder behind me and asked me for my driver's license.

I had a Florida license, of course, but my car had Tennessee tags because I had bought it when I was working for Jerry Lawler in Memphis. So the cop, getting even more suspicious, asked me for my registration.

I said, "Yes, sir," and ran around to the other side of the car to get my registration, which was in the glove box. But when I opened the glove box, I had a gun in it and the cop freaked out.

He pulled his weapon and yelled, "Get on the ground!"

So me and the two Samoans had to get facedown in the snow. I was wearing a tee shirt and no jacket, it was freezing cold out, my hands were handcuffed behind me and I had to lie in the snow for what seemed like forever.

The funny thing is I had never fired a gun in my life. I had never owned one either. But when the wrestlers in Florida heard that I was going to New York, they told me I had to buy a gun to protect myself.

"It's not like here in Florida," they said. "In New York, the fans are crazy. If you're going to be a bad guy, the fans might try to kill you. If they catch you in the parking lot by yourself, you're going to need a gun to scare them with."

So I went out and bought this little .22-caliber peashooter and took it with me to New York. But I hadn't even taken it out of the Western Auto box. I'd just tucked it into my glove compartment and forgotten about it.

What I didn't know was that it was an automatic one-year sentence in New York or New Jersey if you were caught with an unregistered firearm. None of the Florida wrestlers ever mentioned that.

Gorilla Monsoon

I turned to Afa and Sika and said, "Help me out here, guys. Tell these state troopers that I just bought the gun and I didn't know a thing about this law they have here."

But in those days, we were very protective of the wrestling business and the Samoans weren't allowed to speak English. They were supposed to be headhunters, savages who pulled chickens apart with their bare hands and ate raw fish, not civilized people who could explain that they had made a mistake.

So when the cops looked at Afa and Sika, they wouldn't talk. I begged them but they wouldn't say a word. They were afraid they'd get in trouble with Vince.

So I went, "Damn."

Anyway, the cops took us all to this makeshift police

station on the side of the road and handcuffed me to a pipe outside. And again, I was standing in the snow and freezing my ass off.

Finally, a couple of hours later, they hauled me into the station and let me make my one phone call and I called Vince McMahon Sr. When I told him what happened, he said, "Jesus Christ!" and called Gorilla Monsoon, a four-hundred-pound headliner who was a partner in the promotion and lived in that part of New Jersey.

Meanwhile, the cops threw me into a cell and locked me up. And the two Samoans sat outside all night like a couple of little puppy dogs, waiting for Gorilla Monsoon to call in some favors.

Finally, the cops got a call and the next thing I knew, I was free on my own recognizance. All I had to do was come back there once a month for six months to meet with a probation officer. Apparently, Gorilla Monsoon had come through for me.

So I was probably the only person during all of 1979 who got caught with an unregistered gun in the state of New Jersey and avoided that mandatory jail sentence.

Anyway, I finally got out of New Jersey and joined the World Wide Wrestling Federation. But during my first meeting with Vince McMahon Sr., he mentioned that he had an idea. He was going to change my wrestling name from Terry "The Hulk" Boulder to Hulk Hogan.

Why? Because they had Bruno Sammartino for the Italian-Americans, Chief Jay Strongbow for the Native Americans, Ivan Putski for the Polish-Americans, and Pedro

Morales for the Puerto Rican–Americans, but they didn't have anyone to represent the Irish-Americans.

So I was going to be the great Irish hope. The funny thing is I didn't have a single drop of Irish blood in me, my dad being Italian and my mother being part French, part Italian, and part Panamanian.

Anyway, Vince Sr. gave me two bottles of red dye and told me to dye my hair red. And when I was done, I was supposed to look Irish.

Freddie Blassie, a wrestling manager and a close friend of Vince McMahon, went back to my hotel room with me to supervise the dye job. Now, Vince had told me this was the same stuff his wife used on her hair and it wouldn't have any bad effects. But the more I thought about it, the more afraid I was that it would make my hair fall out.

Finally, I told Fred, "I'm going bald-headed the way it is. If I put this on my hair it's all over. I'll be a pumpkin with a big bald spot on my head." So I poured the dye Vince had given me down the toilet.

Fred just freaked out. He said, "Oh my God, you're dead, you're fired, you're never going to work here."

But when I went to tell Vince Sr. about it, he didn't react nearly as negatively as Freddie Blassie thought he would. He said, "Okay, we'll go with it the way it is and see how it works."

And that was the end of the red-hair experiment. But it was the beginning of Hulk Hogan.

Life in World Wide Wrestling

Vince McMahon Sr. brought me into his promotion as a heel, a bad guy. In Allentown, Pennsylvania, that never had a negative effect on me.

It didn't matter to the people there if you were a good guy like Bob Backlund or Bruno Sammartino, or a bad guy like Ken Patera the Olympic Strongman or Ivan Koloff the Russian Bear. If you were a star, they would cheer for you, and they cheered the hell out of Hulk Hogan.

But in the arenas around that part of the country, the fans were more aware of the rivalries that were going on. So in Philadelphia, Pennsylvania, or Albany, New York, or Syracuse, New York, they would cheer the good guys and boo me.

And if that was all they did, it would have been okay. But on several occasions, they let their feelings about me carry over into the parking lot. I had a Lincoln Continental at the time, and the fans would see me park it when I arrived. By the time I came out at the end of the night, my antenna would be broken off, my windows would be cracked, and my tires would be slashed.

And there would be like five hundred wads of spit on the car. It looked like a bunch of kids had sat around for an hour just spitting on it.

The only time I didn't have to worry about my car was when I wrestled in Madison Square Garden. That was because I used to park it at the Ramada Inn on Forty-eighth and Eighth. I was too smart to try driving it into the Garden.

Of course, that meant I had to take a taxi to the Ramada to avoid the fans after I wrestled. But usually, that worked out all right. There was only one time it *didn't* work out, and that was when I came to the Garden to wrestle Gorilla Monsoon.

At the time, Vince McMahon Sr. had Freddie Blassie managing me and showing me how to stay strong in the ring. Before I would give in too much. I would let a little guy punch me up and I'd go down too easy.

But Fred told me, "Forget that stuff. If a guy hits you,

87

don't even move. And if a guy tries to pick you up, don't let him bodyslam you. Just beat people up and throw them around. And don't have any ten- or twelve-minute matches. Beat everybody in three or four minutes."

I was three twenty-five, three thirty in those days, but I looked like three eighty because my waist was narrow. They wanted me to wrestle like a big man, like Andre the Giant. What I didn't know is they were building me up to eventually face Andre in Shea Stadium.

Gorilla Monsoon was a big hero up in New York. He was a four-hundred-pound guy and he was the cream of the New York main-event wrestlers. But because I was on the rise, Vince McMahon had me beat Gorilla Monsoon in thirty-eight seconds.

It was a huge thing back then. The fans in the Garden, who were all Gorilla Monsoon's fans, went nuts. They weren't going to let me get away with it.

So when I left the Garden in my taxi, Gorilla Monsoon's fans got hold of the taxi and actually turned it over. The driver was scared out of his mind. He thought he was going to die. Even the cops who showed up on horseback were scared because they had never seen this before. It was definitely a panic situation.

Eventually, the horses got people to move and they got the taxi right side up again. But I was definitely the Number One Bad Guy in New York.

I was making a name for myself—and not just in the United States. Vince McMahon had a deal with New Japan Pro Wrestling, one of the top two wrestling organizations in Japan, where he would send talent over to them on a regular basis.

I didn't have a family at the time and I was starving for money, so if I had five days off I'd tell Vince to send me over to Japan. And there was nobody bigger in Japan than my manager, Freddie Blassie.

Fred was a legend in Japan. At one time, he had wrestled the big star over there, a guy named Rikidozan. Rikidozan was basically the father of Japanese pro wrestling, and he and Freddie Blassie had some of the biggest wrestling wars in history.

When Freddie Blassie wrestled Rikidozan on Japanese television, Fred had filed his teeth down before the match. And when he got Rikidozan in the corner, he made it look like he was biting him in the head. Then Rikidozan cut his head with a razor blade and Fred started sucking the blood out of the guy's head. And when he was done he backed up and spit the blood back in Rikidozan's face.

It made headline news in Japan because a bunch of elderly people who were watching the match at home that night had heart attacks and died. Nobody in Japan had ever done stuff like that. It made Freddie Blassie a big deal there for life.

So when he showed up with his new find, Hulk Hogan, it put me over with the Japanese fans even before I stepped into the ring. I was on my way to becoming a big star if I didn't screw up.

My first match in Japan was against a guy named Riki Choshu, who had represented Japan in the '72 Olympics. He was on his way to becoming a big star too.

"Classy" Freddie Blassie managed me in the late seventies.

So even though most matches have a winner and a loser, this one was going to be an exception. The promoters wanted us to do a twenty-minute Broadway, which meant we would wrestle for twenty minutes and the match would end up a draw.

Freddie Blassie, who knew Japanese wrestling as well as anyone, said, "Screw that. Kick his ass."

"But," I said, "this guy's an Olympic wrestler."

Fred said, "I don't give a damn. Go out there and beat him up."

So I said, "Okay, I'll try. Should I take my thumb and stick it in his eye socket? Should I go out there and punch him in the mouth and break his nose?" Because Matsuda had taught me how to do all those things.

Freddie Blassie said, "Doesn't matter to me. Just beat the living crap out of him."

So I went out there in the ring with Riki Choshu, and as soon as we locked up I pushed him against the ropes and hit him as hard as I could with my forearm. That was about it. He never recovered from it.

Anyway, I beat the guy up for two or three minutes and won the match. It made unbelievable news in Japan because the sky was supposed to be the limit for this guy, and I had taken him out one-two-three. So that really set me up. In fact, Fred and I didn't pay for food in Japan for the next two years.

There was another reason I was becoming so popular in Japan. The guy known as the Japanese Elvis had bleached his hair blond. I had blond hair too, and I had played music for almost ten years back in the States. So the Japanese people said, "Our Elvis has returned. He used to play music and he's got blond hair, and now he wrestles."

The whole thing was pretty damn weird.

The fans there started calling me "Ichiban," which means Number One. I wore black tights and silver boots there, and the Ichiban symbol on my tights was silver too. And when I came out to the ring I wore a big black Japanese kimono with a silver Ichiban sign on the back. It worked great.

In Japan, wrestling was a different deal than it was here in the States. I had to wrestle aggressively, the way Matsuda had taught me. I had to watch out for guys who wanted to bite my ears or my fingers off.

And from what I could tell, the TV business over there wasn't run by clean-cut executives with Ivy League degrees. Rumor had it that it was run by the Yakuza, the Japanese Mafia. And I heard the same thing about all the wrestling companies.

Over here, we talk about the Mafia but we don't see it. In Japan, it's visible because a lot of the hotshots have the cut-off fingers and the body tattoos associated with that lifestyle.

I ended up going over to Japan a lot. Sometimes it would only be twelve weeks a year, sometimes it would be twenty-two. But I was traveling back and forth it seemed like every three weeks.

As often as I went, it took me a long time to adjust to the culture. I'd never been outside North America, so it was different from anything I had ever experienced. The food was different. The language was different. There were times over there when I'd get lonesome and depressed.

One of those times, I was getting ready to cut a record album with a hot Japanese band called Pink Cloud, and I needed some models for a music video. I called the Ford Modeling Agency over there, but I couldn't understand the receptionist. All she spoke was Japanese.

So I called the number two modeling agency, a place called Folio. The woman who answered the phone spoke perfect English and was really nice to me.

I said, "I'd like to see pictures of the girls."

"Come by the office," she said, "and I'll show them to you."

All the while I thought she was from England or something. But when I got there, I saw she was a beautiful Japanese girl. We became friends and I hung out with her for the next year or so, every time I came back to Japan.

She made life easy. After a while, I didn't want to go home. But of course, I did, because Vince McMahon wasn't going to let me stay there.

The
Deodorant
King

Hollywood

Hulk

Hogan

12

When I was wrestling in New York, I met a guy named Mike Sharpe, who was a second-generation wrestler . . . and the biggest hygiene freak I had ever met.

Mike Sharpe was usually a preliminary wrestler so he would often be in the first match of the evening. But there were times when he would get locked in the building after everybody went home because he was still in the shower, washing off.

Usually, a guy would put a Right Guard deodorant stick under his armpit and go one, two, three, four, five . . . done.

Mike Sharpe would carry on a twenty-minute conversation and swab his arm with the stick the whole time. He would use up the whole damn stick—and then he would start on the other armpit. In fact, if you looked in his bag, he had thirty or forty deodorant sticks sitting in there.

Then, after he was all done using the sticks, he would go back and take another shower. And he would do the same thing over and over again until they kicked him out of the building.

It went on every night. The guy was a total wacko for hygiene.

The Deodorant King

The Hollywood Giant

13

My biggest ambition was to be as big and powerful as Andre the Giant. Of course, there was no way that was ever going to happen. I was crazy to think I could eat and train and get that big.

Andre was billed as seven feet four and more than five hundred pounds. His hands were immense and his feet were size twenty-eights, the biggest feet I've ever seen. And I've got a huge head, but Andre's was about three times the size of mine.

He could be a great guy, but if you got on his bad side it wasn't too much fun. I know, because I was on his bad side for a number of years.

It was all my talk about how I was going to be his size that got me in trouble. I was just saying it because I admired him so much, but it got on his nerves. And where did he take it out on me? Wherever he could.

I remember one time Vince McMahon Sr. sent Andre and me to Louisiana to wrestle in the Superdome. Bill Watts, the promoter in Oklahoma and Louisiana, had wanted me to do a job for—in other words, lose to—his local champion, a guy named Wahoo McDaniels. But Vince McMahon Sr. had told me not to do any jobs because I was supposed to lose to Andre after I made myself look big by beating Wahoo McDaniels.

Well, Bill Watts wasn't happy that I wouldn't lose to his boy, so when Andre got to the Superdome Bill Watts pulled him aside and told him I wouldn't do jobs—not even for Andre, even though I was there for that very reason. Andre was so pissed off he damn near killed me. He messed up my shoulder, screwed my neck up, and suplexed me on my head.

But that wasn't the only time Andre beat me up. It used to happen on a regular basis. In fact, I used to get sick just thinking about wrestling him. On the way to the arena, I'd get so nervous I'd puke. And when we went to Japan and we would ride a bus to the arena, he would sit in back of me and bounce beer cans off my head.

But even then, I looked up to him, and not just because

he was half a foot taller than I was. I just liked the kind of person he was. He had a presence, a mystique about him. And eventually, things improved between us.

I think it was because he couldn't run me off. No matter how much he abused me, I would always sit in front of him on the bus. And when we stopped, instead of him getting off the bus to get noodle soup out of the vending machine, I'd run out and get him all the food he needed. I saw how hard it was for him to get around, big as he was, and I just wanted to help him as much as I could.

Also, a lot of guys who went to Japan would start bitching about their aches and pains after a week or two and haul their asses back to the States. Even when I got hurt real bad, I didn't complain about it or go home. I kept on wrestling.

Andre would go over there a lot because the money was good. And just about every time he went for a four-week tour, I'd be sitting on the bus waiting on him. After a while, he started saying, "Hey, boss, what are you doing here again?"

And I told him, "Just trying to keep up with you, old man."

But I think when he saw that I wasn't going to quit, I earned his respect. Thank God we got around that corner.

After that, Andre and I became really good friends. And the more I got to know him, the more I realized how hard life was for him.

People were real mean to him. I used to walk behind him through airports and hear the type of things people would say about him after he walked by. "What a freak of nature" or "What an ugly person" or "God, he walks like a cripple."

And Andre was never, ever comfortable. Even in a first-class plane seat, he would have to bend his head sideways because it was touching the air vents. Imagine if you had to sit in a three-year-old's tea set all day long. That's what it was like for him.

It was difficult for him to sleep because he was too big for even a king-sized bed. He'd be miserable in it.

Andre's life was hell twenty-four hours a day. But all things considered, he had a tremendous attitude. He knew people were making fun of him and gawking at him and staring at him but he didn't get angry or bitter about it.

The worst was when we had to fly to Japan because the flight would last fourteen hours. Andre used to worry about having time to go to the bathroom before we got on the plane because there was no way he could fit into the john on a plane.

In the hotel rooms, he couldn't get clean because he couldn't fit into the showers. If he needed me to scrub his back for him, I would do that. I just liked the guy so much and felt so bad for him.

One thing that always amazed me was how much food Andre could put away. He was French-Canadian—he had been born in France—so his favorite food was French food, and his favorite restaurant was a place in Beverly Hills where he knew the owners.

I hated French food, but I would sit there with Andre. And

he wouldn't eat just one or two dinners. He would eat every goddamn thing on the menu. Everything. I'm talking about every dish they served. So instead of eating for an hour like most people, we would sit in that restaurant eight or ten hours. That's how long he would take to finish his meal.

And that brother could drink. I remember one time on Andre's birthday, we were in Tokyo to wrestle. It was seven in the morning and I was the last one to get on the bus except Andre. As soon as I swung onto the bus, everyone said, "Hey, did you forget your best friend's birthday?"

I didn't know it was Andre's birthday. So I said, "You've got to be kidding," and I tried to think of what I could do about it. Fortunately, Andre wasn't on the bus yet, so I went running across downtown Tokyo to where a friend of mine had a bar. He lived upstairs so I banged on the door and made him get out of bed. Then I made him give me a case of Pouilly-Fuissé wine, twelve bottles of real strong French stuff.

I came running back to the bus and by that time, Andre was in his usual spot in the back. "Hey," he said, "where you been, boss?"

"I've been getting you a birthday present," I told him.

So I gave him twelve bottles of wine and we all sang happy birthday to him. He opened the first bottle of wine at 7:30 in the morning. At 10:00 in the morning, two and a half hours later, Andre kicked the back of my seat and said, "Piss stop."

I was his monkey. I'd tell the driver when to stop. So I turned around and said, "Don't tell me you drank that whole bottle of wine already."

"I didn't drink one bottle," he told me. "I drank all of them."

Twelve bottles in two and a half hours. And he wrestled that night like he'd been drinking nothing but water.

Another time, Andre came to Tampa and called me from the airport. "Hey boss," he said, "I'm here for about an hour."

I was at my mother's house, which is only about five minutes from the airport, so I raced there and sat down with Andre in the Crown Room at Delta. In fifty minutes I saw him drink a hundred and eight beers. A hundred and eight twelve-ounce beers, brother. It was just unbelievable.

As tough as his life was, Andre always found a way to laugh at it. He always had a hard time in Japanese hotels because the bathrooms are all molded out of one piece of plastic—tub, sink, toilet, the whole deal. I could barely fit inside, so you can imagine what it was like for a giant. And because it was such a tight squeeze, Andre sometimes had to use the bathtub as a toilet. So he got a little creative.

Some mornings when we were checking out of the hotel, he'd be laughing like crazy, and he'd say, "Hey boss, come to my room."

I'd say to myself, What now? What the hell did Andre do this time? Did he pull the curtains off and wipe his ass with them? It was hard to predict.

I remember one day in particular when he called me in my room and he was laughing like hell. "Come here, boss," he told me. So I went down the hall to Andre's room and I could hear his booming laugh all the way at the other end of the hallway.

The closer I got, the more clearly I could hear him laughing—and the more I could smell what he had done. Damn, I thought. Then I walked into his room and saw that he had taken the morning newspaper and spread it all over his bed. And since he couldn't fit on the toilet in that place and his ass was too big to hang over the tub, he just took a huge dump on the bed. It looked like a three-foot pile of horse manure.

And Andre was laughing like it was the funniest thing in the world. He thought it was just hilarious. That was Andre being playful.

Sometimes he was playful in a different way. He had a couple of little waitresses in Tokyo, these two teeny little Japanese girls that were probably four feet eight or four feet ten, and they were in love with him.

Andre would call me during different hours of the night when he'd have them in the room, and he would give me a play-by-play account of the action or make me listen to his girlfriends yelping like a couple of puppies. He used to think it was funny to wake me up at two o'clock in the morning and have me listen to these two little Japanese women screaming for their lives. Whatever Andre was doing with them, he was having a lot of fun, that's for sure.

He was just a different type of brother.

I'll never forget the time I faced him in Shea Stadium in front of a packed house, about 55,000 people. This was in August 1980. The biggest crowd I had wrestled for before that was 20,000 people in Dothan, Alabama. This was a big deal, brother, the match Vince McMahon Sr. had been building me up for.

The top match on the card that day was Bruno

The Giant

Sammartino, who had been the heavyweight champion in New York for many years before he lost the title, against his protégé Larry Zbyszko. The last time Vince McMahon Sr. had booked Shea Stadium, it was for Sammartino to wrestle Pedro Morales in 1972.

But to be honest with you, nobody cared about the Sammartino-Zbyszko matchup. The only confrontation the fans really cared about was Andre versus Hulk Hogan.

Going up against Andre was different from going up against anybody else. Most people will cover you or pin you, and as a businessman you go along with it. You stay with the plan. But you might think your opponent couldn't pin you in a real fight, or that you could kick out of his pin.

Not with Andre, brother. When he laid on top of you, there was no way you were getting up unless he wanted you to get up. That's just a fact of life.

I remember that day at Shea Stadium being really confusing. I'd never been there before and I was driving my own car, and I kept passing the exit and ending up at LaGuardia Airport.

By the time I finally found my way to Shea, there was such a crowd I didn't know where to park. Then I had to find the dugout and the dressing room. It was very difficult, very disorienting. I felt like I was on another planet.

The only time I felt comfortable that whole day was when I was in the ring with Andre. As soon as I got out there, I saw he was smiling at me. Of course, the fans thought he was smiling like the cat who was going to eat the canary. They thought he was going to kick my ass.

But when I saw Andre grinning at me like that, it calmed me down. It gave me comfort to know I was in the ring with someone who knew what he was doing, somebody who was in control. I knew I could trust Andre. If some fan was to jump into the ring and try to stab me, Andre would beat his ass. I can't say that for a lot of guys.

Anyway, Andre beat me in that match. But I came out looking pretty good too. We made it look like I busted him open and he was bleeding like a stuck pig. The fans saw that I had gotten Andre the Giant down and left him lying in a pool of blood, and that just opened up the floodgates to draw more money the next time.

Wrestling Andre that day was my first really big break in the wrestling business. Little did I know that our rivalry was just beginning. We would meet again someday—and with even *more* spectacular results.

At the time, however, it looked like my heel run with Vince McMahon Sr. was coming to a close. It was time for me to move on.

Wrestling was a very territorial business in those days. If you were a good guy, you could stay in one place for a long time. But if you were a heel, you would only stay for six or eight months and then go somewhere else. Maybe the Carolinas for six months, Georgia for six months, California, Portland . . . you moved around as a wrestler. That was the nature of the business.

I had already stayed in New York a lot longer than most heels would have. Of course, behind my back, Vince Sr. was making plans to send me down to some friends of his,

The Giant

the Crockett promotion in the Carolinas, where guys like Ric Flair and Rick Steamboat were wrestling. Then, after I'd been down there six or eight months, he was going to bring me back to New York.

But Vince hadn't told me any of that yet. And even if he had, I was so young and dumb back then I wouldn't have understood that he was trying to help me. So the stage was set for me to go down to work for the Crocketts for a while.

But I'd hardly returned to the United States from a trip to Japan when I got a letter from an unexpected source.

Stranger in a Strange Land

14 We were doing an Allentown TV and I was in the dressing room when I got a note handed to me by Arnold Skaaland, who was a backstage "road agent" for the company. The note said to call Sylvester Stallone.

Yeah, right, I thought. Sylvester Stallone wants to talk to *me*.

I showed it to the guys in the dressing room and they all had a good laugh. So I took the note and threw it away and figured that was the end of it.

Then I went to Japan again for four weeks. When I came back, it was time to do another TV in Allentown, so I was back in the same dressing room and this time Arnold Skaaland handed me a Western Union letter. It said Sylvester Stallone wants you to appear in his next *Rocky* movie.

I had seen *Rocky* and *Rocky II* and Stallone seemed like a god in those movies. I remember sitting there in the theater thinking it would be a dream come true if I could ever be in that type of movie. I'd sweep up behind the horses in a parade to get into one of those movies. And there I was standing in the dressing room with Stallone's letter in my hands.

So I called Sylvester Stallone and on my next day off I found myself on a plane heading for Los Angeles. Later on, I found out who was responsible for bringing me to Stallone's attention. It seems his casting director was a woman named Rhonda Young, whose brother was a huge wrestling fan named Peter Young.

When Rhonda found out Stallone was looking for a wrestler, she naturally went to her brother and asked him who's the biggest and best wrestler of all.

Peter said, "Well, there's this new guy named Hulk Hogan who picks two guys up at the same time and bear hugs them. In fact, I saw him bear hug three guys once. He rag dolls them and just throws them down."

So Stallone got hold of a couple of tapes of me wrestling in Madison Square Garden, grabbing two guys like a couple of rag dolls and throwing them on the ground. And when he saw that, he said, "That's the guy I want."

The end of that story is Peter Young eventually became

my agent and a lifelong friend. But at the time, he was just some fan from Boston who liked the way I wrestled. Lucky for me.

Anyway, as soon as I walked into the studio where I was supposed to meet Stallone, somebody put a big handheld camera in my face and said, "We're filming a documentary, you don't mind, do you?"

I said, "No, I don't mind." I didn't even know what a documentary was.

Then Stallone came over and said hello to me. Funny thing, in the American public's eyes Sylvester Stallone was seven hundred feet tall. In reality, he was only five feet eight and one hundred sixty pounds soaking wet.

Anyway, Stallone asked me to get into the ring with him and move around a little. So I took my shirt off and he pulled on a pair of boxing gloves, and we got into the ring they had set up there in the studio. All of a sudden, Stallone took a swing at me. Not knowing what he was after, I let him hit me.

He said, "No, try to *stop* me from hitting you."

"I don't mind getting hit," I told him, not having the slightest idea what he wanted. "You know, my nose was broken the other day and I haven't gotten it fixed yet. If you want, you can break it again."

Brother, I didn't care what he did. I just wanted to get the part.

"That's okay," he said. "Just try to stop me."

So as soon as he threw his fist at me I reached out and grabbed his left arm and arm-barred it and took him down.

He said, "Wow, you're pretty quick for a big guy."

"Well," I told him, "if we were in a real fight and you ever got close enough to hit me, it would be all over. I could just take you down and break your arm or do whatever I wanted with you. It's like you're playing tennis with someone who's standing on the other side of the net with a bazooka in his hands."

You could see in his expression that he was impressed so far. "Okay," he said, "now hit me on the back as hard as you'd hit another wrestler."

I said, "Nah, I don't think you want me to do that."

He said, "Come on, I'm a tough guy. I can take it."

I said, "You want me to hit you fifty percent?"

He said, "No, give me a hundred percent."

Finally, I only hit him about seventy-five percent, right between the shoulder blades. And as soon as my arm hit his back, his face hit my cowboy boots. Bang splat, real fast.

All of a sudden everybody panicked and jumped into the ring. But Stallone just got up and regrouped and told everybody that everything was cool. Then he said, "Let's get out of the ring."

So I followed him out of the ring. Before I knew it, he was in my face and the guy with the camera was standing there and Stallone said, "All right, you're nobody, you're nothing but a fake wrestler. Now get mad, start talking."

And for the first time that day, I thought I knew what he wanted. He wanted the kind of stuff we did on promo spots. So I said, "Rocky Balboa, I'll break you in half like a little toothpick, I'll turn you into a Philadelphia cheese sandwich . . . " Stuff like that.

Stallone said, "Great, you've got the job."

I said, "Wow, that's unbelievable."

He said, "I'll give you ten thousand dollars to play a wrestler in my movie."

I said, "No, I want fifteen."

Hell, I didn't know what I was talking about. I might have gotten a couple hundred grand, who knows? I just knew you never accept the first offer.

So Stallone said, "I tell you what, I'll give you fourteen thousand dollars."

I took it.

So without an agent, without even reading the contract, I signed something right there on the ring apron. Let me tell you, brother, I was ecstatic.

I went running back to New York and told Vince McMahon Sr. that I got a part in the next *Rocky* movie. I thought he'd be happy for me.

Just one problem. The movie's shooting schedule conflicted with Vince's plans for me to end my career in New York and go to work for the Crockett people in the Carolinas. Of course, he had never told me any of that, so it was news to me.

Vince said, "You can't do this. You work for me. You're a wrestler, not an actor."

But I told him, "I *want* to do this. It's only going to take ten days to film this part. You can spare me for ten days."

Vince looked at me over his glasses and said, "This is

Stranger in a Strange Land

how it works. If you leave to do the *Rocky* movie, you'll never work for this company again."

I said, "Well, then, I guess I'll never work here again." And I left, and a few days later Stallone flew me to Los Angeles.

My first day there at the Olympic Auditorium in downtown L.A., I had to show up at five or six in the morning for makeup. When I came out of the trailer, Stallone introduced me to his stunt coordinator, a guy named Tom Renesto.

As it turned out, Tom Renesto had been working in the Florida Wrestling Office when I first started out. He was one of the bookers there, one of the guys who would put together the story lines for the wrestlers.

I didn't know him very well back in Florida. We just said hello, good-bye, that was it. I was just some kid who was trying to get into the wrestling business so there was no reason to have any more dialogue than that.

And there we were on the set of *Rocky III*. Small world, brother.

Anyway, Stallone and I got into the ring. We weren't slated to film anything the first morning, we were just rehearsing and going through stuff. And the one thing he kept telling me was he wanted everything to be as real as possible.

"I want to do the stunts myself," he said. "I want to take the hits myself."

I was worried, because in the movies you have to do things over and over again to get it just right. I didn't know if Stallone could take that much punishment. But he kept saying he wanted to do all these things himself. He wanted to show what would really happen if a three-hundred-pound wrestler really got into the ring with a boxer.

All morning, Tom Renesto worked with us on the choreography he had laid out. I went through all the motions but I guess I didn't look too happy about it, because at lunchtime Stallone asked me to eat with him in his trailer.

"So," he said, "what do you think of this Tom Renesto?"

I said, "I know him from my days in Florida when I first started. He knows a little bit about wrestling."

Then Stallone said, "What do you think about the match between Rocky Balboa and Thunderlips?"

I said, "It'll be good. He's putting together some good stuff."

And Stallone asked, "How *real* do you think it is?"

"Well," I said, "This guy Renesto is probably a great stunt coordinator, I don't know, but I believe he's appeasing you. He's not showing the audience what would really happen if I was to get hold of you—because if I did, the fight would be over in about three seconds."

He said, "We can't end it in three seconds. We've got to have time on-screen, eight or nine minutes at least. We need ten to fifteen big moves."

"What do you mean by big moves?" I asked. "Do you mean bodyslam over the top rope, five punches?"

He said, "No. In film, one punch is a big move. A bodyslam is a big move. A suplex is a big move."

I said, "You've got to be kidding. You only need fifteen or

twenty of those? Then what this guy is doing is all screwed up. It looks like two two-hundred-fifty-pound guys doing the jazz dance together. It's not even close to what would really happen."

So Stallone asked me if I could set the match up.

I said, "Yeah, of course I can."

So after lunch was over, I did not see Renesto on the set, and I wrote down everything that needed to be done—thirty or forty big moves. First, Rocky would hit me three times. Then I would grab him and hammer him. After that I would back him into a corner. Boom. Big punch, big suplex, big powerslam.

And Stallone did everything himself. But fortunately for him, we got a lot of stuff in one take because I was able to tell him exactly where he was going to start out and exactly where he was going to land.

Then we got to the powerslam, and that wasn't going to be easy no matter what. When you powerslam somebody, you end up landing on top of them—in my case, with three hundred thirty pounds of bone and muscle—and there's really no way to break that fall.

I told Stallone, "That's going to be a stiff one, brother. It's going to be rough, so we should try our best to get it on the first take."

I remember we saved that move for last. When the time came, I picked him up and ran corner to corner, then dove in the middle of the ring. When Stallone hit the canvas and my chest landed on top of his chest, blood squirted out of his mouth.

Hollywood Hulk Hogan

But he didn't bitch about it. He just got up and looked at the cameramen and said, "Camera A, did you get it? Camera B, did you get it?"

They both said, "Yeah, I got it."

So Stallone said, "Print. Good enough. Move on." Then he went back to his trailer and spit up blood for a while.

But he did everything himself. To this day, I've never been around anybody so important to a film who was willing to take those kinds of risks. He wanted it to be real and we got it pretty damn close.

So I did *Rocky III* and made my fourteen thousand dollars, which was no money at all, really. Only then did I have time to reflect on what Vince McMahon had said to me, and how I had lost my job.

Fortunately, I had become a real hot personality in Japan by then, and Vince Sr. didn't have an exclusive deal with the Japanese. So I made a call and booked myself in Japan for eight or nine weeks.

When I came back to L.A., I ran around with Stallone for a while. He and his wife had just gotten divorced, so he was single again and everybody knew it, and because he had just finished *Rocky III* and was about to do *Rambo*, he was hotter than a firecracker.

Women would just come out of nowhere and throw themselves at him. I would meet him for lunch somewhere and all of a sudden we would be surrounded by twenty gorgeous blondes with fake tits and fake noses.

If Stallone decided he liked one of them, he'd leave with her. Then his best buddy here would have his choice

Stranger in a Strange Land

of number two. It was a beautiful thing. Looking back, I don't know now how the hell I ever did it, but it sure was a lot of fun.

Somewhere during that time, I got an idea. I asked Stallone if I could have some publicity stills from the movie. I was standing next to Stallone, holding him over my head, all kinds of crazy stuff. He wasn't supposed to release the pictures yet, but he gave them to me and I sent them to a promoter in Minnesota named Verne Gagne, a two-time NCAA champion who ran the American Wrestling Association.

Verne Gagne called me as soon as he got the publicity shots. He was a shrewd guy. He knew he was looking at a damn gold mine.

"How soon can you start?" he asked me.

I told him I could start right away.

So I went to Minnesota to wrestle for the AWA. But I didn't really leave L.A. behind. I kept coming back for one reason or another.

Anyway, *Rocky III* was just as popular as everybody thought it would be. It made a zillion dollars and everybody got rich—everybody except me, that is. But that was okay. I was getting exposure.

Pretty soon, I would get even more exposure than I wanted. But that would come a little later.

Anyway, Sylvester Stallone was going around promoting *Rocky III,* and of course he wound up on the *Tonight Show*. In those days, Johnny Carson was the host of the *Tonight Show* and he asked about the wrestler in the movie.

"He's great," Carson said. "Who is he?"

Stallone wanted to talk about how many hours it took to film *Rocky III* and how good all the boxing scenes were, but Carson kept asking about the wrestler. He probably asked three or four times. It was pretty funny.

After that, when Stallone went on the *Today Show* and the other talk shows to promote *Rocky III,* he didn't bring up the subject of Thunderlips the wrestler. He didn't want me to overshadow the rest of the movie.

Meanwhile, Johnny Carson called up the firm that was hired to promote the movie and asked *them* about Thunderlips. He drove them so crazy they finally hunted me down and put me in touch with the *Tonight Show.*

Before I knew it, I was sitting backstage in the green room, getting ready to go on with Johnny Carson. I was wearing a black silk tank top, which was good, because you couldn't see the bands of sweat under my pecs. I was real nervous.

But Carson came backstage and was really funny. I guess he was trying to loosen me up because he wanted a good performance from me. And he got one.

He said, "Hey, man, when you're home, what do you do in your spare time?"

I said, "I go lift weights, brother, and eat nails and spit lightning and crap thunder," or something like that.

Carson was at the top of his game. He treated me with a lot of respect. He made me feel comfortable out there.

I was his first guest that night. After I was done, he asked me to move over and sit on the couch. Then Brooke Shields came out. She was about fifteen, a very pretty lady, very friendly.

Actually, I would end up working with Brooke Shields twenty years later, when she had a sitcom called *Suddenly Susan*. But of course, I didn't know that when we were sitting there that day on the *Tonight Show*.

When we were done taping, Johnny Carson wanted to pose for a picture with his head on top of my muscle. Brooke Shields was hanging and kidding with us, and all of a sudden her mother showed up. Talk about overprotective.

She didn't let Brooke get anywhere near me the rest of the time we were there.

Some time after that, I got a call from Stallone. "If you're going to make movies and stuff out here," he told me, "you need to promote yourself. We just got a call from a real high-tone men's magazine called *Oui*. They want to know if I could get ahold of Hulk Hogan to do a photo shoot with four naked girls by a pool."

I was single at the time, but I didn't want to get involved with anything too weird. So I said, "What do you mean *naked?*"

"It's not like *Hustler*," Stallone said. "There'll be four girls feeding you grapes. You'll be in your wrestling clothes. And when the girls take their tops off they want you down to your tights."

Stallone was my mentor as far as Hollywood was concerned, so I said, "What do you think I should do?"

He said, "It'll be great for you, no problem."

So I agreed to do it.

When the day came, I went to Ozzy Osbourne's house and four or five of these girls showed up. We took pictures by the pool for three or four hours. At first, we were all dressed. Then they took pictures of the girls taking my shirt off, and then my boots, and when I got down to my wrestling tights these girls pulled their tops off.

When the magazine came out, there were probably eight or nine different shots of me with these topless girls. And that was it. Boom, done, history, never thought another thing about it.

But those pictures would come back to haunt me, brother. They would haunt me *big* time.

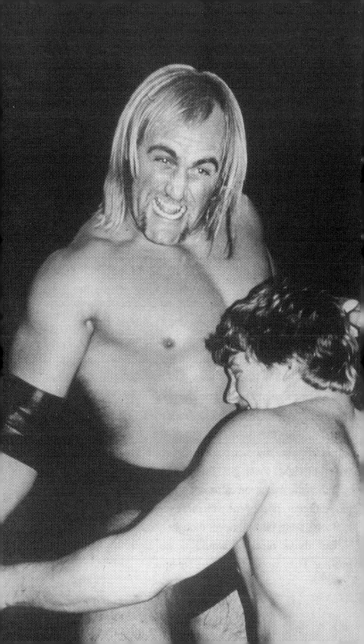

Minnesota
Wants Me

15

If you were a wrestler in the early eighties, Minnesota was the ideal place to work. You would wrestle only three or four days a week and make as much money as you would if you worked seven days in New York. So it was like a dream to go to Minnesota.

Verne Gagne's son Greg was one of the stars there. His best friend wrestled for the company also, and the AWA's World Champion Nick Bockwinkel was Verne's best friend, so it was a real tight clique and it was hard to get in there.

When they saw my pictures as Thunderlips in the *Rocky* movie, they wanted to bring me in as a bad guy. So I came in and for the first three or four weeks, I didn't wrestle. All I did was talk in interviews with my back to the camera.

The TV viewers just saw the back of my hair and my muscles. I didn't have a hole in my hat yet, I had a full head of hair back then. And I would say, "If you want to see my face, you're going to have to buy a ticket to come to the St. Paul Civic Center a month from now."

I was talking like a bad guy, talking like a heel, trying to generate as much heat as I could. It must have worked, because the event sold out.

But as soon as I got into the ring, the fans started cheering and going crazy. I was a heel. They weren't supposed to be cheering me, they were supposed to be booing me.

But my gimmick was I was from Venice Beach, California, and in Minnesota they thought anyone from California was a god. So instantly, I was a good guy, whether I liked it or not.

Verne Gagne panicked. He said, "Oh my God, what am I gonna do? They're cheering him out of the building."

His number one good guy for a lot of years, a wrestler named the Crusher, had just left the AWA. The Crusher was the Minnesota fans' hero, just like Dusty Rhodes was the fans' hero in Florida or Bruno Sammartino was the fans' hero in New York.

The Crusher was from Milwaukee. He used to smoke a cigar and hold a beer in his hand and hit everybody with trash cans. But he was gone, so my timing was perfect. I just came in and took the Crusher's spot as a good guy.

And the wrestler the fans wanted me to beat up more

than anybody was a local boy named Jesse Ventura. Jesse was a bad guy with muscles and blond hair who said he was from San Diego, California, so it was a match made in heaven.

Verne Gagne had finally found somebody who was bigger than Jesse and looked better than Jesse and talked better than Jesse. That was a real ego shocker for Jesse Ventura, but he had to live with it.

After I beat up Jesse Ventura, I became a fan favorite. And when the *Rocky* movie came out, it really put me over. It was the way The Rock is now with *The Scorpion King*. I had that same type of momentum.

Whenever I came out to wrestle, I would play the "Eye of the Tiger" music from the movie. Most fans hadn't seen anything like that before. Very few wrestlers had ever played music on their way to the ring. When the fans heard that, they would go nuts. The whole arena would just start to rock.

Then I would come into the ring and rip my shirt off. That's where that gimmick started, back in Minnesota in the AWA. That's where I started planting the seeds that would grow into *Hulkamania.*

At the same time, I developed a little side business. I started merchandising the Hulk Hogan name and persona with a line of specialty tee shirts that they printed for me at the local mall. Each shirt had a different saying on it.

Now it seems like a no-brainer, but no one in the wrestling business had ever done anything like that before. I sold thousands of those shirts like a pirate out of the back of my truck. The fans just ate them up.

And those same fans wanted me to be the champion of the AWA. Verne Gagne gave me a couple of matches against Nick Bockwinkel, the reigning champion, but Bockwinkel was Verne's best friend and he had been in business with Verne for a long time. Verne wasn't going to turn over the belt to me just like that.

But eventually, it got to the point where fans were saying it was bull for me to wrestle Bockwinkel so often and never win the belt. So all of a sudden Verne Gagne decided that he was going to cancel that month's wrestling slate in the St. Paul Civic Center—because Stanley Black-

burn, Commissioner of the AWA, wanted to be present for the next title match between Bockwinkel and me.

But it really had nothing to do with Commissioner Blackburn being there or not. Verne just wanted to build up the fans' anticipation. And when the next month came, he doubled ticket prices and flew Stanley Blackburn in from Denver, Colorado. And everybody smelled title change.

Verne Gagne, who had basically screwed the fans by raising the ticket prices and making them think the title was going to change hands, came to me in the dressing room that night. He said, "Here's the deal. I'm gonna put the AWA belt on you tonight. But if you keep going to Japan, I want a percentage of the money you make there."

I said, "No, Verne, I'm not going to do that."

He said, "Well, you're going to win the belt tonight. Don't you think that's worth a percentage of your earnings?"

That really got to me. I said, "You know something, Verne? I'm not interested in your belt. As a matter of fact, I'm not interested in wrestling here much longer."

Basically, I was just calling his bluff. I really wanted to stay there in Minnesota. There was no end to my popularity and it was such an easy gig to wrestle a couple of days a week and make that kind of money.

But it was true that I didn't want the AWA championship belt. Because in addition to a percentage of the money I made in Japan, there was another price I would have to pay to get it—namely my status as a bachelor.

Verne Gagne had a couple of daughters and over the two or three months preceding this conversation, it seemed he was always talking about how great his older daughter Kathy was, or inviting me over to dinner with his family, or having Kathy come down and watch us tape TV.

It became a very uncomfortable situation. Probably Verne was figuring if I was part of the family I would never leave. But I didn't want to marry his daughter just to get some wrestling belt.

Anyway, when I told Verne that I wasn't interested in giving him a percentage of my Japanese earnings in exchange for the belt, he got really pissed off and said, "All right, dammit, *you* come up with a finish."

And I did.

I beat Bockwinkel with a legdrop, one-two-three, and

then they handed me the belt. But because I had thrown Bockwinkel over the top rope and out of the ring, Commissioner Blackburn came in all of a sudden and disqualified me, and ripped the belt right out of my hands.

We almost had a riot in the St. Paul Civic Center because everybody wanted me to be the champion. And I could have been—but I just wouldn't do it on Verne's terms.

Bull's-eye on My Back

Hollywood

Hulk

Hogan

16

Fame and success come with a price. For Hulk Hogan, that meant being a target for every wrestler who wanted to make a name for himself.

There were guys who had been in the wrestling business for twenty years and their biggest week had been two thousand dollars. So when they got a chance to wrestle Hulk Hogan, should they have a nice match and do what they're supposed to do? Or should they make a name for themselves by knocking his teeth out?

What would happen if they broke Hulk Hogan's arm? What would that do for their career? Or what would happen if instead of a back suplex they threw my knees up over my head and broke my neck? Goddamn, they might end up with a million-dollar payday.

I knew what I was in for every night I stepped into the ring. These guys in the dressing room would smile and say, "Hi, I'm Billy Bob," but when I stepped into the ring they would try to stick their thumb into my socket and rip my eye out.

I was going to Japan, I was going to South Africa, I would come in there for one day and leave. So a guy's boss might tell him not to hurt me, but if he didn't listen to the boss he wouldn't get fired, and he *might* become a much bigger star. Sounds like a no-brainer to me.

On any given night, I didn't know if a guy was going to give me a clean match or try to bite my damn finger off. All you've got to do is look at all the scars on my fingers to see how often they tried.

I don't think anybody in this business has ever gone through that except me. Nobody else had that extra carrot hanging over their head, take that guy out and you win yourself a pot of gold.

The Girl in the Red Onion

17

One night when I was in L.A., Stallone was busy, so I called Nelson Kidwell, a high-school buddy of mine who was living on the West Coast, and said, "Hey man, let's go out tonight."

Nelson took me to a place in the Valley called the Red Onion, a disco club with Tex-Mex food. I had just appeared in the *Rocky* movie, so all these girls there thought I was an actor. They thought I had just *played* a wrestler, not that I *was* one.

And to tell you the truth, I was going to let them think that as long as they wanted.

That night, I was drinking wine out of the bottle. I had a pretty good buzz on, and I had so many of these blondes hanging around me I didn't think anything of it when another one showed up.

But as soon as she opened her mouth, I could tell she wasn't just another groupie. She said, "I hate to intrude, but I just went to the drive-in with my mother and *E.T.* was sold out so we went to see *Rocky III* . . . and you look just like the guy in the movie."

So I said, "That's right, I'm Mr. T, pity the fool." I joked with her a little, then I said, "You're right, I'm Hulk Hogan and I was in the movie."

She said something to me about dancing but I didn't really have my wits about me, so I told her I wasn't interested. I guess my buddy Nelson Kidwell was a little more clear-headed because a minute later I saw him out there on the dance floor with her.

That's the first time I really saw how attractive she was. She was a really pretty girl with a brown, athletic-looking body and shapely legs. She was like a thoroughbred horse. Plus she had a really nice ass on her.

And here I had just blown her off. What was I thinking?

So when Nelson and this woman came off the dance floor, I took her by the arm and asked her if I could buy her a drink. She obviously wasn't holding a grudge against me because she said yes.

At that point, I put the wine bottle down and ran all the

other girls off and focused on this one woman. It turned out she had a really appealing, upbeat personality, like she didn't have a care in the world. I found myself thinking this was someone I would like to be around.

I asked her if I could take her out and she said, "Well, let's talk about it." That made her even more appealing to me because it was going to be a challenge to win her over. I stayed with her the rest of the night. We talked and danced and I did my best to get her to like me.

Finally, she had to leave. And when she did, it was quick-grab-your-purse-and-go kind of thing. Cinderella didn't bolt any quicker than this woman did. As she was leaving with her girlfriend, I asked her what kind of car she drove, figuring I would beat her out of the parking lot.

"It's an old Volkswagen," she said.

So my buddy Nelson and I went out into the parking lot looking for an old Volkswagen. But as we were searching for it, I saw the woman I was dancing with get into a brand new red Corvette. I said to Nelson, "She lied to me!" Hell, she was taking off without giving me her name or anything.

But I was not to be denied. Nelson and I tracked her down in his old Nova and pulled up next to her at a red light. She and her friend were laughing their asses off because they had tried to ditch us, and almost succeeded.

I said, "Listen, I'm serious. I want to take you out." I told her my name and said, "What's yours?"

She said her name was Linda and she worked at this nail salon in the Valley. "It's in the phone book," she told me, and this time she really hauled ass.

The very next day, I called up the nail shop. Whoever answered the phone said, "It's the guy from the Red Onion." Then I heard Linda's voice saying, "Ask him his name." She had already forgotten it.

Anyway, I got her on the phone and asked her out that night. But I wasn't that familiar with L.A., so I didn't know where to go. I said, "Let's meet at the Red Onion at seven o'clock, since we both know where that is."

Nelson was going to go with me again. But something happened and he didn't come for me in time. Instead of seven, I showed up at a quarter to eight. As I was walking in, I saw Linda walking out, and she didn't look too happy.

"You're late," she told me.

"I'm sorry," I told her, "but it wasn't my fault. My buddy held me up."

It took some doing, but I finally talked her into sticking around. As it turned out, we had a great night talking and dancing. And that was the start of my relationship with the woman who would become my wife.

Of course, when I met Linda, she didn't know a whole lot about wrestling. The promotion in L.A. was in decline at that time, so she hadn't seen a wrestling match on TV and none of her friends had either.

The first match she ever came to was in Denver, Colorado. I was wrestling Nick Bockwinkel, the AWA World Heavyweight Champion. That night, with Linda watching from a ringside seat, Nick hit me in the head with his championship belt and I started bleeding like crazy.

Of course, the blood was really from the cuts I had made

The Girl in the Red Onion

in my forehead with a razor blade, because that's how wrestlers bloody themselves. But at the time, Linda didn't know that. She thought the belt had cut up my face and she started screaming for someone to get a doctor.

But everybody else was cheering, "Yay! Yay!" She looked around at these people and couldn't understand why they were being so barbaric.

Of course, there was an opportunity for me in all this. Since Linda had no idea I'd cut my head with a razor blade, I played my injury to the hilt.

Then we went down to the bar and started drinking with Andre the Giant, who played along with me. He told Linda that she needed to hold ice on my head and wake up four or five times during the night to make sure I didn't bleed to death. He had her feeding me grapes and tickling my toes and giving me more attention than I'd ever been given in my whole life.

Of course, I caught hell for it down the road, when Linda became a wrestling wife and realized I was making a fool out of her that time in Denver. But it made for a memorable night, I'll tell you that.

But in general, it was hard maintaining our relationship. Linda was living in Los Angeles and I was living in Minnesota, and I would really just see her when I went to Japan and back. When I flew into L.A. I would call her up, spend four or five days taking her out and meeting her family, and then I'd leave again.

That went on for six or seven months. Finally, I told Linda, "I'm madly in love with you and I want to spend the rest of my life with you. Would you move to Minnesota so we can get married there first chance we get?"

Linda didn't beat around the bush. "No way," she told me. "I'm not going to move in with somebody."

She made it tough on me, brother. But it was even tougher carrying on a relationship with her living so far away. Finally I said, "I tell you what. I'm going to go out and buy a house. I'm going to get you an engagement ring. And hopefully, you'll think again about moving to Minnesota."

I had never owned a house in my life. That was a big deal, let me tell you. But I wanted to show Linda that I was doing everything right, that I was making an honest-to-God commitment. When she saw all that, she changed her mind and said she would move in with me, but only after we set a date.

So I did it. I set a date to be married. And Linda, thank God, finally gave in and moved to Minnesota.

Weird Wrestling Story

18

One night in the middle of the winter, my partner Ed Leslie and I wrestled in Milwaukee and started driving back to Minneapolis in a bitch of a snowstorm. It was late, two or three o'clock in the morning, and the temperature must have been seventy degrees below zero.

We hadn't gotten very far when I saw something by the side of the road. I said, "I think I see a deer over there."

"Nah," said Ed, "that's no deer. That's a person."

"No way," I told him. "No way there's a person out there in this kind of weather."

But as we got closer, we saw that it was a person. A woman, in fact. And she was as naked as the day she was born.

"Damn," I said, "you're right!"

The naked lady was trying to flag us down. So we stopped and got her in the car, and asked her what the hell she was doing out there. She said this Canadian wrestler had picked her up at the arena and gotten her to drink a few beers, then drove off with her in his car.

She didn't say if this guy had had his way with her or not. All she said was that she had pissed him off somehow— pissed him off pretty badly, apparently—because he ended up throwing her out of the car naked, right into the snow. And if we hadn't come along and seen her standing there, she would probably have died, because the wind was blowing like hell and we hadn't seen any other cars on the road.

She might have lasted fifteen minutes out there, maybe twenty. And then she would have frozen to death.

Anyway, we put some clothes on her and got her to a gas station, and she called some friends to come pick her up. As soon as we were sure she would be okay, we took off. I mean, we had a hell of a long ride ahead of us in that snowstorm.

But more than that, we didn't trust the judgment of a drunk and naked lady to remember which wrestlers helped her that night . . . and which one dumped her bare butt in the freezing snow.

Call Vince McMahon

19 There was a little rumbling coming from Minnesota, and the McMahons could feel the tremors all the way back in New York.

Verne Gagne was thinking in terms of expansion. The AWA already went into Canada, Salt Lake City, Denver, and the West Coast. Now Verne was nosing around the East Coast, trying to buy TV time on Channel Nine in New York.

We had a very strong group of wrestlers—tag-team champions Jesse "The Body" Ventura and Adrian Adonis, "World's Strongest Man" Ken Patera, and four-hundred-seventy-pound Jerry Blackwell. Those guys alone were as major league a crew as anything the McMahons could put in the ring.

And then there was Hulk Hogan, whose popularity was off the scale. I could get in doors most people couldn't.

One night at the Rosemont Horizon in Chicago, I was getting ready to go into the ring. We had a big six-man tag-team match for the fans—me, Greg Gagne, and Jim Brunzell against Ken Patera, Jerry Blackwell, and Sheik Adnan El Kaisse—an Iraqi wrestler who once held the World Wide Wrestling tag-team title as an American Indian called Billy White Wolf. The building was sold out to the rafters.

All of a sudden, Steve Taylor, an old friend of mine from the World Wide Wrestling Federation, stuck his head through the curtains. Steve runs the production crew now for Vince Jr., but at the time he was a photographer.

I was surprised as hell. I said, "Steve, how the hell are you?"

"Fine," he said, "Let me take a picture of you."

"Sure," I told him. "No problem."

So I struck a pose for Steve Taylor and he took the picture. But that wasn't why he had come to see me in Chicago. He handed me a card. On the back it said, "Call Vince McMahon immediately."

I said to myself, *Boy, this is interesting.* I was fired and told I'd never work there again. I guess things have changed.

I wrestled that night, went home, and talked with Linda. I showed her the card Steve Taylor had given me and said, "I don't know if you understand what this means, but this is from Vince McMahon in New York. If I could go back there for just one year, we would have enough money where we wouldn't have to worry about anything."

She said, "Okay, call him back."

So I called him.

But it wasn't Vince McMahon Sr. who answered. It was Vince McMahon Jr.

He told me that he was going to be taking over the company from his father and he wanted to make me the new champion of the World Wrestling Federation (the new name of the company). He had heard about this whole *Hulkamania* thing that I had started in Minnesota and he thought he could embellish it and make it even bigger.

By the time we finished talking, Vince had decided to fly to Minnesota. But Minneapolis was a very small town where everybody knew everybody's business. I didn't want Verne Gagne to know I was talking to Vince yet, so I told Vince that Linda would pick him up at the airport.

Linda had never met Vince but I told her to look for a guy with big shoulders and pads in his suits that made his shoulders look even bigger. "Believe me," I said, "it'll be hard to miss him. He'll look different from anybody else on the plane."

During my first go-around with the McMahons, I used to see Vince at all the Allentown TVs. He was a very young man in those days. You could tell he was a weight lifter because he was all pumped up.

His father had him interviewing people, standing there ringside holding a microphone. He would stand there all day, and he would keep his shoes on or take them off

depending on the height of the wrestler he was talking to.

I used to watch father and son getting in and out of their car at Allentown or Hazelton, Pennsylvania. They were like royalty. They always wore the same suit and you could tell they were there for business. They weren't a bunch of drunken wrestlers raising hell for the thrill of it.

I didn't get to know Vince very well but I had heard that he was a cool guy, that he was wild in his youth and that he would shave his head or steal his dad's car or peroxide his hair blond. At some point, he was even sent to military school.

But we didn't talk very much because we didn't have a whole heck of a lot in common. He was on the other side of

the fence. He was the office and I was the talent. I just knew that he was the announcer, the commentator, and that when he wasn't doing TVs in Pennsylvania he was running rock-and-roll shows and other events out of his own arena in Cape Cod.

Sure enough, when Linda got to the airport, she recognized Vince right away and took him back to our house. He and I started talking about what he had in mind for me and around three or four o'clock in the morning, we shook hands on a ten-year deal for me to come back to New York.

I told Linda, "We're gonna have a ton of heat but I gotta tell Verne Gagne I'm leaving the Minnesota territory."

On one hand, I was handing Verne a problem. I had already booked myself all over the AWA in a series of steel cage matches against Nick Bockwinkel with the world championship belt at stake. Verne had tried to talk me into taking the belt in one of those matches but I hadn't agreed. I had just told him I would think about it.

On the other hand, Verne had it coming to him. When I went to Japan the last time, Verne had made up some Hulk tee shirts because he saw how successful I had been selling shirts on my own. Those shirts were just like mine. They

Call Vince McMahon

had my name, my likeness, and the sayings I had made famous on them. The only difference was that Verne was getting the money.

When I came back from Japan, I found out about it and said, "Hey brother, you sold all those shirts. Where's my percentage?"

Verne Gagne said, "You don't get a percentage. Those are my shirts. I've got a right to sell them."

So even though he had been copying my shirts and selling them, he wouldn't give me a penny. He just told me to screw off. That made my decision to go back east a little easier.

I went up to Verne and told him, "I'm leaving, brother. I quit. I'm done."

He said, "You can't do this to me."

But I could. And I did.

Wedlock

20 **On December 18, 1983, a short time after Vince McMahon came to Minnesota to woo me back to New York, I married my fiancée Linda in Los Angeles.**

I had come back from yet another trip to Japan with a regular entourage, including Japanese wrestling legend Antonio Inoki and a film crew from New Japan Pro Wrestling that was going to record the whole thing.

All my friends from the wrestling business were there—Andre the Giant, Vince McMahon, Adrian Adonis, Ed Leslie (who would later wrestle as Brutus Beef-

cake), maybe a hundred and fifty wrestlers altogether—everybody except Verne Gagne, who I was getting ready to screw over. The wrestlers sat on one side of the aisle and Linda's family sat on the other, wondering what the hell she was getting herself into.

I don't remember much about the ceremony. I was so nervous, it was like an out-of-body experience. I barely knew what was going on.

But I remember the party afterward. It was a damn circus. All the wrestlers raised hell and drank like Vikings. We just went crazy.

At one point, Linda cut the cake and smashed a piece in my face. I overreacted and double-smashed it in hers. Obviously, I had never paid close attention at weddings. I didn't even know the bride and groom were supposed to sneak away before any of their guests.

So instead, I sat at the bar drinking with Andre until they closed the place. Finally Linda, who still had cake on her face, asked me if I was ever going to leave. So I said goodnight to Andre and staggered off with Linda.

I woke up the next morning at about seven o'clock with my tuxedo still on and a New York steak in my hand. I guess I was eating it when I went to sleep without the benefit of a knife or fork.

Linda was sleeping on the bed and I was lying on the couch. And judging by the fact that I was still fully dressed, I guessed that I hadn't consummated the marriage. But to tell you the truth, I was too hungover to really remember.

Linda's mother and father had shelled out a ton of

Hollywood Hulk Hogan

money for the wedding, including a generous amount for booze. But as I was leaving the hotel, they told me the wrestlers had drunk so much we had gone above and beyond our quota.

"How much above and beyond?" I asked the hotel people.

"Twelve thousand dollars' worth," they told me.

Thank God I had some cash money on me from Japan. I paid the tab, but man, that party was a wild one.

So Linda and I left the hotel. But we didn't go on a honeymoon. We flew back to Minnesota. And I went back to work.

Wedlock

Garden
Party

Hollywood

21

So I came back to New York—as a good guy this time—secure in the knowledge that I was going to wrestle for the championship in Madison Square Garden as soon as I had a couple of Allentown TV matches under my belt. At that time, the champion Bob Backlund had just lost his title to a guy called the Iron Sheik, so it looked like it would be me and the Iron Sheik wrestling in the Garden.

Or so I had been led to believe.

The problem was Bob Backlund, who had held the heavyweight title for a long time. He and I had been friends when I had my first run in New York. We had gone to Japan together and trained together and I thought I had earned his respect. But when I came back to New York, it was a whole different deal with him.

Vince McMahon Sr. wanted Backlund to tag team with me, but Backlund balked and said he didn't want to do it. He didn't even want to stand next to me on camera. Then Vince wanted to shoot an angle where Backlund was going to wrestle the Sheik but he got hurt, so he was going to ask his friend Hulk Hogan to wrestle in his place. Backlund didn't want to do that either.

It made it really rough because I was supposed to be getting this big push and it was important that Backlund pass the torch to me. But he didn't want any part of that, because he wanted to wrestle the Iron Sheik himself and get his title back. Finally, it all came to a head at a TV in Allentown, Pennsylvania, a few days before we were supposed to go to Madison Square Garden.

Vince McMahon Sr. called a meeting with me and Bob Backlund and Vince Jr. to clear the air. By that time, Backlund was a nervous wreck. He had red hair and real white skin and he was so upset that he was all broken out in hives.

The first thing he said was, "I don't want anybody who's not an athlete to have the championship belt."

I had been this guy's friend and training partner, and all of a sudden I wasn't fit to wear his belt. I tell you, brother, it shocked me to hear Backlund say that.

Okay, so maybe I didn't have an amateur wrestling background. Maybe I hadn't won any AAU championships or come home with a gold medal from the Olympics. But I wasn't exactly a guy off the street, either.

Besides, there had been a lot of champions who weren't amateur athletes. "Superstar" Billy Graham wasn't an amateur wrestler. Neither was Bruno Sammartino.

The whole meeting, Backlund was itching and scratching like a dog with a bad case of fleas. I'd never seen him so upset.

So Vince Sr. looked at me over the tops of his glasses and said, "You know, Terry, maybe Bob's got a point. Maybe we should wait and see how everything works out, and think about putting the belt on you six months from now."

This wasn't what I had signed on for. This wasn't what I was promised when I shook hands with Vince Jr. and agreed to come back.

So I said, "You know, guys, I burned one hell of a bridge back in Minnesota and I'm going to run back there quick as I can and try to rebuild it. Thank you for everything." And I started to walk out.

But Vince Jr. stopped me. "Look," he said, "my dad's just a little worried. I have to talk to him. But we'll get this thing back on track."

He talked to his father and he told him that he wanted me to have the title shot and the belt, not Bob Backlund. And like that, Vince Sr. gave in.

So Vince Jr. stepped up to the plate and stuck by the agreement we had made back in Minnesota. And the next

Garden Party

thing I knew, Hulk Hogan was getting ready to wrestle the Iron Sheik at Madison Square Garden.

It was shortly after that, maybe the very next Allentown TV, that I saw something that made my heart stop. If you wanted to go to the rest room there, you had to walk up these steps, and when you got near the top step you had to reach out to open the door.

When the door opened, you could see if someone was standing in the rest room already. We never knocked on the door, we would just walk in and out. Anyway, I walked up the steps and opened the door and there was this guy standing there with his back to me—and between his legs was this huge stream of red piss that looked like pure blood.

All of a sudden, I realized it was Vince Sr.

Right away, I closed the door. It took me a second or two to get over the shock. Then I got Pat Patterson, who was Vince Jr.'s closest friend, and I told him what I had seen in the rest room.

Pat Patterson went and told Vince Jr. I don't know what he felt inside. It had to tear him up that his dad was dying. But because of who he was, he kept his game face on and stayed strong for all of us.

Meanwhile, the fans were getting pumped for me to wrestle the Iron Sheik. They had seen the same wrestlers over and over again for a long time, but I was something different. They didn't know what to make of me.

I had wrestled there before, but I had really made a name for myself in the AWA. I was a heel back then, now I was a good guy. Was I going to stay for the long haul or go back to Minnesota? Nobody knew.

They knew the Iron Sheik, though. This guy wasn't just a performer putting on a robe and a turban and calling himself a sheik. He was an accomplished amateur wrestler who had represented Iran in international competition. And before that, he was supposed to have been a bodyguard for the Shah of Iran.

There was a story that he had holes in his head from some type of punishment they inflicted on him. They had hit him with an ice pick or something. That was the kind of torture they supposedly used on the Shah's bodyguards when they weren't doing their jobs properly.

So it was an experience to be in the ring with this guy. And with the Iranian hostage crisis fresh in people's minds, his name and his background really stirred up the emotions of the fans.

Of course, we didn't have Pay-Per-View in those days. What we had was closed-circuit TV. The Garden was always overflowing, so the company would open up the Felt Forum—which was also in the Garden—and run a cable in there with a big screen.

Later on, when wrestling was really hot, Vince Jr. would rent out the Joe Louis Arena in Detroit and the L.A. Forum and simulcast to those places. And then when cable came into its own, he would cut a deal with the cable companies to offer wrestling events to their subscribers on a pay-as-you-go basis.

So Vince McMahon actually pioneered the concept of

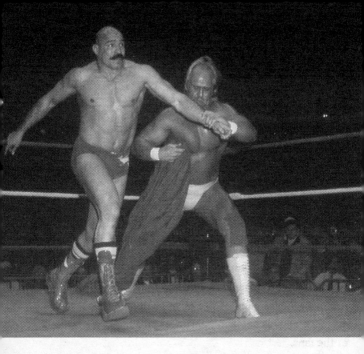

Pay-Per-View. It was his baby. He was the genius behind the whole thing. But that came after January 23, 1984, in Madison Square Garden.

I brought a few things to the party too. One of them was the idea of playing my theme music as I entered the arena. When I suggested it to Vince McMahon Jr., he and his father were on the fence about it. They weren't sure if it was going to work.

But I knew it would work. I had played "Eye of the Tiger" back in Minnesota and I knew it would make the crowd go wild. So I said to myself, "Screw it, I'm going to get this done even if it gets me fired again." And at five in

Hollywood Hulk Hogan

the afternoon, a few hours before we were supposed to go on, I slipped the music tech guy five hundred bucks to play "Eye of the Tiger."

Then, right before show time, Vince Jr. decided to go along with me and play the entrance music. I didn't have the balls to ask for my five hundred dollars back, so I lost it. But it didn't matter. The important thing is I had that music playing when I walked down the ramp.

And it worked, just like I said it would. When the crowd heard that music, almost 20,000 people rose up like the Messiah had come back. It was like the roof of the Garden blew off. It was nuts.

The whole match took five minutes and thirty seconds. Most fans had never seen anyone get out of the Sheik's signature hold, the Camel Clutch. But I did. And then I backed him into the turnbuckle. He tried another hold; I broke it.

I threw him into the ropes. When he came off them, I gave him the boot in the face. He fell in the middle of the ring. I gave him a leg drop, the referee started counting, and *Hulkamania* took off like never before.

After the match, the Sheik was a good sport. Even though he put me over and made me the world's champion that night, he came backstage and gave me a big hug.

Then, in front of Vince McMahon Jr., he said that Verne Gagne—who I had just screwed over—had called the Iron Sheik the night before the match and offered him a hundred thousand dollars to break my leg in the ring.

Gagne knew the Sheik because when the Sheik came over from Iran, he went to Minneapolis to learn professional wrestling. So Verne was the guy who actually broke the Sheik into the business.

Now that the match was over, the Sheik told us what Verne Gagne had asked him to do. But he had decided to not do it. He didn't want to hurt me.

In the end, it turned out to be a good business decision for him. The Sheik was able to keep working as a wrestler and make a ton of money for the next couple of years wrestling me in return matches.

John Stossel

Hollywood

22 By December 1984, wrestling was like a giant wave crashing all over everything. Hulk Hogan was at the crest of that wave.

I was so popular that the TV show *20/20* decided to do a piece on me and on wrestling. They sent out one of their top reporters, a young guy named John Stossel.

He had read an article in one of the New York newspapers that Jackie Onassis could walk down the streets of New York and go almost unnoticed, but when Hulk Hogan walked down the streets of New York it was a mob scene.

John Stossel called and said he didn't believe it. Vince McMahon said, "Come on down and see for yourself."

Stossel and his crew picked me up in New York early in the morning. Then he put me in front of the camera and said, "Where should we go?"

I said, "How about Madison Square Garden?"

"Oh," he said, "that'd be too easy."

I said, "Why do you say that? You think the Garden's swarming with wrestling fans twenty-four hours a day, seven days a week? I don't think it works that way."

But he didn't like the idea of going to the Garden. He said, "I'm going to take you to the Battery. Then we'll see what kind of crowd you attract."

I said, "Okay, sure. Just give me at least a minute on the street, y'know?"

So we went down to the Battery, which is way downtown at the tip of Manhattan Island, and we stood on the corner for about a minute. But it was winter and I was wearing a long, gray coat and a hat. Of course nobody recognized me.

John Stossel checked his watch and said, "Well, Hulk, it's been about a minute and nobody's noticed you yet."

I said, "I'm all covered up, brother. Everybody looks the same when they have the same gray coat on. I know it's freezing, but if you let me take my coat off so people can see me in my tee shirt, you just might get a different result."

John Stossel said, "Okay," and I took my coat off.

As soon as I did that, I swear to God, I was mobbed.

John Stossel

Facing off with Dr. D.

Bang, we got flooded. There were so many people around us it was scary.

So I put my coat back on and we walked back down the street, and the crowd went with us. John Stossel said, "Well, God, Hulk, I guess it's true. We've never had a celebrity on the street before who's had . . . what do you think, three hundred people?"

I mean it was crazy, it was nuts. I said, "It's kind of like this. Wrestling's so hot, that's what happens."

John Stossel looked around at all the people. He said, "I've never seen anything like this on the streets of New York, other than for presidents of the United States."

"I'm the champion of New York City," I said. "I don't know what to tell you."

All of a sudden he pulled something small and sharp out of his pocket and said, "Hey, what's this?"

I said, "Well, John, it looks like a razor blade."

Then he asked me, "Is it true that wrestlers use razor blades on their heads to make themselves bleed?"

It was true. But in those days, we didn't admit it. I said, "That sounds a bit masochistic. I've never heard of that."

Of course, underneath my hat, my forehead was just covered with blade marks.

John Stossel said, "Okay, I just thought I'd ask."

Then he had his crew turn off the camera. He told me he was going home but he was going to come back that night to the Garden to visit with us backstage. Vince had already given him permission to do that.

But we were still very protective of wrestling back then.

John Stossel

So I called Vince and I said, "Red alert, pal. This guy's not out to do a story on how popular Hulk Hogan is. He's trying to reveal whether wrestling is fake or not."

Vince said he would make sure all the guys were in separate dressing rooms that night, the good guys on one side and the bad guys on another. That's the way it was supposed to be in the Garden, the good guys at the north end and the bad guys at the south end. We didn't want them walking down the hallways and talking to each other. We wanted them to be discreet.

So anyway, they let John Stossel into the Garden. Just his luck, the first wrestler he ran into that night was David Shultz, Dr. D.

Not knowing who he was dealing with, he put his mike right in David's face and said, "Let me ask you a question . . . is wrestling fake?"

David went wham, wham, and slapped John Stossel right in the ear. "Do you think that's fake?" Wham, wham, two more real hard openhanded slaps. "Do you think that's fake?"

He hit this guy four times so fast, John Stossel was just kind of out on his feet for a second. Then he recovered and ran for his life.

And I said ring-a-ding-ding, there's a lawsuit right there. Sure enough, we got sued and Stossel said he suffered severe ear damage. I believe it. I saw the hits and I know if anybody hit my ear like that they'd break my eardrum.

23

Before I beat the Iron Sheik, the success of the company had always rested on six or eight pairs of shoulders. But as soon as I won that match in Madison Square Garden and captured the imagination of the wrestling world, the load was placed squarely on the back of one guy . . .

Me. Hulk Hogan.

And because of what happened in the Garden, wrestling was red hot—so hot that we were running two sold out venues a night. If we were in New York on a Monday night, they would also book an event in Chicago. If we were in Boston, they would also book an event in Pittsburgh.

We had A and B towns. The wrestlers used to check their booking sheets to see if they were at the same venue as Hulk Hogan, because they knew I would draw more people and they would make better money.

I was running hard, brother. I started piling up the frequent-flyer miles. That first year after I beat the Sheik, I got on three hundred different flights and wrestled close to four hundred matches. It was crazy, out of control.

And it wasn't just the wrestling I had to worry about. I had all kinds of stuff on my plate, stuff that was just as important as what I did in the ring.

If I was wrestling in St. Louis, I'd have to make a stop in Atlanta, Georgia to take a TV station manager to lunch, then stop again somewhere in Missouri at a children's hospital. Then I was supposed to show up at the arena and be ready to wrestle.

Sometimes I would go to three or four different places before I finally got to the place where I was going to wrestle—prisons, TV interviews, shopping centers, the whole nine yards. It was just 24–7, brother, a nonstop roller coaster ride. I would try to cover all the bases, but it wasn't easy.

I had to walk into a dressing room with twenty wrestlers and be able to fit in on a very barbaric level with these men. And the next morning I would have to attend a business meeting with a thousand people from IBM and tell them about pro rata shares, buy rates, satellite revenue, merchandising, ancillary rights, and business plans. Then I

would have to go meet with a group of women and then a group of children, and in each case I had to talk with them on a certain level.

So I wasn't just some three-hundred-pound wrestler who liked drinking beer and had a tooth knocked out in the front. I was unique. There was no one else in the business who could switch gears like that.

Finally, at the end of the day, I would drag myself into the dressing room and the guys would say, "What did you do today? Fly on a private plane?"

They had no idea where I had been. They would want to talk about the match or what we were gonna do for a finish, and I would say, "Jesus Christ, I'll just see you out in the ring, brother. I'll tell you out there."

Sometimes they would lock me up in a room for twelve hours and I would do two or three hundred three-minute radio interviews. I had that Muhammad Ali rap but I related each interview to a particular town.

If I was going to be wrestling in Los Angeles, I would say I drove down the coast on my Harley-Davidson with a hippie in one hand and a palm tree in the other. If we were going to be in St. Louis, I would say I'll be hanging from the giant arch and doing chin-ups. If we were going to be in Chicago, I would say I'll be throwing lightning bolts from the Sears Tower.

It was like sitting in a sauna when I was doing those interviews. I would come out soaking wet. In fact, I used to sweat so much that the dye from my leather championship belt used to turn my yellow trunks brown. Vince McMahon was buying ten or twelve heavyweight title belts a month because I would just sweat right through them.

At the same time, Vince McMahon Jr. and I were getting the merchandising machine in gear. "Every wrestler should have entrance music," I told him. "And tee shirts too. And toothbrushes. And tennis shoes."

I was in his ear about this merchandise thing, driving him crazy. I had seen what could happen when I was in Minnesota, and I told him there were more ways to make money than just a wrestling payoff. And as soon as he got the ball, he ran with it.

Vince became a monster, the greatest promoter ever, the greatest deal maker ever, the greatest licensing person ever. He did what nobody else could have done—he turned the company into a multibillion-dollar business empire in just a few years.

Every celebrity in the world wanted to get on board. In L.A., you would look out into the crowd and see Gene Hackman, Sean Connery, Johnny Carson, and Wilt Chamberlain. In Boston, it would be a whole other group of celebrities. In New York, it would be the Broadway stage crowd and rock stars. It was a happening thing.

We were so encouraged by this incredible momentum we had, we started doing something that had been a major taboo in the wrestling business. We started crossing territorial boundaries.

If you ran a wrestling promotion, you had always stayed in your own territory. All of a sudden, Vince was buying time in places like Texas and California and Kansas City and broadcasting in those markets.

Every wrestling fan in Kansas City had recognized Harley Race of the National Wrestling Alliance as the world's champion. He had won the belt eight times and owned a piece of the local promotion. Now the World Wrestling Federation was broadcasting in Kansas City and telling those people that Harley Race wasn't what they thought he was, and that Hulk Hogan was the world's champion.

Well, people like Harley Race took offense to that. I told Vince, "One of us is going to get killed, brother. They're going to shoot you up here in your office or they're going to kill me on the road."

Sure enough, when I went to Kansas City, Harley Race was so pissed off that he showed up in the middle of the afternoon when the production guys were setting up the ring, scared everybody off with a gun, and lit the ring on fire. He actually tried to burn down the ring. Then he told the production guys that he was coming back later to break both my legs and put a bullet in each one of them.

When I heard this, I had no doubt that Harley would show up that night. So I went across the street to a place called the Rusty Scupper, drank a bunch of hard liquor, and ate my final supper. I knew Harley Race was a shooter, a hooker, a guy who could break bones, and I was going to be in for the fight of my life.

Later on, at the arena, I was sitting on the toilet when one of the British Bulldogs, Davey Boy Smith, came in. "He's here, he's here!" he told me in his English accent, and I knew he meant Harley Race. So I jumped up, pulled up my pants without even wiping my ass, and ran out to confront Harley Race in the hallway.

The son of a bitch stared me down for a second and said, "I ought to break your goddamn legs for what you've done to me." I thought we were going to fight right there. But the next thing I knew he stuck his hand out and said, "I admire you for what you've done for the wrestling business. And by the way, do you think you can get me a job with your outfit?"

So there was about a year or two where Vince and I were the two most hated men in the wrestling business. We were always looking over our shoulders, wondering when somebody was going to come after us.

But after those couple of years went by, guys started

thanking us. Not just Harley Race, but guys all over the country. With all the merchandising we were doing, we had opened their eyes to all kinds of possibilities.

Instead of just selling hot dogs and beer, they were selling tee shirts and can holders with the likenesses of their local stars. They were capitalizing on the same consumer impulses we were.

So little by little, people started saying to themselves, "Damn, Vince McMahon and Hulk Hogan aren't going to ruin this business. They're making it easier for all of us to make a living."

That went on for a while. But eventually, a lot of the small territories did close up. They just couldn't compete.

The same thing happened with the wrestlers themselves. The guys who survived were the ones who really deserved to survive, the main-event guys who knew their craft and worked hard at it. Instead of making fifty or sixty grand a year, they were making a couple hundred grand a year.

But a lot of underneath guys—guys who would work their job down at Kmart all week and then go wrestle at the Coliseum on the weekend—started to disappear. It was like when God flooded the world and only the good people on Noah's Ark survived. We had flooded out all the beer bellies and the guys who never went to the gym and left only the guys who were really dedicated to the wrestling business.

Hulkamania was running wild, brother, and you never knew what was going to happen next. But out of every possibility, the last thing I expected was that I would become a role model for kids.

The Load

Maybe I should have seen it coming. I was a good guy, and I had the Venice Beach thing going for me, and I was blond and tanned, and in good shape. And one of my catch phrases was to say, "Train, say your prayers, and take your vitamins."

But I wasn't ready for it when, all of a sudden, I saw kids dressing like me for Halloween—and this was before we made any Hulk Hogan costumes. The kids were making the costumes on their own. They were looking up to me and believing in training, prayers, and vitamins.

Then I started getting requests from the Make-A-Wish and Starlight and Dalmation Foundations. Kids who were dying or had handicaps or special needs were asking to see me. I didn't get it. Why did they want to see *me?*

I wasn't ready for the whole thing. I didn't know what to make of it or how to handle it. But whether I liked it or not, there it was.

I would see a kid with a big open hole in his chest and you could see his heart beating. Or a kid who could barely make a sound and you had to lean real close to hear what he was saying. Or a kid who was five years old who looked like he was eighty.

Some kids would live another six months, some would die the next day. It was crazy. And I said to myself, "Man, I better regroup, because this isn't going to stop."

Little by little, I got used to it. I would meet a kid who was dying and there would be twenty people around him crying, but somehow I could keep my emotions in check and give that kid what he needed.

I got real good at it. I saw how Mr. T dealt with them and

Hollywood Hulk Hogan

I learned a lot from him, but I just took it up to that next level.

Seeing these children all the time made me rearrange my priorities. I'd be bitching about my life, and then I'd see these kids whose problems were a whole lot bigger than mine. If they were managing to be so strong and upbeat despite everything they were going through, I could get through my little bunch of problems.

Then, after a couple of years, I wasn't just coping with meeting all these kids. I got to a point where I actually thanked God it was happening, because I realized that I had been given an opportunity.

First I would say to their parents, "You know, I really appreciate your bringing your son to see me. If it's okay with you, I'd like to take some liberties with him—I'd like to talk to him about our Lord, Jesus Christ, who died on the cross to pay for our sins."

And then these parents would say, "Oh, we don't have a problem with that." I would have backed off if they had asked me to, but not one of them did.

So I'd tell these kids, "You say you're my number one fan. That means I've got to wrestle you to find out if you're as big a fan as you think. I've got a lot of people who tell me they're my number one fan, but you look like you might actually be what you say you are."

Of course, I couldn't wrestle them that night because I was already meeting some bad guy in the ring. And after that, I would be too tired to wrestle anybody. And with my schedule as crazy as it was, I didn't know when or where I would finally get a chance to get together with them.

"But I tell you what," I'd say, "now that I know you and we're good buddies, I bet I can think of one place where we're probably going to wind up together."

Then I'd ask the kid if he believed in God, if he believed in Jesus Christ, and if he accepted Christ as his savior. And the kid would either say yes or no.

Now, I knew I was taking it way out there with this stuff, but I would say, "Well, if you do, that's great. And if you don't, here's why you should—because if you believe in your heart that Christ died for your sins, we'll get to go to Heaven together. And then when you bodyslam me it won't hurt so bad, because the clouds in Heaven are a lot softer than this ring over here."

So I'd get my shot in. And it always worked, and the kids would always laugh. And I never had a single kid that didn't accept Christ as his savior.

In some cases, it looked like these kids might not even make it to the end of my match. So I'd say, "I've got to warn you, I'm kind of a thief when it comes to stealing young guys' energy, so you're probably going to fall right asleep as soon as we're done talking. But that's all right because we'll see each other again, I promise you that."

That role model thing was tough, brother. But you can get good at it if you understand they're not really coming to see *you*. They're there because they need faith and hope and if you know that, you can give it to them.

Years later, I would get a trophy from Make-A-Wish for being their most requested celebrity of the decade—more than Michael Jackson, more than Michael Jordan, more than Mickey Mouse. Wrestling was so hot that kids wanted to see Hulk Hogan more than anybody.

But even before that, I got a different kind of reward. I started becoming a better person. The character I presented to the kids was so pure and so positive, it took Terry Bollea, who was about four notches below that, and raised

The Load

the bar for him. I started believing in what Hulk Hogan stood for and trying to be like him.

So it wasn't just the kids that he helped. He helped me too.

The other good thing that came out of my success was I became friends with Vince McMahon Jr. I lived in Stamford, Connecticut, very near his house, and we started to ride motorcycles together.

I actually used to leave there sometimes to go to California to ride a motorcycle, so he bought me one to ride at home. "Hey, man," he said, "now you can hang out here with me more."

We were doing everything together. We were riding, we were lifting weights, and we were blazing new territory in the wrestling business.

We would plan each and every move together. "Well," we said, "we've never been to the NATPE (National Association of Television Program Executives) convention before. How are we going to get in there? How are we going to present ourselves?"

Everything we did was like this *Mission: Impossible* plot to get through somebody's door to pitch our product. And Vince had a better feel for uncharted waters than anybody I had ever seen. He would take his damn house and put it on the line for something he believed in. He would always bet on himself and I'll be damned if the son of a bitch didn't always come out on top.

Hollywood Hulk Hogan

It's Not All Fake

Hollywood

24 Wrestlers get hurt in the ring all the time. Every night somebody tears a muscle or twists a knee or breaks a bone. It's almost always an accident.

But once in a while, there's bad blood between two guys, and the guy who's supposed to lose just says, "I'm beating him." That's when it gets ugly, because it spills over into the dressing room.

I've seen it happen. The worst example I can remember involved a couple of guys named Adrian Adonis and Dan Spivey.

Adrian was one of the boys. He had been up and down the roads, partied a lot and drank and raised hell, and was generally a good-natured guy. But if he didn't like somebody, he could really dish out the punishment—and by that I mean showing the person no respect.

Dan Spivey was a guy Adrian just didn't like. Dan was a tough kid from the streets of Tampa, a guy about my age and size, so I knew him pretty well. He had been a boxer before he got into wrestling and he was real good with his hands.

This particular night, Adrian was leaning on Dan pretty bad and he called Dan something. Dan said something back to him and all of a sudden they were fighting right there in the ring. The fight got broken up before it went too far, but it was a cinch it would continue backstage.

And that's what happened. As soon as Adrian came into the dressing room, he threw a punch at Dan. Dan sidestepped and hit him with an uppercut to the eye that Adrian would need about twenty stitches to close up. Then he hit him with another punch worth twenty stitches. Dan knew exactly what he was doing. Punch by punch, he cut Adrian wide open.

Finally, Adrian went down and Dan kicked him in the face. Adrian was so limp he looked like he was dead. Finally, when Dan backed up to kick the rest of Adrian's face off, we stopped him.

We got flack from the other wrestlers, because you're supposed to let that stuff go in our world. That's our rule: we let it go. So stopping that fight cast a shadow on me and the other guys who interfered for a long time afterward.

It's Not All Fake

"It's a sport ... but it's also entertainment."

Hulk Hogan

25 When I was in the ring, I wasn't just putting my boot in my opponents' faces. I was entertaining the fans in these arenas on a whole different level. I was telling stories in the ring about spitting lightning and crapping thunder and creating havoc with my "twenty-four inch pythons."

I was starting to transcend wrestling. People saw me on talk shows or heard me on the radio and it opened the door for them to go, "Wow, maybe we should watch wrestling. Maybe it's not just a bunch of big men beating each other up. Maybe it's more than that."

Vince McMahon Jr. looked at the character of Hulk Hogan and saw possibilities the rest of us didn't see. He saw that you could go only so far with the formula of wrestling is real and these guys really hate each other's guts. That philosophy was only reaching a certain demographic.

But I was reaching out beyond that demographic. I was getting to people who had never set foot in a wrestling arena.

Vince told me, "It isn't just wrestling anymore with you, Terry. You're entertaining people. It's a sport, but it's also entertainment. It's . . . sports-entertainment!"

As soon as he said that, I knew exactly what he meant. The guy chomping on his cigar in the first row of Madison Square Garden, yelling to see me bleed and get my teeth knocked out, would leave as soon as he heard the phrase "sports-entertainment."

And in that guy's place, the families would show up, the moms and dads and little kids. As soon as people knew it was an exhibition and we really weren't trying to kill each other and the good guy always prevailed in the end, it would become a whole new ball game.

We wouldn't be getting twenty-five bucks for a ticket and a beer. We would have entire families coming in to buy *four* tickets at a time, and spend money on tee shirts and souvenirs.

All of a sudden, Vince started rolling with it. It was like

he was possessed and talking in tongues. It wasn't just about a picture of your favorite wrestler on a tee shirt. It was about licensing, and then an animated TV show . . .

I said, "Whoa, brother! Are you out of your damn mind?"

But he wasn't. Once he came up with the term "sports-entertainment," there was no limit to what he could do with it.

So we kept at it. We kept pushing the envelope every way we could. Eventually, Vince decided the time was right for a really big event—something that was going to be the Super Bowl and World Series of wrestling.

And he was going to call it *WrestleMania*.

WrestleMania:
March 31, 1985

26

The whole *WrestleMania* thing was just larger and more crazy and more intense than anybody ever could have imagined. And naturally, it was going to be held in Madison Square Garden, the mecca of American sporting events.

I was on the card in a tag-team match. My partner was going to be Mr. T, a stocky, trash-talking bouncer from Chicago who had won a Tough Man contest, parlayed it into a role in *Rocky III*, and then become a star on a TV show called *The A-Team*.

I first heard about Mr. T's interest in wrestling from my agent, Peter Young, who was T's agent too. Peter told me that Mr. T had wrestled in high school and would like nothing better than to get into the ring.

The A-Team was real hot in those days and Mr. T was probably the most recognizable face on television. So I told Peter Young that if Mr. T wanted to wrestle, we'd like to bring him into some special event.

Vince McMahon Jr. put the whole thing together. It was going to be me and T against Paul Orndorff and Rowdy Roddy Piper. Little did we know how much that would irritate certain people—and for completely different reasons.

Paul Orndorff—who I had first met when he was a star athlete at the University of Tampa—didn't like the idea because Mr. T wasn't a wrestler. He was an actor, an outsider, and Orndorff, who was a redneck from my part of Florida, didn't think Mr. T belonged in the ring with us. He was so pissed off about the whole thing that he wanted to break T in half, and he probably could have done it.

Dr. D. had a problem with the match, too. But it wasn't because he didn't think T belonged in the ring with us. Dr. D. was fine with the idea of Mr. T wrestling with us. Dr. D.'s beef was he wanted to be in the ring too. Instead of me teaming up at *WrestleMania* with T, Dr. D. wanted it to be *him*.

"Dr. D. and Mr. T," he would say. "Dr. D. and Mr. T." Over and over again, until he convinced himself the whole thing was his idea. But really, he was just bitching because he wasn't part of the main event.

Me and T take
New York by storm.

One night in Los Angeles when we were building up to *WrestleMania,* Mr. T and I were at ringside when Dr. D. power-walked down to the ring. Fortunately, Vince stepped in. Mr. T didn't know how close he had come to a beating. He couldn't tell if David was playing around with him or being serious.

So we were running around the country, promoting the hell out of *WrestleMania.* But at the same time, for about a month before the event, I was training with Mr. T and teaching him what he needed to know to survive in the ring.

He had won that Tough Man contest back in Chicago, so we knew he could be physical if he had to be. But there's more to wrestling than physical ability. I stayed with him day and night, trying to give him a crash course in Wrestling 101.

Mr. T was excited about it, too. He had always wanted to wrestle and this was his big chance, his opportunity to start at the top. But as we got closer to *WrestleMania* and the pace picked up, his attitude changed. He got pissy about everything. He didn't like the hours, he didn't like zigzagging all over the place.

He would say, "I don't want to do the Regis and Kathie Lee show. I don't want to do the Carson show. I'm tired."

Finally, just a few days before *WrestleMania,* Mr. T gave us our first scare. Up to that point I was with him every day, making appearances and working out with him. But that day, he was nowhere to be found. He just disappeared on me.

It turned out that he was sitting in some park with a wino, drowning his troubles. Finally, we found him and put

Hollywood Hulk Hogan

him on his feet again and thought maybe everything was all right. Then he pulled another disappearing act.

But this time, he did it on the day of the event.

We had been plugging *WrestleMania* for weeks. Madison Square Garden was sold out to the rafters. Everybody was looking forward to seeing Mr. T in the ring for the first time. And for some reason, Mr. T wasn't there.

Vince McMahon started saying, "Okay, where is he? Where is he already?"

I called the Helmsley Palace from the Garden and what do you know? T was still in the room. He was just taking his sweet time.

But two hours before the event Mr. T still hadn't shown up, and now we were all thoroughly rattled. We had everything riding on this event, everything we had worked for, and one of our star attractions was still missing.

WrestleMania

Finally, I got a call from the limo garage downstairs. The good news was Mr. T had arrived. The bad news was he was leaving again.

I said, "What? Don't let him leave, brother!" And I ran down to the limo garage as fast as I could.

The problem was that Mr. T had come in with two big white limousines. And instead of him showing up with just his two bodyguards, he had invited twenty other people to come in with them . . . girls, guys, he had a whole entourage. And of course, Madison Square Garden security wasn't going to let all those people backstage.

I got down to the limo garage just as Mr. T's limos were pulling out. T was cussing, saying, "Screw this, I'm leaving!"

But I got in front of his limo and I wouldn't let him leave, because once he left the building I knew we would never find him again.

Mr. T was screaming at me, "Get out of the way, goddammit!"

But I wouldn't move. I said, "You want to get out of here, brother, you're going to have to roll right over me."

Finally, he got out of the car, but he was still bitching and complaining about his friends not getting into the

Garden. I told him, "Look, man, just give me ten minutes to work on it."

Somehow, I got everybody in. But you could tell that T was still agitated, and it wasn't just about his entourage. He was scared of wrestling that night.

He knew he was out of his element and he had a million excuses why he shouldn't go into the ring. Even though we had trained and prepared for the last month, I don't think he had really ever intended to go through with it.

You know, it's okay to talk like a wrestler and act like a

WrestleMania

wrestler and say you're going to be the main event at *WrestleMania*, but when it comes time to lace up those boots it can get a little scary. I can't imagine coming from the world of acting and stepping into a dressing room where you can feel the hostility in the air because we had never had an outsider in the ring with us before.

So Mr. T knew there were some weird vibes going on. I had to talk him down and tell him everything was cool and not to worry. But on the other hand I was begging Orndorff not to break him in half.

Finally, we got to the dance. And when that red light came on Mr. T was a pro, man. He pulled it off beautifully. He was sucking wind and he was in trouble for a while, but he eventually got through it and did a great job.

At one point, he draped Piper over his shoulders and caught him in an airplane spin. Then, after I pinned Orndorff, the two bad guys began to go at each other. The crowd loved it.

We used Mr. T a bunch of times after that, and then when I went down to WCW years later we used him there too. And I never had that kind of trouble with him again.

But that one time, he could have single-handedly destroyed *WrestleMania*. And if he had, there might never have been another one.

Hollywood Hulk Hogan

Three Guys I Never Expected to See in the Same Place

27

Vince McMahon was pulling out all the stops for *WrestleMania*. In his mind, that meant using the open-form scam approach to come up with the biggest, wildest guests he could think of, whether they had anything to do with wrestling or not.

Liberace was one of Vince's wildest scams of all. When Vince brought him in to be our guest timekeeper, he didn't bring him in to be controversial. He did it because he knew it would work. Hell, he would have brought in Groucho Marx if he were still alive.

Anybody else in 1985 would have said, "Are you nuts? What's Liberace got to do with *WrestleMania*? He's a gay guy in a gold lamé tuxedo. What's he going to do, kick his heels up like the Rockettes?"

But all Vince McMahon could say was, "Hell, yeah!" Sometimes he thinks on a higher level than the rest of us.

As it turned out, Liberace was there for only one day. I remember him being very gracious, very eager to please. The only thing that threw me off a little was when he asked if he could hang his robes and stuff in my dressing room.

Of course, I had to say yes. My biggest fear was I thought he was actually going to get dressed in there. I didn't know at the time if he had AIDS or anything like that, but I was a little leery of his persona and all the white pan-cake makeup he wore. I just didn't know what to expect.

But I didn't want to be rude so I let him hang all of his stuff in my dressing room. He turned out to be a very nice person. We even joked around and took pictures comparing all the rings we had on.

I liked Liberace a lot better than Billy Martin, our guest ring announcer. Billy Martin had managed the New York Yankees a few times and was known for being a great base-ball manager, but a real pain in the ass.

He grew up in San Francisco but he struck me as a

stereotypical New Yorker. Right to the point, nothing subtle about him. And even though he was a little teeny man, he seemed to have a lot of pent-up anger. When he was around the wrestlers, he carried himself like the cock of the walk, like he could beat anybody at anything.

He didn't have a clue that he was in the lions' den. He was around a bunch of guys that could be pretty dangerous when provoked. But even if he knew that, he probably wouldn't have cared. He was Billy Martin. He would probably have cussed out Vince McMahon if he didn't like his chair or something.

But my favorite guest of all was Muhammad Ali, one of my favorite sports figures when I was growing up. He was our referee.

I had met Ali a few times before that, so we didn't need

any introductions. Whenever he would see me he would say, "Can I get a picture with the champ? You're the greatest of all time, Mr. Hogan, the greatest of all time. They said it was me but it's really you. When I grow up I want to be just like you."

I asked Ali not to hit anybody when he got into the ring. But brother, he took that refereeing job seriously. When Piper and Orndorff wouldn't listen to him, he got pissed off and took a swing at them.

Luckily, they ducked and got out of the way. I think even then, sickness and all, he would have taken their heads off if he had connected.

Three Guys . . .

I never knew Ali before he became ill, but there's a light in his eyes that makes me think there's a lot going on in his head. He just can't get it out very well.

People attribute that to his career as a boxer. They say he got hit in the head too often. But I've seen all his fights on tape and he hardly ever took a hard shot to the head. He got hit with a lot of body punches, but that was about it.

So I'd be surprised if it was boxing that caused his problems. Of course, I'm no doctor. That's just my opinion.

Richard Belzer

28

Hulk

The hardest part of *WrestleMania* was the road that led to it, with all the millions of appearances Mr. T and I had to make. And the biggest bump in that road came a couple of days before we were supposed to step into the ring.

Our last stop of the day was supposed to be at the Philadelphia Spectrum. We were scheduled to have a press conference there and meet a bunch of local kids because some of the public schools had let them get out early to see us. I remember it was a little controversial at the time to let kids

Hogan

out of school to see a wrestler and an actor, but there they were.

The situation was tense. Mr. T had been bitching all day about being worked too hard. But since this was our last appointment, I said, "Let's just get through this, brother, and then we can relax."

So we showed up at the Spectrum and all these kids were sitting on the floor. Mr. T started talking to them. And the first thing out of his mouth was "What are you kids doing here? You're supposed to be in school! What the hell is wrong with you, missing school to come see Mr. T and Hulk Hogan!"

He hammered these kids. He was relentless. Finally one kid raised his hand and said, "Mr. T, you're scaring us. You're being mean."

"I ain't being mean," said T. "I'm just telling you the way it is. Mr. T *always* tells it the way it is."

I said to myself, *Here we go. His damn attitude again.*

Anyway, it didn't take too long before Mr. T went storming out of there. And there I was, left holding the bag, with all these kids looking to me for an explanation.

I said, "Mr. T's just excited about *WrestleMania*, kids. He's really a great guy. Give me all your papers and I'll get them all signed."

So I smoothed it over with the kids and got them all their autographs. But the whole time I was thinking that something had really gotten up T's ass. It was out of character even for him to talk to kids that way.

After that, we went back to the Helmsley Palace in New

Hollywood Hulk Hogan

York in our separate limousines. And let me tell you, brother, T wasn't the only one looking forward to some rest. We'd been running hard the last few weeks.

But as soon as my wife and I walked into the room the phone rang. It was Linda McMahon, Vince's wife.

"Terry," she said, "I hate to tell you, but there's one more appearance you've got to make today. You've got to go down to a show called *Hot Properties,* a cable show hosted by a man named Richard Belzer. I don't know how it could have slipped off the itinerary from the publicity company but there are fifty kids in wheelchairs down there, a whole busload of them, and they're waiting for you and Mr. T to show up. You've got to go, Terry, it's a live show, and there are all those kids."

Promoting *Wrestlemania* with Vince McMahon, Muhammed Ali, and Liberace.

"Okay," I said, "I'll go."

Then I had the pleasant task of calling my tag-team partner. "Hey, brother," I said, "I'm sorry to do this to you but there are fifty kids in wheelchairs waiting for us to appear on this show."

"Well," Mr. T said, "I ain't going."

I wasn't in the mood to argue with him. I said, "Okay, I'll go by myself."

So I pulled my cowboy boots back on my swollen feet and started to drag myself out the door. All of a sudden, the phone rang. It was Mr. T.

"Okay," he said, "I'm going with you. But that's it."

I told him, "All right, brother, whatever you say." And we went down to Richard Belzer's *Hot Properties* show. So I put on my game face and walked into the studio, and guess what we saw . . . or rather, what we *didn't* see?

Kids in wheelchairs.

They weren't there.

Now Mr. T was pissed off because he thought we had been conned. I was trying to calm him down in the green room when Richard Belzer walked in.

Mr. T had this metal thing with a big spring on it, some kind of exercise bar he carried around and said was a parking meter he ripped out of the ground. He was cranking on it like crazy in the green room because he was so mad.

Richard Belzer said, "Hey, Mr. T, how you doin'?"

Mr. T wouldn't talk to him. He just kept pumping his parking meter.

So Belzer came over to me and said, "Hulk, we're going to bring you guys out there one at a time instead of together."

I said, "Y'know, it would probably be better if we went out there together."

But he said, "No, I want you guys one at a time, it'll be better for you."

"Okay," I said, "whatever you think, brother. You're the boss. We're just here to help you out."

Then Richard Belzer said, "Hey, they forgot to tell me . . . what about this wrestling thing? Is all that stuff fake? You know, choreographed?"

At the time, the mentality in the wrestling business still dictated that you didn't tell anybody wrestling was fake. And if you did, Vince McMahon himself would slap your head off.

Richard Belzer

So I said, "You know something, brother, probably the best thing to do would be to ask me those questions when we're on camera."

So Richard Belzer smiled at me and said, "I see the game you want to play."

And I'm thinking, *Oh boy, this could be a problem.*

Anyway, Belzer got Mr. T out there first and started asking him questions. Mr. T wouldn't talk. All he kept doing was cranking his parking meter. So Richard Belzer said, "I pity the fool, I pity your momma, I pity your momma's fool," trying to get Mr. T to say something.

T still wasn't talking, but I could just about see the steam coming out of his head. *Great,* I thought. I was so worried about what T would do next, the sweat was dripping off my hands.

But just this once, I could see Mr. T's point. We hadn't come here to get abused. We had come to promote *WrestleMania*. This guy Belzer was setting us up. He was taking cheap shots at us.

All of a sudden, they called me out too.

So Richard Belzer started in on me. He was really just trying to be funny. I see that now. If I knew show business then like I know it now, I could have worked with him and made the show great.

But at the time I had my shorts in a wad. I was tired and Vince had alerted me to watch out for guys who wanted to expose wrestling. Like I said, we weren't as relaxed then about what goes on in the ring as we are today.

"Oh," Belzer said to me, "so you think you're a tough

guy? Go ahead and put me in a wrestling hold. Put me in the Camel Clutch, the Iron Sheik's hold."

I said, "Uh uh, brother, that's the Iron Sheik's hold. I don't know how to do that one. Besides, you don't want me to put you in a wrestling hold."

Belzer said, "Oh, yes I do." Then he turned to his studio audience and asked them, "Don't you want Hulk Hogan to put me in a wrestling hold?"

Everyone in the audience clapped—everyone except my wife, that is. She was giving me the eye and mouthing the words, "Don't do it, Terry." I could read her lips. "Don't do it."

She knew I was pissed. She could tell by looking at me. I was about to tell Richard Belzer to forget it.

Then the band started playing funeral music. "Aw, come on," Belzer said, "what are you, chicken?"

Finally, I'd had enough. I said, "All right, come here."

It was a mistake, and a big one. But I walked with him over to a section of hard floor and told him I was going to put a front chin lock on him. If it hurt too much and he wanted out, all he had to do was tap my leg or something.

So I went to put my hand on his back, and when I did—boom—the drummer hit a rim shot and Belzer took a pratfall. It was funny. I should have gone with it.

Now there's a way to put a front chin lock on somebody where it won't hurt, but that's not the way Hiro Matsuda taught me. He showed me the submission hold version of the front chin lock, where you press a bone in your arm against the carotid artery in the other guy's neck. If you do that, you can make somebody pass out in a second with just five pounds of pressure.

By the time I grabbed hold of Richard Belzer, I was pumped to the eyeballs with adrenaline. I reached in, cinched up, and gave him about five pounds of pressure.

And I felt his body go totally limp.

I thought, *I'd better let him go*. But instead of letting him down gently like I should have, I panicked and let him go all at once. He collapsed like a wet noodle and hit the ground— wham!

Then the strangest thing happened. He jumped right up again and looked stupefied, like a dog hit by a car that didn't know which way to run. Finally, he stared into the camera and said, "We'll be right back."

As he said it, the blood was squirting out of the back of his head all over me. I thought, *What'd I do?*

Belzer said, "Hey, that was great, that was really great."

And all of a sudden the producer and his assistant said, "Richard . . . uh, Richard . . . you're bleeding."

Belzer said, "What? What do you mean?"

He didn't know where he was. It was like he was unconscious but still talking somehow. Then they took him over to the makeup chair and put some compresses on the back of his head.

The producer asked me, "How could you do this to him?"

I said, "I did what he asked for. I put a wrestling hold on him." Of course, I knew I had screwed up. I said to Belzer, "I'm sorry, man. I didn't know you would hit your head when I let go."

He told me, "Don't worry, man, no problem. It was great. Thank you."

Yeah, right.

Anyway, the producer asked us to go back on the air and explain what happened. I said sure. So when we were live again, I said, "Look, man, I made a mistake. The guy asked me to put him in a wrestling hold. I warned him against it because I was afraid he'd get hurt. I wanted him to tap my leg but he didn't do that. Then he passed out and hit his head on the floor. I apologize."

And the producer was going with it. "Yeah, this is something you guys shouldn't try at home. Kids, you see how accidents can happen?"

Mr. T hadn't opened his mouth the whole time. All of a

sudden, he decided to talk. "Hell," he said, "that fool deserved what he got. Hulk Hogan is the champion of the world. What's wrong with that idiot?"

I went, *Oh no.*

"Yeah," T said, "he's lucky he didn't get killed." He was on a roll. "Next time we'll get the rest of you stupid fools."

Oh my God. I thought, *Please, T, please shut up.*

No such luck. "The fool should've known better," T went on. "Stupid idiot. What is he, crazy? He should know he's messing with Mr. T and Hulk Hogan, the champion of the world."

He just went on and on and on.

I said to myself, *We're dead.*

On the way back to the hotel, we started laughing our asses off. This thing was so bizarre, it was funny. When we got back to the Helmsley Palace, T started breaking chairs and stuff.

"I told him not to mess with us," he said.

He was going crazy, taking credit for everything that happened. I just thought, *Oh my God, he's nuts. He's out of control.*

About two weeks later, it wasn't too funny because Richard Belzer hit me and Mr. T and Vince McMahon with a multimillion-dollar lawsuit. All of a sudden, Mr. T wasn't laughing anymore.

For months and months, we went back and forth with Belzer's lawyers. Finally, it looked like we were going to have to go to court. Belzer was asking for five million bucks in damages, but we had a feeling the jury would see

Vince and his deep pockets and award Belzer a lot more.

At the time, Vince McMahon's company lawyer was a guy named Ted Dinsmore. He had been with Vince's family for a long time. Just as we were preparing to go into court to fight for our lives, Ted Dinsmore happened to mention that he had been talking to Richard Belzer's lawyers.

He said they would settle the case for a certain amount of money. I can't say how much it was because the settlement agreement we signed prohibits me from doing that.

"But," Ted Dinsmore said, "I think we'll be all right if we—"

I said, "What? *How* much? Jesus Christ, did you tell Vince?"

Ted Dinsmore said, "Oh no, I figured you guys would want to—"

I said, "Are you out of your mind, Ted? Just pay it and get rid of him."

So Vince and Mr. T and I split the money and paid Richard Belzer off. And I thought that was the end of it.

In the meantime, my wife Linda had decided to build her dream house in Florida. She was so into it that she oversaw the whole thing, acted as general contractor and everything. She brought in artisans from all over the world. It was a huge project and it seemed to get bigger every minute.

But when she was done, she had an authentic French farmhouse, almost twenty thousand square feet in size. It looks just like something you would see in Burgundy. The roof on it, which was imported from Europe, is almost four hundred years old.

Three or four years ago, I got on an airplane and picked up a magazine. As soon as I opened it, I saw a picture of Richard Belzer. He was sitting in Nice, France . . . in front of his *authentic French farmhouse*.

I started reading the article. Belzer was saying, "Thanks to the settlement I got in the Hulk Hogan lawsuit, we came straight over here and bought this house."

I took the magazine home and showed it to my wife. She went nuts. It was a good settlement from our point of view, but I guess it was still a lot of money—enough for Belzer to go out and buy a house in France.

According to the article, he named it "Chez Hogan."

Smashing Media Barriers

29

Even before the first *WrestleMania*, there had been interest in Hulk Hogan from outside the wrestling world. When I got to New York, it just exploded.

First I hosted *Saturday Night Live* and did *Fernando's Hideaway* with Billy Crystal. Then I showed up on a soap opera called *Search for Tomorrow*. Imagine . . . a wrestler on a soap opera. It was crazy, brother.

That same week, my picture appeared on the cover of *Sports Illustrated*. That picture gave me a level of credibility no wrestler had ever enjoyed before. It put

me in the same bracket as guys like Mantle and Gretsky, the all-time legends of sports. I was running with the big dogs, boom, in your face.

I still see copies of that *Sports Illustrated*. I must sign five or six of them wherever I go. And when it shows up, it's always in perfect shape. These people have saved it like it's a monument to me.

About the same time, I started my little run on *The A-Team*. The connection there was Peter Young, who was Mr. T's agent. By then, he had become my agent too.

Peter Young, remember, was the wrestling fan from Boston who wound up getting me the Thunderlips gig in *Rocky III*. So even before he was my agent, he was doing good things for me.

Anyway, the producers of *The A-Team* gave me a couple of episodes to start with. I appeared as the salt half of a salt-and-pepper dynamic duo with Mr. T, and the ratings came up on those episodes. After that, the producers talked to me about staying on the show the rest of the year.

But it wasn't just that Mr. T and I worked well together on the screen or drew a few extra viewers. The producers had also seen that I was an effective buffer between Mr. T and George Peppard, the other star of the show.

You wouldn't know it from watching *The A-Team*, but Peppard and T hated each other with a passion. On the other hand, I liked both George Peppard and Mr. T, so I became the peacekeeper on the set.

It all started when Mr. T went to George Peppard's trailer with a copy of *The Hollywood Reporter* in his hands. He was standing outside the trailer, quoting from *The Hollywood Reporter*, and roaring at the top of his lungs.

"Mr. T is not a real actor, is that what I heard? Mr. T is a pompous ass, is that what I heard? Mr. T makes more money than anybody even though he's the worst actor on the set, is that what I heard? Well, get out here, Hannibal, I'll kick your ass."

I pulled Mr. T away from the trailer and said, "Hey, man, calm down."

From that point on, I became the guy who would keep them from killing each other. I would say, "Oh, he didn't really mean that," or "He's sorry he said that," or "He didn't mean to arrive late at the set," or "He's not really trying to steal your scene."

213

Everybody liked to have me around because I calmed all the crap down. So I'd say it wasn't necessarily my acting ability they wanted on the set of *The A-Team*. It was my refereeing ability.

They offered me forty-five grand an episode, which was big money at the time. But I told them I wasn't interested in a long-term commitment. I knew the wrestling business was my base. If I left it to appear in a TV series it could be over in thirteen weeks, whereas wrestling was on a roll—and Vince McMahon was being so good to me, I'd be crazy to give that up.

In the end, I did three or four episodes. That was it.

Meanwhile, we were building on the Rock 'n' Wrestling concept that had started when we brought in Cyndi Lauper, who was a very popular singer at the time.

Cyndi had Lou Albano, a wrestling manager, in the music video for her hit song "Girls Just Want to Have Fun." That was her first real link to pro wrestling.

David Wolfe, who was engaged to Cyndi in those days and was also her manager, was a big wrestling fan. As luck would have it, he lived down the street from me. One thing led to another and all of a sudden singer Cyndi Lauper got even more involved in the wrestling business.

About a month before *WrestleMania*, in February 1985, MTV broadcast *The War to Settle the Score*, where both Cyndi and Mr. T got involved in a confrontation between me and Rowdy Roddy Piper. The fan reaction was terrific.

Two weeks later, I ended up escorting Cyndi to the Grammys, the annual awards ceremony for the music

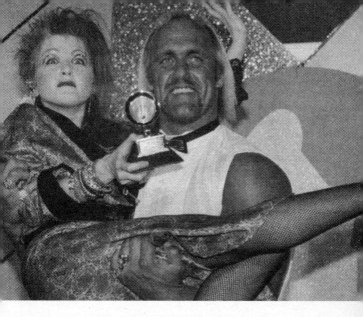

industry. Our seats were in the first row because she had a couple of songs—"Girls Just Want to Have Fun" and "Time after Time"—that were up for consideration that year.

My ass had barely hit my seat when they announced the Best New Artist of the Year. Boom, Cyndi Lauper won the first Grammy. I picked her up in my arms and took a picture with her, Cyndi in her dress and me in my sleeveless tuxedo. She was smiling and carrying on.

From that point on, everybody thought we were dating. But I never dated her. People would ask me how Cyndi was, and I would say, "She's great, man, I love her to death." Which I did. She was and is an awesome person.

Then down the road, when Cyndi wasn't involved with

215

wrestling anymore, they would ask me about her and I'd say, "I had to kick her out, brother. I couldn't take it anymore, there was too much red dye on the pillowcase."

But we were just very good friends. She was great for the wrestling business and her ex-fiancé David Wolfe was a real trouper. I have nothing but good things to say about those people.

Big Matches, Big Gates

Hollywood

Hulk

30

The main event of *WrestleMania II* was scheduled for the Los Angeles Sports Arena in April 1986. Vince McMahon set it up that I'd be facing King Kong Bundy, a guy who was four hundred fifty pounds with a bald head and shaved eyebrows, and was one of the more menacing heels we had at the time.

A few months earlier, Bundy hurt me real bad. I was hunched face first over the turnbuckle and another bad guy named the Magnificent Muraco was

Hogan

I was a heel in my first go-around with the World Wide Wrestling Federation.

Taking down the Iron Sheik in Madison Square Garden.

Back in the late seventies,
Ed Leslie and I wrestled
as Terry and Ed Boulder.

Glorying in my victory over Andre the Giant in 1987.

Bringing the crowd into the match with a cupped hand to the ear.

When Andre grabbed you, there was no getting away.

© 2002 World Wrestling Entertainment, Inc.

Showing the Big Boss Man
who's boss back in 1988.

Getting the best of my pal Ed Leslie, or Brutus Beefcake.

Randy Savage wore red and yellow when
we wrestled as the Mega-Powers.

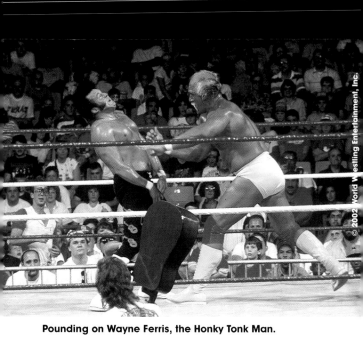

Pounding on Wayne Ferris, the Honky Tonk Man.

Nothing like a steel chair to get your juices flowing.

The title match I eventually lost to Ultimate Warrior.

You got that right, brother—my fifth championship belt!

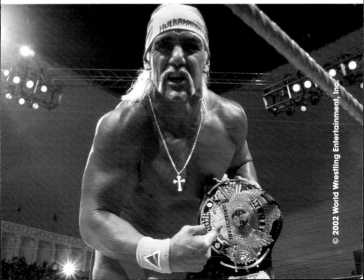

The red and yellow makes a splash in **WCW** territory.

COURTESY PRO WRESTLING ILLUSTRATED PHOTOGRAPHS

Hollywood Hulk Hogan returns to wreak havoc with the WWE.

© 2002 World Wrestling Entertainment, Inc.

The fans went wild for me at *WrestleMania X8*.

Hollywood Hulk Hogan and The Rock—a battle for the ages.

Age before beauty, brother.

The red and yellow is back and better than ever.

standing on the ring apron, holding my arms outside the ring.

Bundy was supposed to run into me and squash me, then back up and squash me a second time. It was supposed to look like he had injured me.

And he couldn't just act like he was squashing me. He had to really do it, or it would look fake. So when the time came, Bundy ran into me full-tilt—all four hundred fifty pounds of him. And it looked like he had injured me because he really *had*.

With my arms being held out in front of me, I couldn't protect myself. All I could do was hold my breath and have everything flexed. But I wasn't sturdy enough to hold back all that hard-charging weight.

Bundy ended up popping my rib cage the way you would pop one of your knuckles. The pain was so bad it made me black out.

They took me to the hospital and checked me out. Fortunately, the X-rays showed I had only suffered a few hairline fractures—enough to leave me wheezing and uncomfortable for a while, but without any serious damage.

It got the wrestling fans going, though. They wrote so many get-well cards and letters—four or five hundred thousand of them—that Vince McMahon had to hire a crew of people to answer them.

That was the buildup for *WrestleMania II*.

The weird part of that *WrestleMania* was how Vince split the crew up at three different venues—Chicago, New York, and Los Angeles. In Chicago, we had a battle royal with all these football players. In New York, we had a box-ing match between Roddy Piper and Mr. T. And in Los Angeles, we had a steel cage match pitting me against the man who supposedly put me out of action.

I remember getting my share of bumps and bruises in that steel cage against Bundy. But in the end, Bundy was a bloody mess. I even got to drag his manager, Bobby "The Brain" Heenan, into the ring. When it was all over, I had won, and *Hulkamania* was running wilder than ever.

By that time, wrestling had become so popular that we were running shows in Toronto once a month, at Maple Leaf Gardens. All of a sudden, in 1986, Vince McMahon tried to get an extra date there. But when he went to book the date, he found out the building was already taken.

We had already announced that we were coming back to Toronto, so we booked an outdoor venue, CNE Stadium, which was really too big for the crowd we had in mind. With a little promotion, we figured we would draw ten thousand people, maybe a few more if we got lucky.

I mean, it wasn't a *WrestleMania* match. It wasn't a Pay-Per-View. It was just the climax of a little feud between me and Paul Orndorff. After the first *WrestleMania*, he had become my tag-team partner, but according to our story line I had pissed him off by outshining him in all our matches. Either I would win the match for us or I would tag him after our opponent was already down.

At a little TV match in Poughkeepsie, New York, he let his jealousy get the best of him and nearly took my head off with a clothesline, followed by his signature sitting piledriver. It surprised the hell out of everybody in the place.

We made it a title match, so there would be an additional reason for people to come see us in Toronto, but we didn't expect much. Then, on August 28, 1986, I got out of the car to walk into the CNE Stadium and got blown the hell away. Instead of ten thousand people in the place, there were almost sixty-five thousand.

A new all-time wrestling attendance record. Go figure.

But the record wouldn't stand for long. Not with *WrestleMania III* pitting Hulk Hogan against his longtime rival, Andre the Giant, on March 29, 1987.

Since my return to the company Andre and I had been tag-team partners. In fact, a lot of fans didn't even remember our confrontation in August 1980, at Shea Stadium. It seemed like the time was getting ripe for another one.

Hulkamania was hot as hell and I was at the pinnacle of my popularity—the biggest attraction in wrestling at the time. And the guy I would be going up against had been the biggest attraction in wrestling up until that time. There was no telling what we could draw with a combination like that.

We built up a story line in which Andre was getting jealous of me. Things really started to heat up at a TV taping in my hometown of Tampa, where I was doing an interview with "Rowdy" Roddy Piper. Andre came out in the middle of it and challenged me to a match. He reached up and ripped the crucifix right off my chest, then threw it on the ground.

I had some Mentholatum on my finger and I was supposed to stick it in my eye to make it look like Andre's ripping my crucifix off had made me start crying. And hell, I *tried* to stick the stuff in my eye. But I was too scared, so I missed my eye and hit my eyebrow instead. I never did get any of the Mentholatum in my eye.

But it was cool because when he ripped the cross off, his fingernails scratched my chest and blood came pouring out. When I picked up the cross a wave of emotion came over me, and the tears started to come out even without the Mentholatum. I didn't expect that to happen, but it's a weird thing to have your cross ripped off.

That set the stage for a battle of the titans between the

Hollywood Hulk Hogan

Giant and Hulk Hogan, who *wanted* to be the Giant.

We knew it was going to be huge, so we booked the biggest venue we could find—the Pontiac Silverdome, where the Detroit Lions played. The permanent seating there alone was more than 80,000. With some temporary seating on the field, we could blow our own attendance record out of the water.

There was a huge buildup to the match, an incredible amount of promotion and planning. The tricky part was keeping Andre and me apart until *WrestleMania*. We wanted to make sure the fans didn't see any physical encounter between us until the night we got into the ring.

All along, I was asking Vince what Andre and I were going to do when the match started, but he kept putting me off and saying, "I'm not sure yet." Vince wasn't the kind to make a snap decision. He would always wait until he heard everybody's opinion and then figure it out.

When it came to my wrestling Andre, Vince ended up listening to a lot of conflicting points of view. Some guys were saying, "The Giant's never been beaten," and other guys were saying, "The Hulk should beat the Giant." Some guys were saying, "Andre's too old and Hulk's the up-and-coming star," and still other guys were saying, "Hulk doesn't deserve to beat Andre."

I didn't expect Vince to make up his mind until the eleventh hour. Finally, at almost twelve o'clock the night before *WrestleMania*, Vince came to me and said, "I want you to win the match."

The only problem was he hadn't discussed it yet with Andre.

As powerful as Vince was in those days, he wasn't the strongest force in the wrestling universe. The strongest force was Andre. If he had said, "I won't let Hogan win," I wouldn't have won. That's all there was to it.

So before Vince went in to discuss his decision with Andre, he wanted to have his gun loaded. "I need to know exactly what I'm talking about," he told me.

For the first time ever, I sat down in advance of a wrestling match and laid it out in detail. I gave it to Vince step-by-step and he wrote it down on a yellow, lined legal pad.

First, Andre and I were going to argue for a while. Then he was going to throw the first punch. I was going to block it and hit him with three big punches of my own. And when I went to slam him, he would fall on top of me.

Andre had a bad back at the time. If he had the mentality of some other wrestlers I've met, that match in the Silverdome would never have taken place. But Andre was old school. Wrestling was his life. When he had to work injured, he didn't complain. He just got into the ring and did his job.

But because I knew Andre's back was bad, I gave some thought to helping him out. When he was on the mat and he had to get up, I made sure he was close to the ropes so he could use them to pull himself up.

So I laid out the whole match. I had Andre bodyslamming me a couple of times and stepping on my back, the whole thing. Then Vince took my plan and went to Andre and told him he wanted Andre to lose the match in front of the largest crowd in the history of wrestling.

I'm sure Andre would have loved to have been fifteen years younger and squashed Hulk Hogan in the middle of the ring. But he was a businessman. He knew that the situation cried out for something special, something the fans had never seen before, and the one thing they had definitely never seen was somebody pinning Andre the Giant.

Andre knew what I was like from all the wars we had fought in Japan. You had to fight for your life over there, and no matter what they threw at me I wouldn't quit. I would jump up like somebody was stealing my children or something. So he knew that out of everybody, I would work the hardest to protect the wrestling business.

So when Vince McMahon asked Andre if he would let me win, out of respect for me Andre said, "Yes."

Without a doubt, the fans were going to see a great moment in wrestling history. But I got a notion in my head that we could take it one step further. Before the match started, I told Andre I didn't want to just beat him. I wanted to really give the people something they could tell their grandchildren. I wanted to bodyslam him.

It was a crazy idea.

I had slammed Andre back in 1980, but he weighed a lot more now. And he was so big that his crotch was at the same height as the middle of my chest. He said he didn't think I could lift him.

I said, "Well, brother, we're going to find out."

When we got to that point in the match, my first move was to get my arm between his legs. That was pretty hard, considering his thighs touched almost all the way down to his knees. Then I had to get him to come toward me so I pushed him into the ropes, and as he came forward again I pulled him in and used his momentum to pick him up.

The problem was, I could only get him up so far. I couldn't turn him because he was too heavy. So I just heaved as hard as I could and turned him the rest of the way. But when I did that, I tore my back out.

If you look at me now, I've got a big hole in my back muscle where it tore right in half that night. That was the price I paid to lift Andre the Giant.

But I got him. I turned him and slammed him and pinned him. It was something that happened once and will never happen again.

If I hadn't made it all the way, I would have been

screwed. Andre would have fallen on me and probably killed me. I had him up so high, he would have crushed me to death.

And there was nothing I could have done about it. If you look at the tape of that match, you can see Andre's knuckles were dragging on the ground when I picked him up. He was so damned big, his leg was almost as big as my whole body.

But somehow, I slammed him.

The funny thing is weeks earlier we had gotten a call from the local promoter recommending that we cancel the date at the Silverdome. Vince McMahon asked him why.

"Because," the promoter said, "the Rolling Stones are going to be here the week before you and the Pope is going to be here the week after. There isn't enough money in the marketplace for people to buy tickets to all the events."

But Vince was willing to roll the dice. "We're not canceling," he said.

The Stones came in and sold 88,000 tickets. Not bad. But Andre the Giant versus Hulk Hogan did even better. We drew almost 94,000 people.

The Pope, God bless him, only filled 80,000 seats. But it was okay. I was preaching the gospel in the ring that day anyway, so whoever came got their dose.

Hulkamania Runs Wild on TV

31 Because the wrestling and rock music idea was so strong, we were approached by CBS and an animation company called DIC to do an animated, Saturday morning TV show called *Hulk Hogan's Rock 'n' Wrestling*. The show ended up running for two seasons, from September '85 until June '87, and it was damn good. Kids loved it. Parents loved it.

No one ever knew it had major talent problems.

The wrestlers who appeared in the cartoons didn't supply their own voices. Actors did them. My voice was done by Brad Garrett, who has a part now on the sitcom *Everybody Loves Raymond.*

But the voice part of it wasn't an issue. The problem was the little live-action ins and outs. Wrestlers like Big John Studd or Junkyard Dog or the Iron Sheik would appear in those spots and give some funny little commentary that led into the next animated segment.

It would be something like "After I washed the elephant, I picked up my car and I threw my back out. Well, watch this and see how it happened."

But Vince McMahon was real strict about certain things. For instance, the wrestlers' contracts said they couldn't cuss in the ring, because kids might hear them from the seats. One of the things Vince was strictest about was drugs. And as soon as you wrote a wrestler into the show, bam, he would fail a drug test.

It was a random test, given every three weeks. You would come to a TV and they would pick ten or fifteen guys to be tested. You would never know who it was going to be. And every so often, somebody failed.

Another promoter might have said, "All right, try to clean it up." But not Vince. He would shoot himself in the foot, bang, and take the guy off TV. And the rule was you had to be on TV to be on the cartoon show.

We had four or five guys who were major players in the cartoon who either quit or died or couldn't pass the drug test. So to keep the cartoon alive you had to keep these

guys walking the straight and narrow. It was a constant grind—but not for me. All I had to do was show up in Baltimore every month to produce my ins and outs.

Even before *Hulk Hogan's Rock 'n' Wrestling* was over, I got involved in another little TV venture. Dolly Parton had a CBS special in the works and she was trying to do well enough to get it picked up as a series.

I guess she wanted me to appear on her show, so she called my house on her home phone and left a message on my answering machine. She told me over and over how much she loved me. "God," she said, "I *love* you, Hulk Hogan!"

Well, I got a lot of heat from my wife about that. She thought it was a fan who had gotten my number and to tell you the truth, so did I. We couldn't figure out why Dolly Parton would call and not her agent or her manager.

Anyway, I called her back and she said she wanted me to be part of her special. She said she'd been having a dream for the last year where she married me, and she wanted to open her show with the same type of dream.

Also, she wanted to produce a music video with me using a song she had written called "Headlock on my Heart." *He had a headlock on my heart, it was a takedown from the start* . . . something like that. It sounded crazy but I agreed to do it.

So when the pilot came out, it opened with Dolly Parton lying in bed reading a wrestling magazine. When she fell asleep, boom, I showed up. We were in a wrestling ring and she got married to me, and her dream came true that she got to marry her hero Hulk Hogan.

I guess it helped her show get picked up for a while. But as I recall, the series didn't last too long.

I found out something about Dolly Parton from that experience. She says "I love you" a lot more often than most people.

When I first got there and she kept telling me she loved me, I thought I was something special. I thought she was genuinely a big fan. Then I saw that she told *everybody* she loved them, from the cameraman to the key grip to the other eighty guys walking around the set.

Apparently, that's her style. "Oh, honey, I love you for bringing me that jelly doughnut, I love you for bringing my car around back, I love you for being so sweet and appearing on my show."

So she loved *everybody*. I wasn't anyone special. But I didn't know that at first. In fact, I didn't have a clue what this woman was up to.

I was also making commercials at the time, both in the United States and in Japan. I plugged everything from Right Guard deodorant and vitamins to tennis shoes and air conditioners.

All of a sudden, CBS, NBC, and ABC started looking at wrestling in a different light. They had always seen pro wrestling as something that belonged on the UHF dial somewhere around midnight. Then along came *Hulkamania* and they said, "Oh my God, these syndicated wrestling shows are pulling better numbers than our prime time dramas. Maybe we should look into this."

Back in 1985, we had been approached by NBC's entertainment honcho Brandon Tartikoff, who was a friend of Vince McMahon, and sports president Dick Ebersol, who was a good friend of mine. Tartikoff said, "Okay, let's do a two-hour special. We'll take *Saturday Night Live* off the air one week, and we'll put on the Saturday night card. We'll call it *The Main Event*."

Naturally, we wanted to succeed, so we used our syndi-

cated vehicles and everything we had going in every marketplace to pump up the numbers on it. And it paid off. We came out of the chute blazing and got some great ratings.

After that, NBC wanted to do a prime-time wrestling show once a month. We did that for a few years and it opened up an even bigger audience to *Hulkamania*.

I was everywhere, brother. I was on network TV. I was on syndicated TV. I saturated the marketplace. A guy sitting with a bent clothes wire on his TV in Botswana might not know who the hell Marilyn Monroe or John Wayne was. But he knew who Hulk Hogan was because I was in his home every week.

Nobody in Hungary knew who eighties' superstars like Michael J. Fox and Rob Lowe were, but even the people in the tiniest town square watching the only TV in town knew who Hulk Hogan was.

So I became the most visible media star of the eighties. It was documented in polls that my face, with the bald head and the bandanna and the blond mustache, was better known than anyone else's.

The time seemed right to try a new medium. That's how Vince McMahon and I got involved in producing a movie called *No Holds Barred*.

32

Vince McMahon and I made *No Holds Barred*, the first feature-length movie for both of us, in 1989.

Originally, I was going to make *No Holds Barred* with New Line Cinema. Vince and the company weren't involved. Then Vince stepped in and said, "I'll produce this movie and I'll pay you the same amount of money that you would have gotten from New Line."

Vince McMahon wasn't movie-friendly in those days the way he is today. I was his shining star and he was worried that I wouldn't be shown in the

right light. But that wasn't all he was worried about. He was concerned that I would make this movie and never wrestle again.

Of course, that was the furthest thing from my mind.

I knew wrestling was my base. I was going to go do the movie and come back like a faithful dog. But Vince reeled me back in anyway, just to make sure he was in control of the situation—making sure he wouldn't lose his golden goose.

Anyway, I was pumped about making *No Holds Barred*. I had done *Rocky III*, so I thought I knew what I was getting myself into. But *No Holds Barred* was different. It was brutal—as Vince and I would find out.

Originally, a writer had been hired to come up with the script for *No Holds Barred*. But when he turned it in, it sucked. Of course, he was going to get credit for it even if it got rewritten fifty times, because that's how the Writers' Guild works.

But Vince and I didn't care about who got credit for it. So we got a hotel room in Redington Beach and sat there for three days, twenty-four hours a day, rewriting this lame script.

I was going to play Rip Thomas, a wrestling champion. And a rival organization was going to try to lure me away. That was the premise. But coming up with the details was a long, drawn-out process.

After a while, I just got delirious. I was spacing in and out. And that's when we had to write the final fight scene between my character and Zeus, the guy we had set up as the villain.

It wasn't happening, though. No matter how hard we worked at it, we couldn't get it right. So I told Vince, "The hell with it. I've got to go to the can."

I was so tired that as soon as my ass hit the seat, my eyes closed and I started daydreaming. And in my daydream the whole fight scene was playing itself out, and you know what? It was great.

All of a sudden I started yelling, "I got it! I got it!"

I ran out of the bathroom and told Vince how it was going to go down, from Zeus coming into the ring to his attacking me to his ripping the ring post in half to his trying to use it like a sword against me.

I told him to write as fast as he could. We didn't have a tape recorder or anything so Vince just scribbled down everything I said.

The hard part for me was keeping my eyes closed and

trying to spit everything out before I lost it. But when I was done, and Vince had gotten it all down, we had the type of fight scene we wanted.

Next, we had to cast all the parts, especially the part of Zeus. So we went out to Los Angeles and saw all these monster actors. We were looking at them one after another but none of them felt quite right to me.

Then this huge African-American guy showed up. He had his wrestling gear on, his boots and this huge belt. One of his eyes had been blinded so it was gray, and his other eye was crossed, and he had one eyebrow straight across his head. He was hitting himself in the chest and screaming like he was on fire.

He told us his name was Tim Lister Jr. His nickname, strangely enough, was "Tiny."

I said, "That's the guy. Just tell everybody else to leave."

Vince knew right away, too. The guy just blew us away.

Making *No Holds Barred* was tough on Vince because it was his money that was at stake and because he was doing two things at once. During the day, he was filming with me, and at night, as I was getting my three or four hours of sleep, he was up booking wrestling and trying to keep his business alive.

It was tough on *me* because I was in front of the cameras every day, almost every waking minute. I had taken a leave of absence from wrestling to do this, never dreaming that making a film could be a lot harder than being in the ring.

The good thing about working that hard was that it developed a bond between Vince and me. No one but us

Whatever It Takes

could understand what we were going through or the sacri-fices we were making.

When we finished working our eighteen-hour days and we were ready to drop, we would go train at Lee Haney's Animal Kingdom in Atlanta. (Lee Haney was a bodybuilder, a six-time Mr. Olympia.) And when we were done training, usually at about three o'clock in the morning, we'd pop the trunk of our car and drink a beer.

Vince would call it our "heart attack beer." We would drink it to calm our nerves. Then we would go to sleep for three or four hours and be back on the set at six A.M.

We were like cyborgs, brother. Sleep was our enemy. We would just change the battery in our forearm and keep on going. That's where Vince and I got the motto "Whatever it takes."

Finally, we finished our little, low-budget film and took a deep breath. We figured the hard part was over. All we had to do was sit back and see how much money we were going to make.

That's when we found out we couldn't get the film into the theaters.

We had no idea that was going to happen. We didn't know that we could go to twenty different theaters that would love to have our film and get turned down by every damn one of them.

Because if they took Hulk Hogan's one little film, Paramount and United Artists and Twentieth Century-Fox, who gave them a hundred films a year, could say, "Well, we're not giving you *our* films anymore."

So we found out that we couldn't peddle this thing out of our trunk. We had to have a distributor. And the one we finally hooked up with was New Line.

Of course, they cut themselves a rich deal. They weren't going to have any production costs because Vince McMahon had already paid for all of that stuff, so it was all profit for them.

New Line was a small company at the time, but they got the movie in a thousand or twelve hundred theaters the first week. I thought my fans would say, "It's just a wrestling film. We can see Hulk Hogan wrestle on Saturday for free. Why should we go to a theater to see him?"

But for some reason, they came to the theaters to see me. Maybe they were people who had seen me eight years earlier in *Rocky III* and liked what they saw. I don't know, brother. But I remember we blew the doors off the theaters.

I mean, the critics didn't like it. They said I couldn't act and there was nothing good about it. But this low-budget thriller that cost seven or eight million to make was up there with the big boys at the box office.

In fact, in the second week it was out, it finished ahead of *Ghostbusters II*. I said to myself, *That's interesting*. This little film that nobody thought would make a ripple was doing better than a major motion picture.

That opened New Line's eyes. They said to themselves, "Maybe this Hulk Hogan character is marketable. Maybe he's got a following." And they signed me up to do two more films.

But Vince and I learned a valuable lesson about making

movies. We learned that to get back to dollar one, you've got to bring in about two and a half times your investment. So if you put ten million in, you have to make twenty-five back before you break even—which meant that the wrestling business was a lot more lucrative.

Meanwhile, Vince got an idea. The character of Zeus was so popular, he decided to take the actor who played him and bring him into the ring for a Pay-Per-View.

The guy wasn't a professional wrestler but he had wrestled as an amateur, so he was easy to train. I only took him into the ring maybe five or six times. And on this one occasion, you could say a match was choreographed.

But for good reason. The guy was so big and strong, I wanted to make sure his strength wasn't mistaken for meanness. I mean, if he hurt one of the wrestlers accidentally, they would have gone, "You son of a bitch!" and gotten even with him.

I didn't want this naïve newcomer to come in there and have some guy pull his other eye out. So I made sure he handled the wrestlers with kid gloves, and I begged them to help me get through this.

They weren't exactly thrilled about me bringing in an outsider. It was hard to explain the benefits of it to them. Then, at our *SummerSlam* in 1989, Brutus Beefcake—who was my old friend Ed Leslie—teamed up with me to defeat Zeus and Randy Savage. When the other wrestlers saw the ton of money we all made from the Pay-Per-View, they were happy.

My next film came out of nowhere. It started when my agent called me up and said, "Steven Spielberg wants you in his new movie. It's called *Gremlins 2: The New Batch*. It's not a very big part and there's not a lot of money in it, but you're going to work with Spielberg. If I were you I wouldn't turn it down."

I said, "I'm there."

They told me it would be two days of filming. Just a cameo role, really. But I could handle that. Hell, I was going to work with Steven Spielberg!

When I got there, I saw that the dressing room they had set aside for me wasn't much more than a broom closet. It was no big deal. I was so excited about meeting Spielberg that I didn't care.

"Okay," they told me, "put your Hulk Hogan clothes on.

Whatever It Takes

You're going to run the gremlins out of the theater." Cool.

So I changed and went running out to the set, all ready to mind my Ps and Qs and do the humble bumble double probation routine, and not really minding at all—because in a minute, I'd be talking to Steven Spielberg. Then I would have a chance to show him I wasn't just a yelling, screaming, bald-headed, peroxide-blond maniac. There was more to me than that.

I was hoping he would say, "Hey, this guy might have something. Maybe I can make him a transvestite or a bad guy in my next film, or a transvestite *and* a bad guy. Maybe I can stick a couple of bolts in his neck and make him the next Terminator."

So I went out onto the set and I started looking for Steven Spielberg. But instead of Spielberg, I saw this other guy telling people what to do. I saw him telling the cameraman when to roll and when to cut. And I realized . . . I was with the second unit director. Steven Spielberg was with the stars of the film directing the money scenes.

So I went all the way out there and worked on *Gremlins 2* but I never got to meet Steven Spielberg. That was just a carrot they dangled in front of me.

In the end, though, it was cool. I took my kids to see the movie, and when they spotted their dad in it their eyes popped. And that was just as good as meeting Spielberg. Maybe even better.

Anyway, by then I was in the process of making another film—the first of the two I had promised to do with New Line. They had a script lying around called *Urban Commando*. They tweaked it a little here and there and tailored it to fit me, and the result was a pretty good low-budget kids' film called *Suburban Commando*.

Technically, I was the movie's executive producer. But really, I didn't do anything. It just meant I got an extra check in the mail.

Suburban Commando came out in 1991, lasted two or three weeks in the theaters, and made money—not a ton of it, but enough that I didn't get branded as somebody who couldn't push a film. My costars were Christopher Lloyd and Shelley Duvall, who had gotten their starts in TV sitcoms.

Shelley Duvall was very steady, very even-tempered. She would say things like, "We can do it, no problem." Nothing bothered her.

Christopher Lloyd was pretty businesslike too—while he was on the set. But after work, it was a whole different story.

He was going through a divorce at the time, so my wife and I decided to take him out at night and keep him company. He took us down to Melrose Avenue and led us into all these bars where everybody had spiked, orange hair.

I was scared to death. But the kids all said, "Hey, Christopher, what's up? Come here, man, drink this. Smoke some of this."

He knew everybody in every bar up and down Sunset and Melrose. I said to my wife, "This guy's not what we think he is."

I ended up becoming really good friends with him and I felt bad about seeing him go through his divorce. But what

247

a survivor he was. He strolled through the whole mess with ease while we were shooting the movie.

A little while later, it was time for my third film with New Line. They gave me a handful of scripts and treatments. "Here's A, B, C, D, and E," they said. "Pick the one you like best."

But I met with a guy named Bob Shaye, who was one of the executives there, and pitched my own treatment. "What about *this*?" I asked.

He looked at me. "You write your own stuff?"

"Not really," I said, "but I kind of know what works for me."

He thought about it and decided he liked my idea, but it needed some work. "I'm going to send you to New York," he told me. "There's a guy there named Michael Gottlieb who wrote a movie called *Mannequin*. But if you don't think you can work with him, we'll find you somebody else."

So I went to New York and met with Michael Gottlieb. He was a real skinny guy with buck teeth and big round glasses. We sat in the lobby of the Plaza Hotel and I laid this thirteen-page treatment on him.

Right away, he started hitting me with ideas. What about this? What about that? "What about a tea party with the girl and they put curlers in your hair? What about the kids torture you?"

I said, "Okay, brother, you're the guy."

So he wrote *Mr. Nanny*.

Of course, it was another low-budget film, so they didn't give us much to work with. We had only one toilet seat to break over my head, only one anchor to hit the guy in the face with, only one pair of jeans to dye red in the swimming pool.

But we turned out a hell of a little film. It did well in the theaters and then it had an incredible shelf life. It went to video, it went international, it turned a bunch of money. I still keep getting big checks in the mail from it, so it had a tremendous back end as well as a front end.

So my first few movies were moneymakers. Of course, I hadn't bodyslammed the movie business like I did the wrestling business. I learned it was more political connections than talent and I didn't have a lot of either.

But I had done well enough to draw some attention. It would give me the chance to appear in other movies and TV shows down the line.

That would turn out to be a good thing *and* a bad thing.

The Trump Plaza WrestleManias

33

WrestleMania IV at Trump Plaza in Atlantic City was different because Vince McMahon was going to put the belt on somebody new—"The Macho Man" Randy Savage.

In February, I had lost the heavyweight championship belt to Andre the Giant in my first unsuccessful title defense, but the championship was declared vacant when it turned out Andre's "friend" Ted DiBiase—who was playing a greedy rich guy called "The Million Dollar Man"—had "paid off" the ref to give Andre the victory. So Vince set up a sixteen-man tournament for the championship belt, which Randy was supposed to win when it was all over.

Randy Savage was pretty darn hot at the time. He and his wife Elizabeth, who was also his partner, had taken a baby-face turn and had lots of momentum.

The agreement was that Randy would take the belt and keep it until I was done making *No Holds Barred*. Then I was going to get the belt back. And Randy was comfort-able with that. He was a horse's ass sometimes, but when it came to business he was always on the money, always ready to give and take.

One thing I remember about that *WrestleMania* is getting a call from Randy Savage at three o'clock in the morning. Randy was a night person. If somebody told him his hair should be longer or maybe he shouldn't drop an elbow before he covered a guy, he would pace the floor all night long.

Hell, sometimes he would stay up pacing worrying about what color shoelaces to put in his boots. He would drive his wife crazy because he'd never lie down, he'd never go to sleep. He was just weird that way.

Anyway, he called me at three in the morning because he was thinking about an idea I came up with for a finish. Randy said, "We've got to call Vince and wake him up."

So we called Vince and told him the idea, and he bought it. I was going to hit Ted DiBiase with a chair to help Randy win the belt. But I think Vince would have preferred to hear my idea after sunrise, not at three in the morning.

Anyway, Andre and I met in the first round of the sixteen-man tournament. I guess a lot of people thought I was going to beat Andre and eventually win the belt back. But Andre and I wrestled to a double disqualification because we bashed each other with chairs, so the road to the title was wide open—and Vince McMahon had taught the fans that Hulk Hogan's destiny was still unpredictable.

When Randy Savage faced Ted DiBiase in the final of the sixteen-man tournament, I sealed Randy's victory by smashing DiBiase with a chair. It made sense. He had screwed me out of the title and I was getting my revenge.

At the time, certain fans asked why I had to be involved in the finish of the match. They wanted to know why I had to have a hand in everything that happened.

What these people didn't understand was that Vince McMahon was just trying to make the most out of what he had. At the time, we didn't have as many Superstars as we do today, so he was using me everywhere he could.

It wasn't me who made those decisions. It was Vince McMahon. When he told me he wanted *Hulkamania* to run wild and for me not to lose a match, I did what he told me. It wasn't my job to argue with him. My job was to get into the ring and make Hulk Hogan as big and strong as I could.

Another thing I remember about that *WrestleMania* is how different the atmosphere was from all the other *WrestleMania*s I had been to. I didn't see or hear any real wrestling enthusiasts in the first seven or eight rows. The people there weren't cheering and screaming at the top of their lungs and stomping and making the building shake.

They were Donald Trump's friends and the high rollers

who frequented his casino—people who didn't follow the wrestling story lines and didn't know what was going on—so it was a much more sedate and unemotional atmosphere. We had to work extra hard to get a rise out of that crowd.

Usually, all you would have to do is point at a guy to get a reaction. That night, I had to slap his face, stomp his feet, kick him in the ass, and then point at him to get the reaction I wanted. It just didn't feel comfortable.

So of course we went back the next year.

At *WrestleMania V*, we had the same kind of crowd. I figured Vince must have cut one hell of a deal with Donald Trump, because the venue and the atmosphere just weren't conducive to a big wrestling event, much less a *WrestleMania*.

While Randy Savage held the championship, the two of us formed a tag team called the Mega-Powers. Our manager was Randy's real-life wife, Miss Elizabeth, a good-looking brunette who went over big with the fans.

The story line was that Randy got insanely jealous of my friendship with Elizabeth and our argument escalated to a showdown at *WrestleMania*—where we would meet with the Macho Man's heavyweight title on the line.

Unfortunately, Randy wasn't in any shape to wrestle.

He had burst the bursa sac in his arm, which is located between the tendon and the bone. At the time, I told him to go get a hole cut in his elbow and have the fluid drained out of it. It would take a few days, maybe as much as a week. But if he didn't do it, it would swell up and get infected. I knew that because my bursa sac had ruptured once too.

253

But Randy didn't get the drain put in. And sure enough, his arm got infected and swelled up like a balloon.

Even then, the Macho Man was old school and he figured he could beat the infection with a bunch of antibiotics. But a couple of days before *WrestleMania V*, the temperature of his arm had gone up to about 120 degrees.

Finally, he gave in and let the doctors drain the poison out of his arm. But he waited much too long. His arm was so full of poison that he was in danger of losing it. The last thing he should have done was wrestled.

I remember worrying that Randy wasn't going to be available for *WrestleMania*. But he was a second-generation wrestler. He kept saying, "Don't worry about The Macho Man, I'll be there."

And he was.

His arm was full of blood poisoning from his ruptured bursa sac, but he got into the ring and wrestled me for the belt. And brother, we had one hell of a match.

It was much better than that crazy tournament thing they had the year before. The tournament just confused people and bored them to death. At *WrestleMania V*, Randy Savage and I stole the show.

In the time he held the belt, Randy had done about the best anybody except Hulk Hogan could have done with it. He had given me the time I needed to make *No Holds Barred*. But when *WrestleMania V* rolled around, Vince McMahon wanted me back in the spotlight so we could have everything working for us when the movie came out. He wanted *No Holds Barred* to do the best it possibly could.

34

In the late eighties, my family life was a roller-coaster ride. Peaks and valleys, brother. Good and bad. The bad came first, in 1987, when I got word that my brother Allan had passed away.

Allan had had a long history of problems, starting with his weekend fighting back in Tampa and going on from there. He had been in and out of prison in Florida, violated his parole, and ended up going to Texas under a different name. He just took off and started another life, leaving his wife to raise their three kids, Michael, Vickie, and Melissa.

Then he got into trouble in Texas and ended up moving to L.A., where he got remarried and had a child named David Bollea. But trouble found him in L.A. too. He ended up partying a lot and running with the wrong group of people.

At one point, Allan tried to pull himself together and went through a drug treatment program. I saw him right after that.

I dropped him off at his house in L.A., gave him money for his rent, his van, and his motorcycle, and asked him if he wanted to come up to San Francisco to watch me wrestle at the Cow Palace. He said he wanted to stay in L.A., so I went up to San Francisco on my own.

I had just finished my match and come out of the ring when I was handed a note saying there was an emergency. By the time I called the number and got hold of somebody at the hospital, my brother was dead.

He was in a hotel room all by himself when he died. The official cause of death was a heart attack, but I have my doubts. There must have been a catalyst. It's pretty rare for somebody to just lie down in a hotel room and have a heart attack.

I was close with my brother Allan at a couple of points in my life. The first time was when I became a teenager and I got old enough to drive cars and drink beer, and he started seeing me as somebody he could hang out with. The second time was in the last few years of his life, when he was living on the West Coast with his new family.

The news of his death rocked me pretty good, but my parents took it even worse. I remember how devastated

Hollywood Hulk Hogan

they were. But I'll tell you, brother, they weren't surprised. We had all known that we would get the call someday. Watching Allan struggle with his life was like watching somebody die of cancer for ten years.

He had a heart of gold sometimes. But he also had a dark spot in him that finally killed him. Where it came from, I don't know.

We all thought that Allan's death was the worst news we could get. But it wasn't. Right after Allan died, his first wife—who was raising their three kids in Florida—was murdered. It was like a one-two punch. And all of a sudden, their three kids were without a mother or father.

It was pretty stressful on my parents and on me because my mother and father were living on a fixed income at the time. Thank God I had started to make some money in the wrestling business, or it would have been even worse.

As for Allan's kids . . . his two girls took it really hard. They cried and carried on the way you would expect. But Allan's son Michael reacted differently. His whole demeanor changed after his parents died. All of a sudden he stopped showing emotion. He was just stone-faced.

Michael was about twelve years old when I took him on the wrestling circuit with me for a little while. We went to Chicago and Madison Square Garden, and all the wrestlers he met were really nice.

The first guys he met were Vince McMahon and Hercules Hernandez. We got off the elevator and there they were, these two big guys and this skinny, skinny little kid. They said hello to him and brought a smile to his face.

He told me after that, "I'm going to be a wrestler someday."

And he *did* become a wrestler. He wrestled for about twelve years as Horace Hogan, all because of how nice the guys were to him. But it took us all a long time to get over my brother's death.

The good news started in 1988 with the birth of our first child, a baby girl we named Brooke. It bowled me over to think I had a daughter. All of a sudden, my whole life was different.

For one thing, having Brooke at home meant I lost my partying buddy. My wife, Linda, had gone everywhere with me. She was my best friend. She was always up for another city and another workout in the gym and another beer at the end of the night. So we were a team.

But now I was alone out there and it was harder than I thought it would be. The whole time I was on the road I was wishing I could be with my wife and my baby daughter. But I didn't have that luxury. I had to keep chasing the almighty dollar because I didn't know when this *Hulkamania* opportunity might end.

I told Linda I'd keep at it until it affected my daughter. As soon as Brooke said one thing about me leaving, I would start to wind things down. And that's what happened. When Brooke was about two years old, I was leaving the house and she started crying. It just tore me up. So I approached Vince about giving me a little more family time, and he did what I asked.

Then, a couple of years later, my son Nicholas came

along. At that point, I was really overwhelmed. A daughter *and* a son—it flipped me out. In one way, having two kids made me want to work harder. But in another way it made me want to be home more. And because I was still the main guy, I had to be really visible. But once again Vince cut me some slack so I could be with my family.

family

Terror in
Aisle Two

35 About ten years after I did
Rocky III, I was in the local supermarket,
pushing my daughter Brooke around in
a shopping cart. My wife, Linda, was
walking ahead of us, looking for something on the shelves. As Brooke and I got
to the end of the aisle and passed the
row of cash registers, I caught a
glimpse of some tabloid rag and saw
the headline: "Hulk's Porno Past."

I thought, *What's this?*

Sure enough, they had my picture
underneath the headline. I'm relaxing
in a lawn chair at poolside and I'm with

those four girls I posed with at Ozzy Osbourne's house, except they all have black stripes drawn across their chests.

And that photo shoot I did for *Oui*—the one Stallone said would be a good idea, no problem—was all of a sudden coming back to haunt me.

I broke out in a sweat like I had typhoid fever. But somehow, I managed to keep going. As I walked down that aisle and up the next one back toward the cashiers, it felt like the longest walk of my life. I knew that when we got to the checkout line Linda would see the headline.

My mind was racing, but I couldn't think of a way out of this. I figured my only hope was if my wife decided to go to the produce department. Then I could try to grab all two hundred of the suckers and throw them out so she wouldn't see them. I know it sounds crazy, but there was nothing else I could do.

But Linda didn't go to the produce department. She walked right up to the cash register and saw the tabloids. Right in front of my daughter, she grabbed one of them and said to me, "What the hell is this?"

She had me shaking. "Well," I said, "that's something that happened about six months before I met you. And—"

Linda didn't even let me finish. She just grabbed my daughter out of the shopping cart and stormed out of the store. "I suggest you come home," she said, "as soon as you're finished checking out."

I just stood there like an idiot. I couldn't talk, I couldn't walk, I couldn't do *anything*. And as I watched my wife get into the car and drive off, I realized I didn't even have a ride home.

Terror In Aisle Two

Linda finally got over it, but it took her like twenty thousand years. When I told Vince about it, he laughed his ass off. Real funny. Of course, he wasn't the one that had to get home from the supermarket.

More Big Matches

36

Along with the Pontiac Silverdome, the other big crowd in the *Hulkamania* era was in 1990, at *WrestleMania VI* in Toronto SkyDome—the same place where I would face The Rock twelve years later in 2002. This was a title match between me and Ultimate Warrior that drew almost 68,000 fans.

Ultimate Warrior was the most chiseled bodybuilder to come into the wrestling business. He was ripped, brother, cut to the bone. I was always thought of as a bodybuilder, even though I was really just a weight lifter. But when this guy came in, he blew me

away. He had been dieting his whole life while I was out drinking and raising hell with the boys.

Also, he had an interesting mystique about him. He talked about "the mighty warriors in Heaven" and stuff like that. He had a pretty good rap.

But when he got into the ring, after he ran in and shook the ropes and stuff, he had no game. He had no wrestling psychology. And that's what it's all about—creating emotion. Great guy, nice guy, but really just a flash in the pan.

Vince McMahon wanted Ultimate Warrior to beat me for the belt. I didn't agree with him. I didn't think the guy could carry the load. Then again, maybe I didn't give Vince a choice in the matter.

By that time, my mind wasn't focused on wrestling the way it should have been. Seven years of carrying the load as the main guy had taken its toll on me. I was tired and I was starting to get hurt a lot. I was beat.

I should have told Vince that I needed a break. I should have said I'm hurt. Everybody else took time off. I should have looked in the mirror and said, "Hey, man, you're human. You can only push yourself so far."

Instead, I kept wrestling. And the more it ground me down, the more my attitude started to suck. So when Vince wanted to hand the title to Ultimate Warrior, it was because he could see down the road to a time when he might not be able to depend on *Hulkamania* and would need to switch gears.

I agreed that I would lose the belt to Ultimate Warrior. But I made sure we had a hell of a match. Just when it

265

looked like it was over, I kicked out of his finish. Then I pinned him and he kicked out of my finish.

At the end of the night, the referee was supposed to get the belt from the timekeeper and give it to Ultimate Warrior. But this was my chance to steal back everything that he had gotten from me. So I zipped over to the timekeeper and ripped the belt out of his hand. Then I walked up on the ring apron with the belt, looked up to God, shook my head yes, walked into the ring, and handed Ultimate Warrior the belt.

As I left the arena, 68,000 people in SkyDome watched me go. Ultimate Warrior held the belt over his head in victory and no one cared.

It turned out I was right about Ultimate Warrior. He

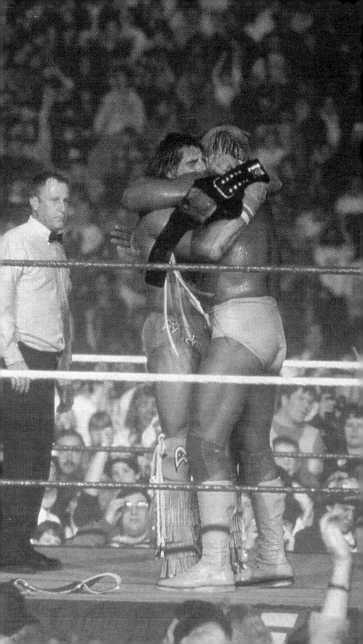

couldn't carry the load as heavyweight champion, not the way Hulk Hogan had. Vince's attempt to move in a different direction hadn't been the success he had hoped it would be. Eventually, he decided he would have Ultimate Warrior drop the belt to Sergeant Slaughter, a guy who had been portrayed in his career as a patriotic drill instructor.

The plans for *WrestleMania VII* took place when we were in the middle of Operation Desert Storm in Iraq, so it seemed like perfect timing to feature a guy like Slaughter. But I didn't know if Vince McMahon was going to let me wrestle him and get the belt back.

I mean, I had been working almost straight through from day one. I went through my career with all sorts of injuries and never stopped. But I would complain and bitch about them, and I'm sure listening to me wasn't any fun for Vince McMahon. I'm sure he was saying, "Oh my God, how can we move beyond this guy?"

So I really didn't know if I was going to get the belt back from Sergeant Slaughter or if Vince was going to try to move ahead and give it to somebody else.

Then I got an idea. I said to Vince, "You've had good results going against the grain. You took a policeman—the Big Boss Man—who's supposed to be good and turned him into an evil character. Why not do the same thing with Slaughter? Let's turn him traitor to his country. And who better to wrestle a guy like that than the one who took down the Iron Sheik in Madison Square Garden?"

Vince liked the idea, especially because he could capitalize on the headlines to boost our numbers. So he took

Hollywood Hulk Hogan

Sergeant Slaughter, who had been an American patriot, and turned him into the worst kind of heel you could have had in those days—an Iraqi sympathizer.

Sergeant Slaughter announced his allegiance to Saddam Hussein and at a *Royal Rumble*, he beat Ultimate Warrior for the championship. That set everything up for *WrestleMania*.

Instead of me wrestling Randy Savage for the hundredth time, I went into the ring as the defender of America, ready and able to take down the traitor Slaughter the way I had taken down the Iron Sheik back in 1983. By the time the match was over, I had become the first three-time champion in World Wrestling Federation history.

Unfortunately, we caught a lot of heat for the Iraqi sympathizer angle from the press, with people saying we had no right to exploit a real war. But that was nothing com-

More Big Matches

pared to the fan reaction. I understand Sergeant Slaughter had a couple of close calls and some wackos even threatened his family. It was a tough time for him.

Believe me, it wasn't what I had intended.

We even ended up moving the venue. For security reasons, we abandoned the idea of using an outdoor stadium and ended up in the L.A. Sports Arena. I've heard people speculate that we made the move because ticket sales were disappointing, but my understanding of the situation is that Vince was concerned about security in an outdoor arena.

Undertaker

37

Back in 1991, when I was making *Suburban Commando*, I was playing a guy from another planet and I needed a couple of alien bounty hunters to chase me to Earth. We had one big guy named Tony Longo to play one of the bounty hunters, but we were looking for a second big guy.

All of a sudden I thought of this guy named "Mean" Mark Calloway, a six-foot-ten wrestler who I had seen working for WCW. I said, "This guy would be great."

So I called him and brought him down to do the movie. As we talked on the set and I got to know the guy, I saw some star quality in him. I asked him if he was interested in going to New York to wrestle and he said he was.

First chance I got, I called Vince McMahon. I said, "Hey, brother, there's a guy here making this movie with me . . . he's a wrestler, he's a nice guy, and he's like six foot ten. I think I can draw some money with him."

Vince said, "Well, let me see him."

So as soon as I could, I left the movie set and brought Mark Calloway to see Vince McMahon. Vince looked at the guy for about five minutes and said, "Okay. We'll call him Undertaker."

I said, "Are you out of your mind? We talk about training, prayers, and vitamins. We don't talk about *body bags*. Come on, Vince, you're nuts. It'll never work."

Boy, was I wrong. Vince stuck with his idea for a gimmick and a wrestling superstar was born.

But Undertaker is more than a gimmick. I've always loved working with him in the ring because he knows where he is every second of the match. He doesn't rush or do a bunch of little punches that don't mean anything. There's a reason for every move he makes. He's got the new-school mentality of knowing the match has to move and you have to get off your ass, but he also has the old-school approach of "Let's paint a picture for the audience."

The first time I wrestled Undertaker was at *Survivor Series 1991*. The match ended when Ric Flair, a newcomer who had been the champion of both the National Wrestling Alliance and World Championship Wrestling, slipped a chair into the ring. Undertaker hit me with a piledriver on the top of the chair and took away my title.

He also screwed up my neck something fierce. It wasn't his fault; he took care of me and made sure my head didn't hit the mat. But the jolt of my neck being stretched like that sent me right to the hospital.

I was in there for a couple of days. Everybody wanted to fuse the disks of my neck together, but I decided against it. It would be years before I got all the feeling back in my arms. But six days later, I was wrestling Undertaker again in a special Pay-Per-View rematch called *Tuesday in Texas*, because Ric Flair's interference had made the title null and void.

I won the belt back at that match. But because Ric Flair interfered again and accidentally knocked out the referee, the title was declared vacant. That springboarded us into *Royal Rumble 1992*, where to everyone's surprise Ric Flair emerged with the championship belt.

So first Undertaker got the belt and then Flair got the belt. I thought that was interesting—two more examples of how Vince McMahon was trying to switch gears and expand the identity of his company.

Undertaker

Steroids

38

By 1991, people were starting to learn that Hulk Hogan was human.

Up until then, I had been wrapped in this superhero mystique. People accepted it at face value when I told them to train, say their prayers, and take their vitamins.

Then, little by little, they found out that I did more than train and say my prayers. I liked to drink beer and raise hell at night.

So I got into a little bit of trouble here and there. The fans started to turn on me and I got booed a lot. And then I gave them something else to boo me about, because it wasn't just vitamins I was taking.

I probably started taking anabolic steroids in 1975.

But at the time, every wrestler I knew took them. In fact, they were being used by athletes in every sport—baseball, football, hockey, right across the board.

The most commonly prescribed steroids were testosterone, decadurabolin, and Dianabol. They were part of my generation. I'm not making excuses but they were everywhere. And a lot of that had to do with what we knew about them, which obviously wasn't enough.

One thing we *did* know about steroids was that they enhanced the way you looked and the way you performed. They made you bigger, stronger, and faster. What was especially important to wrestlers was that steroids helped you put on muscle mass.

I had always gotten my steroids from a doctor because I felt like I didn't know enough about them. But they were also available in the gyms I went to and a lot of wrestlers bought extra bottles there on the side.

It's hard to blame them. Steroids were legal at the time. And we were told that taking steroids was safer than putting sugar into your body. This stuff is safer than sugar? Well, I take sugar into my body. Why wouldn't I want to take this—especially if it makes me bigger, stronger, faster, and helps me make more money? Wow, I'm in.

That was the attitude. Nobody said, "Here, stick this in your ass or eat this pill, it'll kill you." Nobody told us that if you took steroids for thirty years it could be harmful to your long-term health.

Hollywood Hulk Hogan

I never had a question about whether I would take them. It was part of my daily regimen. Did you take a shower today? Yeah. Did you brush your teeth? Yeah. Did you take your steroids today? Yeah. Okay, let's go.

That was the deal. It was how I lived.

I'm two hundred eighty pounds now, but back then I weighed three hundred thirty, three hundred forty, because my body was full of water weight. My face was huge and puffy, and my arms were so bulky I couldn't touch my shoulders.

Some people say steroids cause personality changes. They didn't do that in my case. I didn't have fits of temper or anything like that.

But they did affect my day-to-day life. For one thing, they increased my appetite a lot. I was always eating, so it always felt to me like my stomach was full and my clothes were a size too tight.

For another thing, the steroids made me sweat. I'd be sitting at a table in a restaurant with normal people, saying, "God, it's hot in here, isn't it?" But nobody in that restaurant would be hot except me.

Anyway, the Feds began an investigation of steroid use. All of a sudden, instead of Burt Reynolds and Lonnie Anderson's divorce being front-page news, the papers were talking about steroids.

Before I knew it, I had gotten dragged into it. They could have gotten Lyle Alzado from the Oakland Raiders, who for all I knew was taking ten times the amount of steroids I was. But no, Hulk Hogan was the most recognizable athlete-entertainer in the world, so they put my neck on the chopping block.

In my mind, everything I had done was legal.

But the Feds didn't really want me. They wanted the money man, the boss, the brains behind the brawn. They wanted the guy who had made a name for himself as the Einstein of the wrestling business. So they dragged Vince McMahon into it. It was very unfair.

The Feds were trying to say that Vince McMahon distributed steriods to me, and if a judge found him guilty they were going to put him away for a long time. But they didn't have a case. Vince didn't distribute drugs to me or to anyone else. The Feds were just trying to bury him, to drag him through the mud and destroy his business.

So they told me they weren't going to go after me, even though they had trashed my name already. What they wanted was to go after Vince—and they wanted me to be a government witness at his trial.

They said, "All we want you to do is tell the truth."

So in my mind, I was really cool. I wasn't going to get into any trouble. And if I told the truth, Vince wouldn't get into any trouble either. That worked for me.

Boom, all of a sudden my communications with Vince were cut off. I think his attorneys told him not to talk to me anymore because I was going to be a government witness. He may have thought that I had turned on him.

I would never have done that. But not being able to speak with him at that time put a tremendous strain on our relationship. And we didn't talk for a long time after that, even after the trial was over.

My Biggest Mistake

39

In July of 1991, I was invited to go on The *Arsenio Hall Show*, which was a very popular nighttime talk show.

There was really only one reason for Arsenio to have me on his show at that time. He knew it and I knew it, and it didn't take long for him to get around to it. He wanted to know about my steriod use.

So I told him, "No, I do not take steroids."

If it was just my own reputation I had been concerned about, I might have been a little more honest. But I was worried about destroying all the good I had done with the Hulk Hogan character. Because of me, kids were living by the code of training, prayers and vitamins, and I didn't want them to think that I'd given them bad advice.

I mean, training, prayers, and vitamins is the right way to go. And you can attain your goals without taking steroids. It may take a little longer, but you'll be a better person for it because you haven't taken a shortcut to get there.

So I was afraid all those kids would lose faith in me and what I'd told them. And that was why I rationalized the situation and told Arsenio Hall that I didn't take steroids.

I thought that maybe he would let me slide at that point. But he went on. "Aw, come on, you experimented with them, didn't you?"

And I said, "Yeah, I experimented with them a few times," which was a hell of an understatement. But in my mind I was saying to myself, he's asking me if I'm an abuser and I'm not. I just took what the doctor told me.

But I was very nervous and I kept using the word "basically." Every time he'd ask me a question I'd say, "Basically, steroids are this" and, "Basically, I did that," and you could just tell I was full of it.

So "basically," I got killed. I got buried. And everybody thought I was a liar.

Vince had advised me not to go on the show. He told me it wasn't a good idea. But I said, "No, I feel like I've got to explain myself." Great. Instead of explaining myself, I had outsmarted myself.

Hollywood Hulk Hogan

I see now that I should have taken all of the bullets out of Arsenio's gun and said, "Yes, I used steroids to bulk up." I should have come clean. It probably would have hurt my career but not as badly or for as long a time. So I screwed myself.

It was the biggest mistake I've ever made. I should have just been man enough to fess up, and if it ruined me then it ruined me. As it was, I almost ruined everything I had accomplished, and that was more important to me by far.

My Biggest Mistake

Flattening Out

Hollywood

40

When you come off anabolic steroids, you're supposed to do it very gradually. You're supposed to wean yourself off them little by little. But I didn't do that. I just went cold turkey.

I had been on steroids for so long, it was like letting the air out of an over-inflated tire. My body just flattened out. It had no definition. It took a year for me to come around to the point where I looked normal.

Unfortunately, some guys *never* stopped taking steroids. Despite Vince McMahon's trial, despite what they learned about the negative side effects, they continued to take them.

The funny thing is that some of these guys were getting the big push. They were visible. But they could still get away with steroid use.

I was a different story. They were watching Hulk Hogan like a hawk. If I were to quit drinking beer and go on a Richard Simmons diet, somebody would claim I was back on steroids. I couldn't even make the attempt to look good or they'd point a finger at me. That's how bad it was.

I think I'm okay now, but I wouldn't say that about everybody who took steroids. The guys who abused the drug, who would get a doctor's prescription for a bottle of testosterone and then go to a gym and get four more bottles, might be in a little trouble.

Just for the record, my opinion of steroids is completely different from what it used to be in the seventies and eighties. I didn't know much about them then. Now I do.

If a doctor prescribes steroids for a patient with arthritis or AIDS or dwarfism, that's one thing. But anybody who uses drugs to run real hard and have his body weight fifty to a hundred pounds over the normal level is a total idiot. It's not healthy. It's not safe. It's just plain stupid.

There are valid reasons for people to take doctor-prescribed steroids. Becoming a wrestling hero isn't one of them.

Fall from Grace

41   It wasn't just my body that was flattening out in the early nineties. Interest in wrestling was flattening out too. The numbers weren't what Vince McMahon might have hoped they were.

And for the first time, I was getting some negative vibes when I climbed into the ring. Fans were holding up signs that said, "Hogan, did you take your shot today?" or "Hogan is bald because he takes steroids!"

When I went back up the ramp, I would hear adverse comments from the audience—not from everybody, of course, but they were there. I hadn't heard that kind of reaction since my first run with the McMahons in New York.

It didn't help that I looked so scrawny compared with the wrestlers who were still taking steroids. And it didn't help either that I was off making movies from time to time, pursuing a screen career while my wrestling career suffered.

My relationship with the company was becoming strained. Vince seemed to be trying to distance himself from me and from the steroid controversy.

At the beginning of my second run with the McMahon promotion, when Vince and I were on the same page, we had talked every day, sometimes two or three times a day. Now we wouldn't talk for weeks at a time.

Still, I was looking forward to *WrestleMania VIII* at the Hoosierdome in Indianapolis, where I expected to wrestle Ric Flair for the championship belt he had won at *Royal Rumble*. Hogan-Flair was the match fans had fantasized about for years. It could have been as big as *WrestleMania III*—the battle of the century.

When Vince booked the match, I said, "Brother, we're going to draw some money *now*." If anything would kick wrestling back into overdrive, it would be me going nose to nose with Ric Flair.

But a few weeks before *WrestleMania*, Vince changed his mind about the match. He put Randy Savage against Flair for the heavyweight belt, then had me wrestle Sid Justice— a real pro in the ring and a guy who would do whatever you asked of him, but he didn't have the stature of a Ric Flair. Flair and I were dumbfounded by the move.

So I wrestled Sid and did the best I could, and Randy Savage defeated Flair for the championship belt. But the people had really wanted to see Hogan-Flair. Anything else was a letdown.

Vince also had me announce that I was retiring at the end of my match with Sycho Sid. It was supposed to just be a break for me because I was always bitching about how hurt and overworked I was. But it would also be another chance for Vince to see if he could move beyond *Hulkamania*—to see if his company could go on without me just like it had gone on without all the other stars who left over the years.

If they would have gotten behind me and pushed *Hulkamania* as hard as ever, we may have gotten the company's momentum back. Instead, Vince chose to go a different way. But he didn't have anything as exciting as *Hulkamania*, so everything gradually started to come crashing down.

Then the federal government really started to put the pressure on Vince. They tore the guts out of his business and he had a hard time regrouping. So it all just hit bottom—the industry, the numbers, fan interest, and my future with the World Wrestling Federation.

By mutual agreement, I was gone for almost a year. During that time, I filmed *Mr. Nanny*. I also started wrestling again in Japan, where the fans still loved me regardless of the steroid mess.

It was a refreshing change, brother. I didn't have to cup my

Fall From Grace

hand to my ear to get the
crowd behind me. I didn't
have to do the boot in the
face and the legdrop to get
a big cheer. I could just go
out to the ring and wrestle.
It was fun.

But back in the U.S., the
wrestling business was just
getting worse. Finally, it
seemed Vince McMahon
was willing to put me back
in the spotlight, if only for a
little while.

I was going to wrestle at
WrestleMania IX at Caesar's
Palace in Las Vegas—not
in the main event, but in a
tag-team match. It would be me and Brutus Beefcake against
the team of Ted DiBiase and Irwin R. Schyster, who called
themselves Money Inc.

The main event would pit Yokozuna, a seven-hundred-
pound challenger, against the champion, Bret Hart. Yokozuna
was slated to win that match and take the heavyweight belt.

But when I got to the building, I told Vince, "Look man,
we both know I'm done here. The moment has passed, the
love affair is over. But I've got an idea that will allow me to
pass the torch."

"And what's that?" Vince said.

"After my tag match is over, when Bret Hart gets beat by Yokozuna, how about if I come out to protest the way Bret lost? Yokozuna's manager, Mr. Fuji, can challenge me to get into the ring against Yokuzuna—and boom, I can beat Yokozuna to win the title. Then I go to the next Pay-Per-View and drop the belt right back to Yokozuna, and I'm out of here."

That was the deal. Vince agreed to it and I thought, *Boy, I just stole me a couple more big paydays.* And I didn't mind doing a job for Yokozuna because I loved the guy to death. It was all set.

Fall From Grace

On April 4, 1993, at *WrestleMania IX*, I took the belt from Yokozuna for my record fifth championship. I pinned him one-two-three, paving the way for our rematch.

But before we got to *King of the Ring* a month later, Bret Hart got in my face and said, "You son of a bitch, Vince McMahon told me you won't drop the belt to me."

I said, "Brother, I'm dropping the belt to Yokozuna. That's the deal I made."

And Bret said, "That's not what Vince told me. He said you wouldn't drop the belt to me because I'm not in your league and I couldn't lace your boots up."

I said, "Well, how about you and me get in a room with Vince right now?"

Finally, the three of us—Vince, Bret and myself—wound up in a room together. Bret said to Vince, "Didn't you tell me that Hulk Hogan wouldn't drop the belt to me?"

And Vince said, "Bret, that's just what you *thought* you heard."

I had a feeling that Vince wasn't going straight up with Bret, and I think Bret felt the same way. But Vince was the boss, so there was nothing Bret could do about it except fume a little.

I was fuming a little myself. To tell you the truth, I didn't care if Bret Hart got the belt or not. It just pissed me off that Vince had told me one thing and then told Bret another, because everybody thought it was my decision not to drop the belt to Bret. It made it look like I wasn't a team player.

A month later, just as I had agreed in my discussions

with Vince McMahon, I dropped the belt back to Yokozuna at *King of the Ring* in Dayton, Ohio.

Then I left World Wrestling Federation.

I wasn't fired and I didn't quit. It was a mutual agreement that I would no longer wrestle for the company after I lost the championship to Yokozuna. I would just pursue other interests.

There wasn't any animosity between me and the company. I just walked out and that was it. But to tell you the truth, brother, it was a relief to move on.

The drama had just gotten out of hand, with people bashing me left and right, calling me selfish for some of the things I had or hadn't done in my career when it was always the promoter who had asked me to do those things. I had been down a long, hard road and it was nice to finally take a breather.

Fall From Grace

The
Hollywood
Jet Ski
Incident

42 Actually, my career almost ended just *before WrestleMania IX*— along with my life.

The day before I was supposed to leave for Vegas to wrestle Yokozuna, I got the bright idea to go jet skiing in Tampa with my old friend Ed Leslie and Ellis Edwards, the stunt coordinator from *Baywatch*.

I had just gotten off a plane from England and I'd been drinking beer the whole time we were in the air, so I had a twelve-hour beer buzz going. I really should have just laid down and gotten some rest. But instead, I called Ed and Ellis and said, "Come on, man, let's go jump some waves."

Both of them were more agile than I was. Ellis was a small guy, maybe a hundred forty pounds, and he jumped horses and rode motor cross and all that stuff. Ed was like a cat. Out of the three of us, I was the clumsy one—and that day, I proved it.

It happened that Ed Leslie had a brand-new Polaris ski, which was smaller than mine and a lot faster. It had trim tabs that kept the front end down and prevented it from dolphining out of the water.

Ed asked me, "You want to give it a shot?"

I said, "Sure, brother."

So I traded skis with Ed, and after I had been riding it for a couple of minutes I thought I was pretty much used to it. Then we filled it with gas. That twelve or fourteen gallons of gas in the front end made it stay down a lot more. I didn't need to use the trim tabs anymore with all that extra weight in front, but I wasn't used to riding Ed's ski so I left the tabs down.

Along came a big wave and I jumped it. But instead of riding up over the second wave, the front end of the jet ski dug in and launched me headfirst over the top of it. I knew the jet ski was coming after me, but I thought I'd be okay because I was underwater and I thought I could stay there for a second. Then the ski would go right over my head.

I forgot about my life jacket. The damn thing bobbed me right back up—directly in the path of the jet ski. It hit me right in the face at a speed of forty miles an hour. It's a miracle the thing didn't kill me.

If it had hit me in the side of the head, I'd have been dead. If it had center-punched me right between the eyes, it would probably have ripped the top of my skull off. But instead, it hit me underneath the eyeball and broke my orbital socket.

I was in pretty bad shape. My eye was messed up. My jaw was messed up. I was a disaster to look at.

The funny thing is there's a rumor that I didn't get hurt in a jet skiing accident after all—that I got punched in a bar fight by Randy Savage. Brother, I *wish*. Getting hit in a bar would have been a lot easier than getting slammed in the face by a seven hundred-pound jet ski.

I actually lost consciousness and wound up lying there facedown in the water. If Ellis Edwards hadn't seen me and used all of his hundred forty pounds to pull me up onto his ski, I'd have been a goner. But somehow, he got me onto his ski and saved my life.

When the doctors saw me and stitched me up, they told me I'd be crazy to try to wrestle. They didn't even want me getting on a plane. But I told them it would take more than a crushed eye socket to stop me. This was a *WrestleMania*, brother. I wasn't going to stay home for anything.

The only problem was the athletic commissioner up in Las Vegas. If he knew how bad I was hurt, he wouldn't let me get into the ring. And I was all bruised and battered. I looked like hell.

But when I saw him, I told him I was wearing makeup.

I said it was all just a work—a put-on. And the guy believed me.

So I swerved the commissioner and I got to wrestle Yokozuna at *WrestleMania IX*. It was pretty painful, but I got through it.

The Jet Ski Incident

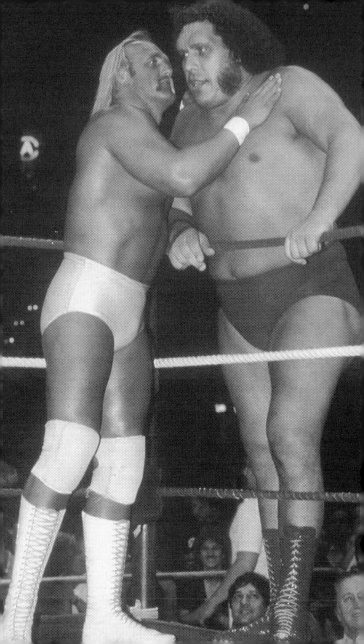

Last Days of the Giant

43 Andre had a condition called acromegaly. It was a pituitary problem. That was why he was such a huge person, and why his hands and feet and head were so big in proportion to the rest of his body.

After I pinned him in the Silverdome, he needed back surgery again. Then it was just a steady downhill roll for him over a period of several years.

I remember in the early nineties Andre wore those crutches that clip onto your forearms. He was walking with them and it just about broke my heart, because he was in pain and just drenched with sweat, covered from head to toe with it.

The worse he got, the more he drank. You could tell because he smelled of alcohol and he was always unhappy when you talked to him. He was in a lot of pain. There was just nowhere the guy could be comfortable, especially now that he was crippled and hurt. His life was just miserable.

Finally, he passed away in January of 1993. The wrestling word lost a titan, a guy that will never be replaced. I lost a friend.

Turning Forty with the Fifties

44

It was August 1993. I had just left the company when my wife surprised me with a fortieth-birthday party at the Rockaway Grill, a fifties-diner-style restaurant in Tampa.

The auto club had parked maybe twenty '57 Chevys around the place to decorate it on the outside. And one of the "decorations" inside was a miniature prototype for the All-Star Sports Café that would eventually open in mid-town Manhattan.

Robert Earl, the president of Planet Hollywood, was the main guy behind the All-Star Café concept. He had lined up five or six star athletes from different sports and was trying to talk me into getting involved. He even had pictures of me posing in the prototype.

I didn't end up joining Earl in his new venture. It just seemed like a risky business to put my name on, and my lawyer, Henry Holmes, advised against it.

All my friends in the wrestling business were at the Rockaway Grill too. They were raising hell, so naturally there was a lot of gossip flying around.

Whenever you leave a place, people tell tales about you. I heard people were dumping on me now that I wasn't with World Wrestling Federation—saying that I wasn't a team player, that I wasn't a good wrestler, that I didn't talk to people backstage, that I was basically an asshole.

It was like a bunch of women bitching in a beauty parlor. I might have had an argument with my wife or my son could have gotten run over by a car or I might have been thinking I had yellow ganja leprosy coming out my butt. But I didn't say hello to somebody one time, so I'm an asshole.

The only bit of gossip that really interested me was the stuff about Vince McMahon. Some of the other wrestlers were saying he was really unhappy with me and thought I hadn't left gracefully.

One of the guys there was Davey Boy Smith, one of the British Bulldogs. He was saying how much he hated Vince McMahon because Vince had screwed him over and that he was going to kick Vince's ass first chance he got.

Some of the other wrestlers at the place thought that was a good idea. They wanted a piece of Vince too.

Well, who should surprise us by walking into the party but Vince McMahon? He was wearing an Elvis-type leather suit and his wife, Linda, was dressed fifties style too. I remember thinking how nice it was of them to make the trip and show up.

Vince was cool. He fit right in. And all these big, tough-guy wrestlers who said they wanted to beat him up suddenly lost their nerve and didn't say a word to him. I thought it was pretty humorous.

Vince McMahon will fight you. I could say I'm gonna beat your ass and if you want to back down, that's cool. But if you say that to Vince, he's going to fight you, whether he's got a chance against you or not. That's how he is.

So it was kind of funny to see how it all went down.

Thunder in Paradise

45

When I was still in the World Wrestling Federation, I was approached by the producers of *Baywatch*, Doug Schwartz and Greg Bonann, to star in the pilot of a TV series called *Thunder in Paradise*. It was about two ex-Navy SEALS with a high-tech boat, a kind of *Mission: Impossible* on the water.

I did the pilot with costars Chris Lemmon and Carol Alt, but it didn't get picked up by any of the major networks. It just sat there. So in my mind I put it on the back burner and concentrated on wrestling.

Then Rysher Entertainment, the company that had produced *Lifestyles of the Rich and Famous,* said they wanted to make *Thunder in Paradise* a series—but they wanted to do it as a syndication deal. So a year and a half after we did the pilot, with the black cloud of the government's steroid investigation hanging over my head, I left World Wrestling Federation and started to shoot the series.

And I wasn't just the star of the show. I was also executive producer.

I had held that position before, but all it had meant was an extra ten grand in my paycheck. In *Thunder in Paradise,* executive producer wasn't just a title. I was really in the trenches, making sure I was getting good deals on honey wagons and catering and lighting equipment.

If I could stay on budget, I would make money. If I brought in the wrong stunt people and shot too much film, it had a direct effect on my income. Return on investment became the equation of the day instead of how much fun I could have.

I felt like *Thunder in Paradise* was my chance to make it without a safety net. I'd always had a promoter or a bunch of other wrestlers to use as props. This was the first time that I was actually out there on my own.

I did all the music for the show with Jimmy Hart, "The Mouth of the South." Jimmy had been a member of the Gentrys, the group that came out with hit records like "Keep On Dancing" and "Cinnamon Girl" when he was still in high school. Later on, he had gotten into wrestling as a manager, which is how I met him in Tennessee back in 1977.

We had been real close friends ever since. Jimmy had managed me, and I knew he had a great ear for music, so when I got the *Thunder in Paradise* gig I brought him in right away. His main job on the show was to write music, but he also ended up with a small acting part as a lounge-band leader.

At one point, they wanted me to do the show in Hawaii. They weren't filming *Magnum* there anymore. They weren't filming anything.

The Hawaiian government was willing to bend over backward for us. They said they would give us good deals and pick up some of the production costs. They even offered me a liquor license so I could open my own club there.

But I told my wife I couldn't see moving to Hawaii if I was going to have to work fourteen- or sixteen-hour days and never go to the beach. So I didn't want to take the show to Hawaii. I just stayed in Florida.

When the first show aired, it did a staggering number in New York, like a 9.1 share. Vince McMahon and I weren't on the best of terms at the time but he sent a fax to my house. "Well," he said, "congratulations, Monster. It looks like you really are the thunder in paradise."

After that, *Thunder in Paradise* continued to do well. But because it was a syndicated show, we were at the mercy of the individual stations and what time slot they decided to give us. All we could do was watch our pennies and try to put something exciting up on the screen.

Unfortunately, we ran into a problem in that area— and it revolved around nepotism. My partner Doug Schwartz was one of the producers. His nephew, Michael Berk, was another producer. And his brother-in-law, Greg Bonann, who was a lifeguard before he got involved with *Baywatch* and would rather have been back on the beach in L.A, was also a producer. They were all one big family.

So when Doug Schwartz made a deal, no one spoke up and questioned it. They just went along with it, even if it didn't seem like the right deal.

My partner was making some apparently questionable decisions on how to spend our money, like bringing guys in from L.A. instead of hiring local. I probably should have nipped the problem in the bud, but I had plenty else to keep me busy. I mean, I wasn't just the executive producer—I was also the star.

I was in almost every shot, which made my days long and brutal. We were trying to pack a seven-day schedule into five days, so it wasn't unusual to roll for sixteen hours at a time. Because I didn't have time to train, I lost weight. A year into the series, I was down to less than two hundred fifty-five pounds. I felt great but I didn't look like Hulk Hogan. I looked like Hurricane Spenser, the Navy SEAL character I played.

Jamming with Jimmy Hart (fourth left).

Thunder in Paradise

And I was making money, but it wasn't wrestling money. I was starting to miss being in the ring. I was starting to miss the rush I had gotten from the crowd when *Hulkamania* was at its height. But I didn't even consider walking out on *Thunder in Paradise*.

Until fate took a hand.

Since the day we started working on the show, we had been filming on Soundstage A at the MGM Studio in Disney World. It was funny because MGM had a backstage studio tour where 3,000 people an hour went through a glass walkway and saw all the TV programs that were being shot there.

Sometime after we started, Ted Turner's World Championship Wrestling began shooting one of its syndicated wrestling shows next door to us, on Soundstage B. And actually, the way it was set up, the lettering was backward—so the people on the tour saw Soundstage B before they saw Soundstage A.

In order to whet their appetites, the tour guide would say, "Come backstage and watch Hulk Hogan film his new show." Naturally, everybody thought it was a wrestling show. It didn't occur to them that I would be making *Thunder in Paradise*.

So they walked past Soundstage B and they saw Ric Flair—who had returned to WCW—and Sting and Arn Anderson and all these wrestlers. But they didn't see me, so they would ask their tour guide, "Where's Hulk Hogan?"

Some 3,000 people an hour were coming through the place asking for Hulk Hogan. It drove the tour guides nuts.

Then they walked past Soundstage A, and they saw me

Hollywood Hulk Hogan

with a machine gun and my Navy SEAL coat and Chris Lemmon and Carol Alt, and they went, "Oh, now we get it. *Thunder in Paradise*. But really, we want to see him wrestle."

Some 3,000 visitors an hour were hounding the people from the Turner organization and asking where I was. The next thing I knew, Ric Flair came nosing around while I was eating lunch with my partners, Doug Schwartz and Greg Bonann.

We were talking about some overseas TV deals we had going and Ric Flair said, "Hey, Hulk Man, you wanna dance with the Nature Boy? You want to make some money?"

I said, "What are you talking about, Ric?"

And he said, "I'm talking about WCW. I've been speaking with Ted Turner and he said if we can get Hulk Hogan it'd be like getting lightning in a bottle. We can go unleash it on Vince McMahon and beat his ass."

I said I'd think about it, maybe someday. But I still considered Vince my friend, even though there was some distance between us. And truthfully, I didn't think anybody could beat Vince's ass in the wrestling business.

But Ted Turner wasn't about to let it go just like that. All of a sudden, Eric Bischoff, the executive vice president of WCW, started talking to me. Eric was a Minnesota boy who had been a fan of mine back when I was working for Verne Gagne at the AWA.

His family was in the meat business and when I was wrestling in Minnesota, he was driving a truck around, going from door to door selling frozen meat to people. He and his wife were sleeping on a box spring on the floor,

Thunder in Paradise

trying to put together a future for themselves. And his dream had been to meet Hulk Hogan.

"Because if I could meet Hulk Hogan," he told me later, "I could tell him about my idea, a new sandwich called the Hulk Hoagie. I figured it would make millions."

Well, he never did meet me when I was up there. But after I left the AWA, he became an announcer there. He was a good-looking guy and he had a cadence to his voice that sounded good on TV.

One time, he flew east to audition for World Wrestling Federation and Vince McMahon briefly popped into the room, then left. Bischoff didn't get the job because, as he says, he was terrible at the time.

But he stayed in the business and ended up down in Atlanta with WCW. He started out as an announcer and worked his way up the ladder. By the time I had heard from Ric Flair about joining WCW, Eric was the executive vice president of the organization, actively going around and recruiting new talent.

Even during the steroid controversy, he still believed in Hulk Hogan. And he was just as instrumental as Ric Flair, if not more so, in getting me to think about joining WCW.

But I still wasn't ready to make the switch. Not yet.

Then, after we had put about a year and a half into *Thunder in Paradise*, a guy named Keith Samples came to me from Rysher Entertainment and said, "Look, Terry, we want *Thunder in Paradise* to keep going, but we need to break up this little family business."

Keith didn't like some of the deals that were being

made, and he wanted some people in there who might actually at least ask questions. His suggestion was that we bring in a producer from *Robocop*—and hold off on deals until the guy got there.

I told him that was fine with me. I said, "We'll send Michael Berk and Greg Bonann back to L.A., and I'll just run the show with Doug Schwartz. And I promise you, we won't make any more deals until the guy from *Robocop* shows up."

But money still kept getting spent on questionable stuff. Keith told me the only way we could keep going with *Thunder in Paradise* was if I took full responsibility. But by then, I had had enough. I was beat up, burned out, and tired of Hollywood. All I wanted was to go home.

I said, "The hell with it. Pull the plug. I don't care."

So the show was canceled.

Word spread like wildfire. All of a sudden, I had these Turner people all over me, asking me to get involved with WCW. I said if I was going to talk about this, I wanted to do it with Ted Turner.

So I went up and met with Ted and a guy named Bill Shaw, who was the president of WCW and Ted's right-hand man. I came out of that meeting feeling good about what I was getting into. I decided WCW would be a good move for me.

Hell, I was getting back into the wrestling business, the thing I did best. What could *possibly* go wrong?

Steroids: The Trial

46 Vince McMahon's trial for steroid possession and distribution started in July of 1994 and went on for about two weeks in Uniondale, New York, on Long Island.

There weren't very many people in the courtroom that whole time. Those two weeks were like the preliminary matches on a wrestling card. Everybody was waiting for the main event.

Finally, Hulk Hogan showed up, and everything was different. There were news trucks in the parking lot and reporters with cameras, and people fighting for ringside seats in the courtroom. It was quite an event.

I had a three-piece suit on, but I was also wearing a black bandanna. I wasn't trying to make a statement. The bandanna was just part of me.

Nobody in the press said I looked nervous, but I was. I knew what I was going to say and all that, but I didn't know how the jury would react. I didn't know if they were going to take what I said and decide Vince was guilty, even if he really wasn't.

I mean, Vince was a cocky son of a bitch. He didn't give an inch. And in a court of law, you never know what the jury's going to think. They may have watched wrestling and decided that Vince was a rich guy who didn't deserve a break. You never know.

Anyway, I got on the witness stand and they swore me in. Then the district attorney asked me if Vince McMahon had ever sold me steroids. I said, "No." They asked me if Vince McMahon had ever injected me with steroids. I said, "No."

At that point, the courtroom just about came apart.

They had hoped I would say that Vince was a drug dealer. But I told the truth, just like they asked me to. And when I did that, the government's case against Vince went down the drain.

That didn't mean the case was over. The government had spent millions and millions of dollars trying to prosecute Vince McMahon, and they may have wanted to justify all that cost to the taxpayers by continuing. If they missed

Steroids: The Trial

nailing Vince, I felt that there was a chance they would make me a target of the investigation instead.

I saw what Vince was going through. It was hell. Would the Feds try to lay the same rap on me that they had laid on him, and ruin my life for another three or four years? Or maybe even longer?

But when the Feds thought about it, they realized they had no case. They hadn't come close. Vince had been acquitted of all their charges.

Thank God it didn't continue beyond that, brother, because it then could have become a witch-hunt—and there was no telling where it might end.

When the trial was over, Vince came out on the steps of the courthouse and said something that surprised me. He said he was upset I didn't tell the truth.

And here I thought I *had* told the truth. That became a bone of contention between us that wouldn't go away for quite a while. It wasn't until years later that Vince told me what he was talking about was my appearance on *Arsenio*.

Ted Turner's Traveling World Championship Wrestling Show

47

WCW knew the only way they could compete with Vince McMahon was to sign Hulk Hogan, so they brought me in—even though I had the stigma of the government's steroid trial hanging over my head. They showed faith in me and it wasn't long before they were rewarded.

On July 17, 1994—three days after I testified in federal court on Long Island and five days before Vince McMahon was acquitted of the charges against him—I was in Orlando, Florida to face my old pal Ric Flair for the WCW heavy-weight title in an event called *Bash at the Beach*.

I felt great, like twenty million pounds had been lifted off my shoulders. I felt cleansed. And I was looking forward to working with Ric Flair.

To help promote the match and the significance of Hulk Hogan's joining WCW, Disney World—where I had filmed *Thunder in Paradise*—agreed to give me something I had never had before: a red-and-yellow ticker-tape parade. I sat in my red-and-yellow Viper, drove through the Disney property with my arm waving, and finally wound up at the MGM theme park.

A couple hundred people showed up, but it was shot in such a way that it looked more like a couple thousand peo-ple, and I had my plants in the audience screaming how great Hulk Hogan was while they were throwing confetti. It was all planned and staged, but it looked good on TV.

And the parade did what it was supposed to do—it drew attention to my championship match with Ric Flair.

The first time I met him was in 1978, but he probably doesn't remember because he was already a big star and I was just starting out. Then I wrestled him in '83, when I began my second run in New York. That's when we got to be friends.

The real Ric Flair is a toned-down version of the extrav-agant character you see in the wrestling shows. He's always wanting to fly first class. He's always got a nice suit on. He's always in the bar buying drinks or ordering champagne.

What I like about him is he thinks about wrestling twenty-four hours a day. It's his life. He never gets tired of it.

When I met up with him at *Bash at the Beach*, he was riding high with WCW. But as soon as I stepped into the ring, the crowd cheered me so hard the building shook. And when I beat Ric Flair for the title—the first of six I'd win in WCW—the reaction was deafening.

Shaquille O'Neal is a good friend of mine. He was playing with the Orlando Magic and just starting to get hot at the time I wrestled Ric Flair for the belt. Shaq was sitting ringside, his eyes as big as saucers, when I finished Ric off.

All of a sudden, Shaq jumped into the ring, gave me the belt, and held my hand up. It was awesome, brother, especially since I had been out of the ring for a while and didn't know what to expect.

So I had the steroid trial in my rearview mirror and a long, bright stretch of open wrestling road ahead of me. I was on Cloud Nine.

And I had set myself up to make a lot of money with my new employer. During my *Hulkamania* run, I had pulled in several million dollars a year. My deal with WCW might allow me to make millions more.

The guys at WCW were just getting into merchandising. But after Minnesota and my time with Vince, I knew how to cut a merchandise deal with a saber. My legal counsel, Henry Holmes, convinced WCW that I should receive more than half of the gross merchandising revenues from

Hulk Hogan products and that I would share with WCW a percentage of gross revenue from all other WCW merchandise after expenses.

I also got a hell of a guarantee for each Pay-Per-View— seven hundred grand minimum each time I laced my boots up.

Everybody had thought, Oh my God, the World Wrestling Federation is a monster and when you leave it's like being thrown off a Royal Caribbean cruise liner into hurricane waters without a life jacket. There was no question that you would drown. But I got lucky. I washed up on the beach in Shangri-La. It was a dream deal!

48

When somebody is coming into a company like WCW, a good announcer tries to help them make a splash. It just makes sense. You talk about how big a star they are, how tough they are in the ring, and how terrific their movies are. That's what I expected when I agreed to come to WCW.

But one of the company's announcers at the time was my old pal Jesse "The Body" Ventura from Minnesota, and he wasn't exactly laying out the red carpet for me. I watched him talk about me on television, and he was saying, "Hulk Hogan makes nothing but cheap, low-budget movies—not like *Predator,* the major motion picture I made with Arnold Schwarzenegger."

Predator was a major picture and Jesse *did* have a great part in it. But he wasn't doing good business by saying those things. He was knocking the hell out of me.

So I called Eric Bischoff and I said, "Listen, brother, I'm not interested in coming over if you're going to stick a knife in my back before I get there."

Eric told Jesse to cool it and be part of the team. Of course, Jesse got really pissed off but there was nothing he could do about it. Eric was his boss.

From that point on it was a downhill slide for Jesse. He would show up at all the TV events and all the other announcers would have their suits and ties on, but Jesse would be asleep in the corner looking like he was hungover or something. Eric Bischoff didn't know what Jesse was doing in his spare time, but he was worried. Hell, we were all worried.

Jesse was a real good announcer. But he would go a long time without shaving and I thought he looked like hell. It was like he had stopped taking care of himself, and that was bad for business. Eventually, he got himself fired.

I had nothing to do with that, but he blamed me for it. And it reminded me of what wrestlers had told me about Jesse even back in Minnesota.

In the AWA, he was always nice to me—at least to my

face. But Jim Brunzell and Greg Gagne always told me how jealous Jesse was of me, and that he would talk trash about me as soon as my back was turned.

I didn't believe it. Jesse was such a man's man. He was a Navy SEAL and a Vietnam vet, even though he wouldn't talk about details because he said it would be a national security breach or something.

I did know that Jesse didn't like to lose a match, not to me or anybody else. He'd bitch and complain about it all the time.

Then we got to New York and again guys told me he was jealous of me. And again I didn't believe it.

Then Jesse got a radio show in Minneapolis. And all he did, week after week, was talk Hulk Hogan down. I used to get calls from people in Minnesota telling me how much Jesse hated me.

But I can only think of one thing I ever did to make him feel that way. When he started out in politics, he was campaigning to become the mayor of Brooklyn Park in Minnesota. I was up there for a boat show with my buddy Irwin Jacobs, who owned a bunch of boat companies, and I happened to run into Jesse.

Jesse was real nice to me. He asked if I would come support his campaign for mayor because he needed the help.

I said, "Well, I'm in town for Irwin, but I'll think about it." Then later I called Jesse and said, "You know, I really would love to help you, but I'm busy with stuff for Irwin, so I can't."

I guess that really pissed him off. He has been openly against me ever since. He has taken unprovoked shots at me whenever he can.

Of course, he became mayor of Brooklyn Park without my help. And he became governor of Minnesota without my help. But it didn't make him hate me any less.

I see now that Greg Gagne and Jim Brunzell were right. I believe that Jesse's a bitter guy and I feel that he's always been jealous of me and hated me.

Of course, I've always done better at everything than Jesse. But the reason that's happened is he made it that way. He would always knock himself out of the box before we had a chance to compete with each other.

So don't invite Jesse Ventura and Hulk Hogan to the same dinner party, because the guy's not likely to show up if I'm there.

Two Good Years and Two Better Ones

Hollywood

Hulk

49

Hogan

Almost immediately, WCW went from being the minor league of wrestling to one of the major leagues. The arenas where we wrestled went from having 1,500 spectators or maybe 2,000 to 15,000 or 20,000 spectators. And our TV numbers were going through the roof.

Hulkamania was driving WCW like it had never been driven before. And it went on driving it for two very good years.

For me personally, it was great. Henry Holmes had made a great deal for me. I was making a ton of money. WCW was paying for Lear jets, hotels, limos . . . and they were giving me a per diem, just like a movie deal.

Best of all, I had an opportunity to get to know my family again. I had been away so much making *Thunder in Paradise,* it was nice to fit back in finally.

Then all our momentum kind of leveled off. The TV numbers and the Pay-Per-View numbers hit a plateau, and the plateau wasn't high enough. And the question became, what do we do about it? How can we get the numbers going up again?

And we came up with a wild idea . . . turning Hulk Hogan into a bad guy.

I had talked to Vince McMahon about the idea of me turning heel even before I left his company. He told me I could never be a bad guy, it just wouldn't work. But still, I had this thought in my mind.

So when WCW started floundering a little, I went to Eric Bischoff and I said, "Look, brother, if I looked at these kids and I said, 'For years I been telling you to train, say your prayers, and take your vitamins, but guys, I did it for the money,' that simple statement would shock the wrestling world. It would turn me into a heel."

Eric liked the idea so he ran it by Ted Turner. I don't know how the hell Eric got him to agree to it, but Ted Turner said, "Okay, give it a shot. Just leave yourself an out if it blows up in your face."

So we did it.

It fit in with something else we were doing, which was bringing some new talent into the fold. First Scott Hall—who had been Razor Ramon—came to WCW and said, "Hey, I'm from New York and I'm coming into this minor league promotion to take it over. And guess what? My buddy's coming with me."

People were wondering who was going to show up next. Then the next week Kevin Nash appeared. Nash was the former heavyweight champion. Oh my God, the fans went crazy. Hall and Nash were branded stars, straight from Madison Square Garden. They acted like they were pulling off a hostile takeover of the company.

They picked up Eric Bischoff, the executive vice president of WCW, and powerbombed him through a table on TV. Then they set up this big match, *Bash at the Beach*, in July 1996 in Daytona, Florida. It was a six-man tag-team match with Randy Savage, Sting, and Lex Luger against Nash, Hall, and a partner they hadn't named yet.

Hall and Nash fought two against three until the end of the match. They had already taken Lex Luger off on a stretcher and Randy Savage was basically in there fighting all by himself. All of a sudden I came walking down the ramp and everybody expected me to come to Randy's aid.

But instead, I turned on Randy and helped Hall and Nash beat him. I told my fans I had done it all for the money. And that night I joined with Hall and Nash and I said, "This is the future of wrestling . . ." We called ourselves the nWo, the New World Order.

Then I tagged "Hollywood" on the front of "Hulk Hogan" to give myself that bad-guy flair. I told the fans that I didn't need the wrestling business, that I could make movies if I wanted and leave wrestling behind.

I told them I had made sixteen motion pictures—which was true—and that I had bodyslammed the movie industry the same way I had bodyslammed the wrestling world. Of course, I didn't mention that I only had cameos in eight of those movies and that the rest were low-budget films.

It didn't matter. All that mattered was that we got the fans' attention and made the nWo the hottest thing going.

It wasn't the first time there had been an invasion of bad guys in the wrestling world. It had happened before over in Japan, when five or six wrestlers would go from one company to another and upset the applecart.

I don't know if Eric Bischoff was thinking of what had happened in Japan when he came up with the New World Order. What I *do* know is he was telling me about a phrase in the Bible about the order of things to come, and how people come and go but there's a certain set of rules that will prevail at the end of the day, and the Latin words on the dollar bill that mean "new world order."

New World Order. It seemed like the perfect catch-phrase for the element we were trying to bring into WCW.

After years of morality plays featuring good-guy wrestlers and bad-guy wrestlers, Kevin Nash and Scott Hall introduced the idea that it's cool to be bad, it's cool to do dirty stuff, it's cool to go out there and make these hand signals for West Coast rap and East Coast rap and have their bandannas tied on backward. They were on the edge, brother. They were happening.

People loved Nash and Hall even though they were bad guys. But they didn't love *me*. I was a different story entirely.

My turning heel had shocked the wrestling world, just like we intended. But to tell you the truth, it kind of shocked me too. The Hulk Hogan character was so great, the red-and-yellow guy with the training, prayers and vitamins . . . you could get hooked on being that character. And I *had* gotten hooked on him. I had come to believe in what he said. It was a real positive road to follow.

The heel thing was negative; it was going against the grain. Sure, I was good at it on camera, and I milked it for all it was worth. But as soon as the TV camera was off, that good feeling I'd had with the other character was missing.

I didn't feel comfortable looking at a kid and saying, "Yeah, I'll give you an autograph, but then get out of here!" I was a bad guy so I had to keep that edge, but it just didn't feel right to me.

My family was sentimental about the red-and-yellow guy too, but only to a point. They said, "We trust you. We know this is a business decision. You're not really a bad guy. It's just your job." They were smarter than I was, brother. I was too close to it.

But thanks to the nWo, WCW was off and running again. In fact, we were doing better than before. We started kicking ass in the ratings.

Vince McMahon and his people had to scramble to fight back. They came up with skits depicting me as an old guy

A new nWo member, Horace Hogan

with blond hair and a walker. The guy was saying, "Getting old, brother, getting old."

They were trying to make fun of me. But it backfired on them because people would see the skits and then they would switch over to the WCW channel to see if I really *was* that old. So it actually gave us even more exposure.

Every time we would put an nWo tee shirt on some wrestler, we would make him a star, that's how strong the nWo was. My nephew Michael Bollea came in, and wrestled for the nWo as Horace Hogan, and did real well for himself. Other guys came in too, it seemed like one every week.

We had the Midas touch, brother. Everything we touched turned to gold.

Son of
the Giant

50 **You never know where you're going to come across wrestling talent.**

About a year after I joined WCW, I got a call from the owners of the Chicago franchise in the Continental Basketball Association, which is like the minor league of professional basketball. These guys said they were having trouble selling tickets so they came up with a new half-time promotion—a series of one-on-one celebrity basketball games.

And they wanted Hulk Hogan and Mr. T to be the first two celebrities on the court.

"No problem," I told them.

Before I knew it, I was playing Mr. T in a half-court basketball game. Let me tell you, brother, I smoked him.

I humiliated him. But that wasn't the best thing that happened during intermission, because at one point I happened to look up into the seats and saw one of the biggest human beings I'd ever seen.

He was about seven feet tall, maybe even a little taller, and he weighed about four hundred eighty pounds. He looked like a Clydesdale moving through that crowd.

I elbowed my wife in the ribs and said, "Look over there, Linda. You see that guy? He's got a big dollar sign painted on his back." I thought if the guy were a wrestler he would be an instant success.

Anyway, when intermission was over and I was in the locker room getting dressed, there was a knock at the door. All of a sudden, the giant I had seen before was standing there, and he had a manager named Jimmy. I don't remember his real last name but what I called him was Jimmy Jams.

"Hey," said Jimmy Jams, "this kid wants to meet you. His name's Paul Wight and he's a big fan of yours."

I went to shake the big guy's hand and it was trembling. I could see he was scared to death even though he was huge, half a foot bigger than me.

So we talked for a minute and he told me he played basketball somewhere. I wasn't really listening to him. I was

Son of the Giant

just thinking about how much money he could draw in a wrestling ring.

I asked him, "Have you ever thought about wrestling? I mean, you're so big."

Jimmy Jams said, "Go ahead, do the Hulk Hogan interview."

So Paul Wight said, "Let me tell you something, brother," and did the whole Hulk Hogan rap as if he were me doing an interview.

So I said, "That's very flattering. It's nice to see you come out of your shell. But let me think about something for a second." Right away, I ran to the phone and called Eric Bischoff. "Jesus Christ," I told him, "you ought to see this guy, how big he is."

Eric said, "Well hell, then, let's see him."

So I brought Paul Wight with me to the next place WCW was doing a show and I introduced him to everybody. He had the big Andre the Giant–type hands, the big fat sausage fingers, and the real big body. But he wasn't proportioned the way Andre was. He didn't have the twenty-eight-inch feet, he had normal size-sixteen feet.

Still, he was a giant, and we wanted him to wrestle for us. We put him in the Power Plant, which was WCW's wrestling school, for about a year. That's where he learned how to hit the ropes and fall and run around.

But we didn't leave him in there too long. We didn't want him to learn too much because he would start working like a two-hundred-pound guy instead of a five-hundred-pound guy. So we waited just long enough and then we pulled him out of there.

Then we called him The Giant and shot an angle that he was Andre's son, because he did look a lot like Andre. But unlike Andre, he had long hair.

The fans seemed to like him and we made him a star as fast as we could. When he met me in a title match at *Halloween Havoc* in October 1995 and won the belt from me, it started one of my bigger rivalries in WCW.

At the *Road Wild* Pay-Per-View in August 1996, I beat The Giant and got my belt back. But I'll tell you what, brother, he looked even better after I was done beating him.

In wrestling, you can't humiliate your opponent. You've got to make sure he's okay because you're going to need to work with him again. That's why I've always had a revolving door of people to work with. I make my opponents look good. After you've wrestled me, people are going to think you're a god.

As for The Giant . . . he's wrestling for WWE now under the name Big Show. I wish him luck. He's one of the nicest guys in the business.

Son of the Giant

Three Rounds with the Champ

51 George Foreman and I are good friends, but that didn't stop him from almost killing me one time.

I met George in the early nineties through my attorney and longtime friend Henry Holmes. Henry was George's lawyer too and we just hit it off right away. So when George asked me to help him raise money for charity at this youth center he runs in Houston, I said I would do whatever he wanted.

Little did I know what he had in mind.

When I got there, the first thing I noticed was that the place didn't have any air-conditioning. Here it was the middle of the summer in Houston, Texas. It felt like about a thousand degrees. And there's no air-conditioning.

The second thing I noticed was this boxing ring in the middle of the youth center. Then I found out that George had told the kids I was going to box him three rounds. This wasn't Rocky Balboa, brother. This was George Foreman, former heavyweight champion of the world. And I wasn't going to be a wrestler like I was in *Rocky III*. This time, I was going to do it with boxing gloves on.

So anyway, we got all geared up. I put on the big padded jock. I put on the gloves. And then I saw George putting on some headgear. I said, "Hey George, buddy, where's *my* headgear?"

He said, "Oh, you don't need any headgear."

I looked at him. "What do you mean I don't need it?"

And George said, "I'm not going to hit you in the head. You're my friend."

"Well then," I said, "why are *you* putting it on?"

"Because you're wild, man. You're probably going to hit me in the head."

"You *sure* you're not going to hit me in the head?"

"Don't worry about it," George told me.

Okay. We got into the ring after that and started talking to all these inner-city kids, and I was so nervous I could hardly talk because I knew George was going to kill me. Just for the hell of it, he was going to murder my ass.

The local newspapers were there. The TV stations were

Three Rounds with the Champ

there. And they were all going to watch me get killed.

So against my better judgment, I started boxing with George Foreman. The first time I tried to hit him, I didn't even come close. Then I tried to hit him again, and again I missed him.

You think George is slow when you watch him on TV. You think he's moving like molasses. But let me tell you, brother, when he starts with his bobbing-and- weaving, you wouldn't believe how fast he is.

No matter what I did I couldn't hit him and it was pissing me off. But George wasn't trying very hard to retaliate, so I was doing all right. Then, just as we got near the end of the first round, he got me in the corner.

I put my arms up to protect myself, figuring I could get through the last few seconds of that round if I stayed there like that. George was screwing around with me, going at me with these little baby punches. Then all of a sudden, he stepped back and threw a left hook at me.

Wham! His hook hit me in the right arm, up by the shoulder. And he hit me so hard, my whole leg went numb. That freaked me out. He hadn't hit me in the leg, but my leg had no feeling in it.

I hobbled out of the corner and said, "George, I swear to God, if you ever hit me that hard a second time I'll never talk to you again."

George thought it was hilarious. But it actually took the whole minute between rounds for the feeling to come back in my leg. I couldn't imagine him hitting me in the face with that hook. I'd be dead.

Anyway, he took it easy on me the next couple of rounds. But by the end of the second one, I couldn't even hold my gloves up. In the third round, it just became a comedy routine, because I couldn't box anymore.

The kids who were watching us had a good laugh. I'm glad for them, because *I* certainly wasn't laughing.

Three Rounds with the Champ

Hulk
Rules

Hollywood

Hulk

Hogan

52 In 1995, I came out with an album called *Hulk Rules* by Hulk Hogan and the Wrestling Boot Band. But really, the album was born back in 1992 at Wembley Stadium over in England.

Before the show, which was sold out to the walls, I met a Make-A-Wish kid with cancer. He had a doctor and a nurse with him, a whole medical entourage.

He was supposed to be sitting ringside when I went out to wrestle, but I didn't see him there. After the match, I came back and said, "Where's the kid?"

They told me, "Oh, he died before the match got under way."

Jimmy Hart was with me that night, so we sat down and wrote a song right away in the dressing room. Another *Hulkamaniac* in heaven, there's one empty seat in Wembley, the little *Hulkamaniac* that came to see me. It's a ballad, a slow song.

Anyway, we sat up and wrote ten or eleven songs that night, because once we wrote one we were on a roll. When we recorded the basic sound track, we didn't even use a drummer. We put the songs to a little Rhythm Master, a machine that played different funky beats. Then we plugged in guitar, keyboards, and base, and played around it.

At the studio, we had a couple of horn players and some chicks to sing backup, including my wife. Linda ended up sounding so good, we pulled one of the vocal guys off and gave her a couple of songs, which ended up better than the rest of the stuff.

The profits from the record sales went to the family of the kid who died. They were having trouble paying his medical bills, so we helped out.

Hulk Rules

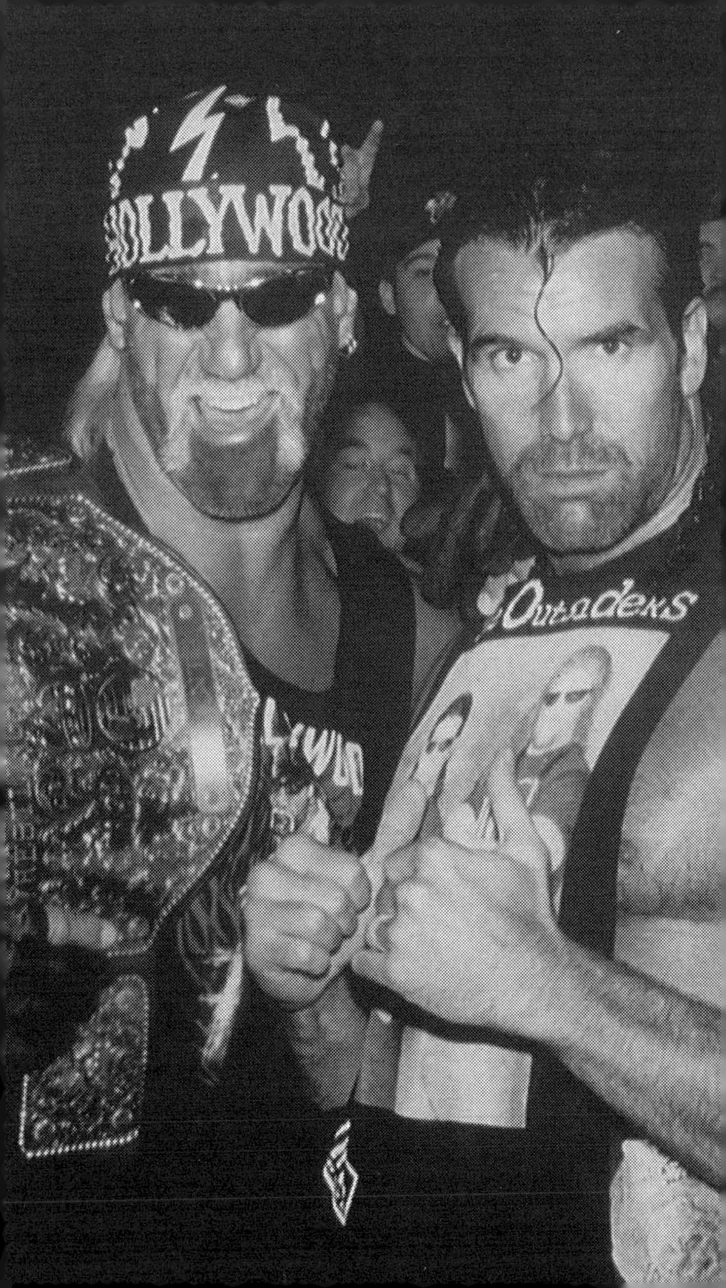
OLLYWOO

The
Hasselhoff
Position

53

While the nWo was taking over the wrestling world, it was only fitting that somebody named Hollywood Hulk Hogan spend at least part of his time back in Hollywood making motion pictures.

In '96, I came out with a couple of low-budget kids' films called *The Secret Agent Club* and *Santa with Muscles*. Then, building on the success of *Thunder in Paradise*, I went the action-adventure route in '97 with *The Ultimate Weapon*. Like all my other films, it made money.

After that came a couple of two-hour movies of the week for Ted Turner's TNT channel. *Assault on Devil's Island,* which was originally supposed to be a pilot for an ongoing series, hit cable TV sets in '97. The sequel, *Hunt for the Death Merchant,* showed up a year later.

I played a Navy SEAL named Mike McBride who would do anything to survive. If he had to smoke dope with the Vietcong to steal their gun, he'd do it. Whatever it took. McBride was a great character.

Funny thing—I found myself working with the same guys again. Schwartz, Berk, and Bonann, the *Baywatch* boys. Basically, they saw these TV movies as a way to make money during their off-season.

I had the "Hasselhoff position"—25 percent of the company, just like I'd wanted. David Hasselhoff had 25 percent of *Baywatch*. But my partners, as good producers do, were always trying to talk me into taking less and less money because they needed it "on the set." They would say, "You know, it's your company too. We'll make money on the back end."

Anyway, the first movie was a pleasure to work on. My costars were Carl Weathers, Shannon Tweed, and Marty Kove, and they were all pros. We shot in Key West, the Bahamas, and Tortuga Island.

The second movie had a lot of the same actors, but it wasn't nearly as pleasant as the first one. Of course, we weren't in the Bahamas anymore. We were in Vancouver, Canada.

The only reason we even considered Vancouver was to

save money. They said if we had enough Canadian content and enough Canadian actors, we could get a hell of a break on all our production costs.

"Everybody's coming to Vancouver," they told us.

So we went up to Vancouver and we scouted locations there. We checked out the prices on trucks and equipment and honey wagons and catering, and sure enough they had all these fantastic deals to offer us.

It was great. We could put more money into the film. So we decided we were definitely going to Vancouver and we didn't give it another thought.

Nine months later, when we went up to Vancouver to start shooting, all of a sudden these deals were no longer available. There were twenty other films being shot in Vancouver at the same time, so the light that we were going to get for a hundred bucks a day had become five hundred bucks a day. The steadycam we were going to get for two hundred a day had become two thousand a day.

Supply and demand, brother. They were right about everybody coming up to Vancouver. It was just that we didn't know how limited the supplies were, and of course no one told us.

The weather was miserable. When it wasn't snowing, it was raining. I just remember slogging through the mud the whole time. And somehow, my partners managed to turn what was supposed to be a twenty-eight-day shoot into a fourteen-day throw-something-on-the-screen. But then, the boys from *Baywatch* were notorious for frugality and getting all they could from people.

Even then, the movies did really well. TNT liked the premise and they liked the ratings, and they wanted to make a third one.

But after slogging through the mud and not making a lot of money, I said I wasn't interested.

Hollywood Hulk Hogan

Showdown at Mega Mountain

54 In 1996, I was in Denver, Colorado filming a movie called *Three Ninjas: High Noon at Mega Mountain* with Loni Anderson and Jim Varney.

WCW had overtaken the World Wrestling Federation in the TV ratings. We were stomping Vince McMahon into a mud hole and the word on the street was that WCW wanted to re-sign me to another two-year deal. How could they do anything else? No matter what people thought about some forty-five-year old guy wobbling around the ring,

I got big TV ratings, and was still drawing money everywhere I went.

Anyway, we were shooting the movie at night, and it takes your body a while to adjust to that type of nocturnal, vampire-like lifestyle. By the time we finished the second night of filming and I got back to the hotel, it was six in the morning and I was dragging my ass big time.

I still had my makeup on. I even had the wig I wore in the film still glued to my head. I hadn't let the makeup artist take any of it off because I was so beat. I said, "It's okay, I'll just rip it off when I get to my room. It'll leave a ring of glue around my forehead but I don't care."

As I crossed the lobby of the hotel to get an elevator, I heard somebody yell, "Monster!"

Only one guy's ever called me that. I turned around and sure enough, I saw Vince McMahon relaxing in a chair in the lobby.

He told me he was in town on business and he was staying in the hotel across the street, but he had heard I was staying in this one. I said, "Brother, let me go up to my room and get this wig off my head and get this makeup off, and then I'll come back down."

So I joined him down there a little while later, and we sat and had a cup of coffee and talked. Mostly we talked about the crap we had pulled on each other.

Why did you do that to me? Well, why did *you* do that to *me*? Well, why did you say this? Why did *you* say *that*? That kind of bull, on and on for about two hours. But at least we straightened it out.

Then we started talking about me going back to work for him. I could have done it, too. I had a window of about thirty days before I re-signed with WCW.

I said, "Well, I'd love to. It seems like the right place to end my career." There was just one problem. . . .

I didn't think that Vince could afford to pay me the money I was negotiating for from WCW. My lawyer, Henry Holmes, was asking for multimillions of dollars a year for a reduced schedule. We believed that maximizing my impact was more important than the number of days I worked. WCW was dominating the TV numbers and I didn't think it was the right time to make a change.

Anyway, we talked and talked and finally I said, "Brother, I've got to go back to work. I've got another all-nighter ahead of me."

Vince was very understanding. He said, "Hey, some other time, then."

I said, "Yeah, man, some other time."

Helicopters

55

What scares me more than anything else in the world?

Helicopters, brother. Helicopters scare the *crap* out of me.

My wife's father was the chief helicopter pilot of the L.A. Police Department for twenty or thirty years and he's gone down a couple of times. The second time he barely lived through it.

But it's not just what happened to my father-in-law. Helicopters just spook me in a way nothing else can.

That's why it was kind of funny when I was making *Thunder in Paradise* back in 1994, and Michael Eisner made me an offer he thought I couldn't refuse. At the time, Eisner was the chairman of Disney, and he knew that I couldn't stand the commute from my home in Tampa to the studio in Orlando.

In order to be in the makeup trailer by six o'clock in the morning, I would have to leave the house at three-thirty and drive a hundred and fifty miles on my bike on an empty interstate. So if anything happened to me, I'd be a dead man.

Of course, my family was sleeping when I left, so I wouldn't see them in the morning. Then I'd get off work at seven at night and by the time I got back to Tampa it would be nine, so my kids would already be going to bed. It's not hard to see why I didn't like that commute very much.

So Michael Eisner said, "Let's fly Hulk to work in a helicopter."

He knew I had a little landing strip attached to the back of my property. A helicopter could pick me up there in the morning and fly me back and forth, he said, and then I'd stop complaining about not seeing my family.

But I had this feeling in the pit of my stomach that the helicopter would fall out of the sky. I was so afraid I told Eisner, "Forget it. I'll just drive the damn interstate."

My helicopter phobia got even worse when I was filming *Assault on Devil's Island* a few years later. We had a scene where Carl Weathers and I were running through the jungle and this big black chopper was coming after us.

My stunt double and my good friend Ed Leslie were both dressed in all-black Ninja gear and were hanging out of the helicopter on either side, holding on to its struts. They had a former Vietnam pilot flying the thing and his instructions were to fly it low to the ground, following a hundred feet behind me along this path in the so-called jungle, and they had set up all these pods that would explode as I ran by.

I didn't want to do the shot because it was so windy that day and the helicopter had to fly so low. But against my better judgment I agreed to give it a try.

This pilot was so good he was able to cut underneath the trees and make it look like he was almost on the ground chasing me. So I'm running hard and the pods started going off, bang-bang-bang. So far, so good.

Then I heard a loud sound like a weedeater from hell. I looked back over my shoulder and I saw that the helicopter was trapped underneath this palm tree. The wind had just lifted it up all of a sudden and the rotors were cutting through the tree and the pilot was trying like hell to get himself free.

Thank God, the helicopter finally cut its way out of the tree. But even then, I saw the chopper slide sideways and almost lose it. As I'm holding my breath, figuring somebody's going to get killed for sure, the pilot pulled up somehow and finished the goddamn shot.

My partners were going, "That's great, that's really great! Let's do it again!"

I just shot them the bird and said, "We're not doing that shot again. Let's move the camera and get out of here."

It's weird when it comes to helicopters, brother. I'll never go up in one and that's a promise.

Dennis
Rodman

56

One day I got a call from a buddy of mine, Tony Carlini, who lives in Newport Beach, California. One of his neighbors in Newport Beach was Dennis Rodman, who was a forward for the National Basketball Association's World's Champion Chicago Bulls.

Rodman was red-hot at the time. He was pulling all kinds of crap, dying his hair like a rainbow and wearing wedding dresses and all kinds of stuff. He was also a big wrestling fan, a big mark. He was dying to get into the ring so he asked Tony Carlini if he could meet me.

"No problem," I told Tony.

I ended up meeting Rodman at the Newport Beach Ritz-Carlton. I figured we would have a quiet conversation, talk a little about what he wanted to do and how we might be able to use him.

Little did I know it was going to be a testosterone fest.

Rodman had all his boys there, his posse. Right off the bat, he started up. "What's the big deal?" he said. "I can do that wrestling crap."

I saw how it was going to be, so I looked him in the eye and said, "You can't even make a basket, brother. How the hell are you going to wrestle?" Before he could say anything, I gave him the other barrel. "How many points you score last game, brother? Two? *None*?"

Rodman saw he wasn't going to outtalk me, so he changed tacks. He said, "Drink some drinks with me, man. Kamikazes." And he got a waiter over and ordered the drinks. Then he took a seat at one end of a long table and held court with all his boys and his girls, and I wormed my way down to the other end of the table.

The kamikazes came and I swear, there must have been fifty of them. I said to myself, "Oh man, I'm in trouble here. This guy is a hard liquor fanatic."

By the time I was on my way to my sixth kamikaze, I was starting to get a little sick. Okay, I thought, I'm not going to be able to hang with this guy.

So because I was at the end of the table, I started taking the kamikazes and dumping them. I was dumping them in the plants, on the carpet, down the stairway to the kitchen . . . I don't know how the poor waiters didn't slip and fall. As far as Rodman knew, I was drinking every one of those suckers.

But he was relentless, he kept on coming. So finally, I said to myself, *Okay, I'm going to get even with him.*

I called upstairs and got hold of Brian Knobbs, who wrestles as one of the Nasty Boys and is a really good friend of mine.

"Get down here," I told Brian, "I need some help, bro. I got Dennis Rodman down here and I want you to humble him."

I could hear Brian Knobbs snickering on the other end of the phone. "I'll be right down," he said, "don't worry."

A couple of minutes later, here he comes, man. Brian swings through the door, slaps Rodman in the head two or three times, and yells, "You want to drink some drinks? I'm the Nasty Boy. I'll drink with you. You want to wrestle? See if you can keep up with me."

To make a long story short, Brian Knobbs drank Rodman under the table. Then he took Rodman's agent outside and slammed him on the hood of my car. Then he took Rodman himself and started throwing him around like a rag doll in the parking lot.

It was hilarious. It was a scene from the damned Keystone Kops. Brian just abused these guys so much. The next day Brian Knobbs was on the plane with me and he asked, "Did I do good?"

I said, "Brother, you did great."

After Brian had humbled Rodman's ass, we gave Dennis

the chance he wanted. We brought him down and booked a tag-team match at *Bash at the Beach '97*, and made a deal with his agent. But we couldn't just let him get into the ring unprepared, so we arranged to work out with him for a couple of days.

The first of those days, I had Lex Luger and the Giant down there at noon, because those were the guys who were going to be in the ring with us. Rodman was late. Hours went by.

The Giant was pissed but he was a young guy and he was going to do what I told him. But Lex Luger, who was two hundred eighty pounds without an ounce of fat on his body, wanted to kill Rodman. He wanted to just break him in half.

I said, "Lex, let's just get through this. We'll never see this guy again."

Finally, Rodman sauntered in. He was supposed to be there at twelve and he had kept me and the guys waiting till four. Fortunately for him, Lex Luger and the Giant were able to keep their tempers in check and work with this guy.

So we showed Rodman the ropes for a couple of days, but he was real lackadaisical. I had no idea if he was really going to be able to pull it off.

Funny thing—if Rodman seemed lackadaisical to us, he must have seemed even worse to the Chicago Bulls. It turned out he was missing the team's practices to be in the ring with us. Chicago was headed for the NBA Finals again and Rodman was blowing off their practices to work with me, Lex Luger, and the Giant.

Of course, once he got to the Finals, he had more rebounds than anybody. He came out smelling like a damn rose.

And that's pretty much what happened when he got to the wrestling venue too. When the red light went on, he

Dennis Rodman

pulled it off masterfully—just like Mr. T and other guys who had surprised me from time to time. He was a pro.

Still, I swore to God after that I'd never work with him again. He'd about given me a nervous breakdown. That was it for me. Never again.

But the next year, at *Bash at the Beach '98*, we needed a main event and Rodman was still hot. So despite all my misgivings, I ended up working with him a second time.

The good news was Karl Malone wanted to get some action this time. So we made it Hulk Hogan and Dennis Rodman against Diamond Dallas Page and Karl Malone.

Malone was the exact opposite of Dennis Rodman. If Rodman was in great shape, Karl Malone was in ten times *better* shape. This guy was *ripped*. I wouldn't have believed it, but with his shirt off he was like a bodybuilder.

And he was strong as hell. He took me into the ring and threw me around in places I wasn't planning on going. He was gifted. I can't say enough good things about him.

So there was Karl Malone on one side of the fence and he was training hard, brother. He was doing sit-ups, he was running, he was jumping. He was taking classes to get himself in even better shape than before. Diamond Dallas Page, who's such a detail freak he's nuts, had Karl Malone pumped enough to jump to the moon.

Then there was my tag-team partner Dennis Rodman on the other side of the fence, and he wasn't doing a damn thing except getting drunk.

I said, "Man, we're going to get killed."

One night, Rodman wanted to stay out all night drinking. But we were supposed to do the Howard Stern show in the morning, so I told him that wasn't a good idea. I said he should be in bed by midnight.

But he promised me that if I let him stay out late, he would still get up in the morning and do the Howard Stern show. So against my better judgment, I let him stay out until five in the morning. And of course, I stayed out with him.

The next morning, I pushed myself out of bed and went to wake up Rodman, but he wouldn't get up. He said, "Screw Howard Stern. I'm not going on that show. I don't want to get out of bed."

I said, "Well, Dennis, we made a commitment. You prom-

Dennis Rodman

ised me if you stayed out all night you'd still go, so now you're going. Get your ass up."

I actually had to drag him out of the bed. He had his pants on from the night before, but no shoes. I didn't care. I dragged him out of there and threw him into the car. It was a damn circus.

Anyway, we got to Howard Stern by 6:30 A.M., which was when he had asked us to be there. But Rodman was pissed because I wouldn't let him sleep, so he wouldn't talk. He just clammed up and wouldn't say a thing. I had to do all the talking to Howard Stern.

When we finally got to the event, Rodman got into the ring and messed up two or three moves. He wasn't as good as the year before, but on the whole he was okay.

Then we used him one last time against Randy Savage at *Road Wild* in Sturgis, South Dakota. It was an outdoor event and Randy just beat the hell out of him.

He didn't like the fact that Rodman was being lazy in the ring, so he put knots all over Rodman's head. Then he walked Rodman out of the ring, put him in one of those portable johns, and pushed it over with Rodman in it.

We hadn't seen Rodman since, but now he's talking about wanting to get back into wrestling. He doesn't have much going on so he sent the word out to me. He lost some weight, maybe thirty pounds, but he's going to get back in shape and he wants another chance in the ring. At least that's what he said.

I'll see if he's serious or if he just called me after about fifty gin and tonics.

Hollywood

Jay Leno

57

The first time I met Jay Leno was on a Love Ride for Muscular Dystrophy in Los Angeles. Everybody who's anybody goes on this ride. You make your way through the canyons for half a day and end up at somebody's ranch, and all the money's donated to muscular dystrophy research.

One year, they asked me to lead the Love Ride, and the guy who was riding with me was Jay Leno. I found out later that he always leads it. Anyway, we talked while we were up there and became friends, and one of the things I learned about him was that he was a wrestling fan.

When I told Eric Bischoff this, he said, "What the hell, everybody else is jumping in the ring. Why not Jay Leno?"

We asked Leno if he was interested in appearing at *Road Wild*. He said, "Yeah, man, absolutely. But only if I can do it well."

So we set up a ring at NBC studios and we had Billy Kidman, Chris Kanyon, and Sugar Shane Helms stay out there to work with Jay Leno. I told them what I wanted and they worked with him every day, leading him through it one step at a time.

He was going to grab his opponent's head and run the guy into the turnbuckle. And after the guy hit the turnbuckle, Leno was going to take him and throw him to the other corner. You would never script a main event that way, but we did it because we were going to have Jay Leno in the ring.

Finally, Eric Bischoff and I went out there to see what kind of progress they were making. Kidman, Kanyon, and Helms said Leno was doing great. They told me all the stuff he could do.

I said, "Really? That's unbelievable. Let's see it."

To tell you the truth, I was expecting a damn nightmare. But surprisingly enough, Leno was a good athlete. He moved in the ring like he had done it all his life.

I said, "This guy is taking to it like a duck to water."

With that big melon-head of his, he could have been a wrestler and used his head to butt his opponent for the finish. His signature move would have been a headbutt in the gut that made everybody pass out.

Leno looked like he knew what he was doing, so I got into the ring with him. When we locked up, he was supposed to take my arm and make it seem like he was twisting it real hard. Then I would have made a face and said, "It hurts, I give up, brother!"

But instead of just grabbing my arm and holding it loosely, he twisted it so hard he almost ripped it out of its socket. I yelled, "Hey, man, loosen up!"

He turned pale and said, "What did I do wrong?"

I said, "Jesus, you almost took my damn arm off, that's what you did. I'm working with you here. I'm your buddy. Take it easy, brother."

I told him all he had to do was twist my arm real easy. Then I would act like he was killing me. I said, "Nobody knows if you're grabbing me this hard or THAT hard. It's up to me to tell them how much it hurts."

After I explained it, he got it.

About a week before the Pay-Per-View, we were supposed to promote the match on the *Tonight Show*. The scheduled guests were Diamond Dallas Page and Karl Malone, who were going to team up against me and Eric Bischoff.

All of a sudden, we got this idea. We wanted to take over the set and throw Jay Leno off it, then put our feet up on his desk like it was *our* show all of a sudden.

Gary Constantine, who was Jay's producer, said, "No way."

But when we told Jay about it, he said, "Hell, let's go for it."

So Eric Bischoff and I came out of the audience unexpectedly and took over the set of the *Tonight Show*. Then I sat down in his chair and Eric sat down next to me and I started interviewing him like I was Jay Leno and he was a guest.

So basically, the nWo had taken over the *Tonight Show* the same way we had taken over the wrestling business. We were saying that no one could stop us.

Then Jay Leno showed his face again—but this time he had his two friends with him, Diamond Dallas Page and Karl Malone. Page and Malone jumped me and Eric and kicked our asses. It was pretty wild. We got some good ratings that night.

So the stage was set for the tag-team match at *Road Wild*. When the time came, Leno and Page teamed up against Bischoff and me. Leno did a great job. He was even better than he had been at the rehearsals. It was like he knew he had to make the moves bigger and ham it up. In the end, he pinned Eric Bischoff for the victory.

I could have let it go as "The guy beat us." I mean, it was respectable. But when he went back on the show, he made fun of it. He got a few laughs with it. He didn't say he knew what he was doing.

But he did. He had it down, brother.

Hollywood Hulk Hogan

Hogan for President

58

Jesse Ventura became governor of Minnesota by following a simple formula—he knew a little bit about everything, just enough to debate the established politicians and nail the issues straight on.

Then he put the icing on the cake by telling people he would extend ice fishing season another week. Instead of catching twenty walleyes they could catch twenty-two. Hey, brother, Jesse's the man!

Eric Bischoff looked at Jesse and said, "Terry, you could run for President of the United States."

And Ted Turner agreed.

I told Ted, " I'm not a politician. I'm a wrestler."

He said, "You don't *have* to be a politician. It's a popularity contest."

Maybe he was right. I had already shown I was better than Jesse in the wrestling business. If he could talk the people of Minnesota into making him their governor, maybe I really *could* get myself elected president.

So one night, I went on the *Tonight Show* and told Jay Leno I was going to retire and run for president. People went crazy.

Ted Turner actually did surveys—five thousand people in Fulton County, Georgia, five thousand people in Orange County, California, and five thousand people in Minnesota. We asked them a hypothetical question: if they had a choice of Bill Clinton (even though he couldn't run again), Hulk Hogan, or Ross Perot, who would they want to be elected president? The only reason Perot was in there was he was a friend of Ted Turner.

About seventy percent said they would rather elect Hulk Hogan than either Bill Clinton or Ross Perot. I said, "Oh my God, this could happen."

A little while after that, I checked into some hotel in Atlanta and saw that I was in the "president's suite." I called my wife and said, "This must be destiny, Momma." I'm such an idiot.

But people everywhere were asking me about it. It wasn't a joke anymore. It was starting to get real.

Hollywood Hulk Hogan

Ted Turner wanted to go for it. He was willing to put up money to finance my campaign. Eric Bischoff was saying it would be a tremendous publicity stunt, but Turner was saying, "Shoot, it might work."

Finally, I sat my kids down and talked to them about it. I said, "If I win, I'll be President of the United States and we'll have to move to the White House. How do you guys feel about that?"

My kids said, "Two things, Dad. First of all, won't you have to take a cut in pay?"

I said, "Well, yeah. I won't make the kind of money I'm making now."

Then they said, "If you become president, won't people be trying to assassinate you?"

That hadn't occurred to me. I said, "Yeah, you might be right about that too."

I was all excited about it for a total of two weeks. Then I realized it wasn't going to work. It wasn't just the stuff my kids had brought up—I was going to have to read the paper every day so I could at least know a little bit about everything the way Jesse did, and that was too much work for me. Besides, if I won I wouldn't be able to hang out on the beach all day.

So Jay Leno called me back to his show and said, "Okay, Hulk, what's up? You said you were retiring."

I said, "No, Jay, you misunderstood me. I said I was tired, not *re*tired."

That got a big laugh. And I was off the hook when it came to the presidency of the United States.

Hogan for President

A Slippery Slope

For a couple of years, the nWo kicked Vince McMahon's ass. We were flying high. But eventually, the situation started to fall apart.

I think Eric Bischoff could really do a good job running a company now. But at the time, he got hit with so much so fast it was like he was riding a motorcycle and he had just accelerated from sixty to a hundred and sixty. Choom! He was hanging on to the handlebars for dear life and his feet were sticking straight back. He was just trying not to get thrown off.

One problem was that he had a huge company to run, but couldn't find enough qualified people to help him run it. The wrestling business isn't just about what happens in the ring. That's maybe two percent of it. The rest of it is television deals, public relations, knowing how to maintain momentum. And to accomplish all that, you need employees with experience and ones you can depend on and trust.

Vince McMahon's people had been working for him for a number of years, so they knew the wrestling business inside and out. They had what we called Titan Training, which means you don't punch a time clock. You bop till you drop. If you have to yawn, do it in the bathroom so no one sees you. And make sure you finish the job, no matter how long it takes.

The "Titan" in Titan Training came from "Titan Sports, Inc.," which was the real company behind the WWE brand name.

At WCW, lots of the secretaries would go home at five o'clock and you couldn't find them after that. When Vince McMahon's executive assistants go home, I've got all their numbers—home numbers, cell numbers, whatever, so I can find them if I need them.

Vince McMahon could be making love to his wife at four o'clock in the morning and if I call him to talk about *WrestleMania* he'll put me on a speakerphone and let me talk to him. No question about it.

Just the other day, I was talking to Debbie Bonnanizo at WWE who was working on my new *Hulkamania* logo. She

Hollywood Hulk Hogan

said, "This is weird. I was working on this same logo twenty years ago."

That's the kind of person Eric needed.

The other problem was that Eric started listening to Scott Hall and Kevin Nash. They were of the opinion that wrestlers should talk more and not wrestle so much. Then Kevin Nash brought some of his friends in and they didn't fit in real well, so it became a bunch of bull instead of business.

After a while, we split the nWo brand into two groups. There was the original black-and-white nWo and there was the red-and-black Wölfpac. And we brought in Sting and "Macho Man" Randy Savage and Lex Luger, even though none of these guys had a clue what "nWo cool" was all about.

Then we split the brand again and had the Latino World Order with all the Latin guys wearing nWo shirts but in red, green, and yellow. And slowly but surely, we watered the whole concept down.

Meanwhile, Vince McMahon had found a new way to compete with—Jerry Springer-style wrestling. Stone Cold Steve Austin was shooting the bird and telling his boss to shove it, which was what all of America would have loved to do. Vince's wrestlers were getting the women in the audience to pull their tops up. He was pushing the envelope—and he blew right by us like a damn freight train.

Our ratings were down. The bottom line was hurting. And of course, it all fell on the shoulders of Eric Bischoff.

One night, I got a call from the guy. He said, "I'm sitting here with six of my best friends, trying to figure out how to get the nose back up on this thing." In other words, he was

sitting there drinking a six-pack all by himself, trying to find a way to boost WCW's numbers.

"If this was your company," he said, "what would you do?"

I said, "That's easy, brother. If it were my company, I would put the belt on Bill Goldberg."

Bill Goldberg was a guy who had played noseguard at the University of Georgia, then gone on to play profes-

Hollywood Hulk Hogan

sional football for a few years. After an injury took away his football career, he tried wrestling—and thrived at it.

When Bill Goldberg came out of wrestling school, he had a snap to his work that you don't see very often. The WCW immediately put him on a winning streak, trying to get him up to a hundred wins as soon as possible to make him somebody special.

I was scheduled to wrestle him in a dark match—a match that would be seen by the people in the arena but not on TV. I told Eric Bischoff to switch gears, televise the match, and let Bill Goldberg win.

I said, "Nothing would have more impact now than Goldberg beating Hogan for the belt. He seems to be a great guy. Why don't you give him a chance?"

Eric Bischoff made a call and it was all arranged.

The match went off and Goldberg beat me. Good sport that I was, I put the belt on him myself. People in the state of Georgia were happy that I got my ass beat by their homeboy.

Unfortunately, nobody else in America seemed to feel that way. The numbers didn't change. The only thing that was different was that Bill Goldberg had the belt—and that turned out to be another type of problem.

All of a sudden, he became this monster who didn't ever want to lose a match. He just stopped like a mule in midstream and said, "I'm not losing."

You have to be flexible in the wrestling business. You have to be able to go in different directions. When a guy's one-dimensional, you can't do anything with him. You can't write

A Slippery Slope

Running wild on Sting

story lines and create emotion when somebody refuses to do business.

So working with Bill Goldberg became a nightmare. Nash and Hall were saying things about me and I was saying things about them. And a lot of guys got hurt all at once, maybe ten top guys all at the same time.

Eric Bischoff was out there all by himself, without any

Hollywood Hulk Hogan

experienced people to lean on. He did his best to keep us going, but it was an uphill battle.

Finally, they took the reins of WCW away from Eric and gave them to a bean counter, a guy from accounting named Bill Busch. This guy didn't have a clue what wrestling was about, but they put him in charge.

One day, he called me up and said, "I hired away a couple of show writers from the World Wrestling Federation, Vince Russo and Ed Ferrara. What do you think?"

I said, "I don't know them, but anything's better than what we got."

So he brought these writers in.

What I didn't know was that Russo and Ferrara had already sold Bill Busch. Russo had claimed he was the one responsible for the success of the World Wrestling Federation. He said he had told Vince McMahon what to do, what moves to make, and forged their whole attitude in the nineties.

When I heard that later on, I said, "No way. It's just my opinion, but Vince McMahon's the guy responsible for the success."

But it was already too late. Russo was in.

The other thing I didn't know about Russo was that he was on a mission to get rid of me and bring in guys who weren't established yet. Even before he met me, he walked into a creative meeting and said he wanted to get rid of Hulk Hogan.

So I never had a chance with this guy. He said I was too old to wrestle anymore. I couldn't draw money. Over the

A Slippery Slope

next two years, Russo made my life miserable. He hung me out to dry every chance he got.

One of his big ideas was something called The Millionaires' Club. He took all the WCW wrestlers who were over forty or who had made it in the business and stuck them in the Millionaires' Club. Then he took all the young guys who hadn't established themselves yet and called them The New Blood.

It was Vince Russo's way of trying to create new interest in WCW, but it didn't work. He was trying to separate the lettuce from the tomatoes but you really need a mixture of both to make the salad work. You need established guys and younger guys working as allies.

The worst part of The Millionaires' Club was you could see Vince Russo's agenda in it. He was putting all of us veterans in this club to say we were rich, pompous prima donnas whose best days were behind us.

But when he would have one of the young guys in The New Blood beat a guy in The Millionaires' Club, the idea would backfire on him and the fans would boo the young guy. Vince Russo said he just couldn't understand why the fans would do that. He later dropped the whole thing.

The older guys tried to make the idea work. We tried to make the younger guys look good. But we were going against the grain of the fans' loyalties and expectations. They loved the guys they knew.

Ric Flair would lose a match to one of The New Blood guys, but they would still cheer him and boo the guy who had beaten him. Ric made it look like his opponent had stripped

Hollywood Hulk Hogan

him of his pride and his honor, but the fans knew it was a work. As far as they were concerned, Ric was still The Man.

One time Russo told me he was trying to make a name for Billy Kidman, one of the newer guys in WCW, and he wanted to get me involved. I said, "Sure, brother, I'll do whatever you want."

So Russo had me lose to Kidman, who weighed about a hundred and eighty pounds, two or three weeks in a row. Finally I got "lucky" at a Pay-Per-View and beat this kid. It made me look ridiculous, but I went along with it.

At the end of that, Billy Kidman was supposed to get this big push. But a week later, Russo had him in a Viagra-on-a-pole match, where the loser had to take a whole bottle of Viagra—and Kidman lost. Then they took him off TV.

So why did they sacrifice Hulk Hogan and let Billy Kidman beat him three, four weeks in a row if they weren't going to make Billy Kidman a star? It didn't make any sense to me.

And I wasn't the only one involved in Russo's stuff. On one occasion, Russo himself won a championship belt. Another time, Mike Awesome threw Chris Kanyon off a three-story-high, triple-threat steel cage.

It should have been a main-event story line, Chris Kanyon versus Mike Awesome, the kind of thing that could have gone on for six months. Chris Kanyon should have shown up in a wheelchair.

But the very next week, Vince Russo had Mike Awesome and Chris Kanyon shaking hands and becoming friends. Again, to me, it made no sense.

A Slippery Slope

The more I saw of Russo, the more I realized he was a guy I totally disagreed with. But he was accomplishing one thing. He was doing what he said he would do—slowly but surely driving me out of the wrestling business.

I'll never forget when Russo had me lie down in the middle of the ring at *Halloween Havoc* in 1999, without wrestling even for a second, and let Sting put his foot on me to win the match. Russo said he had some great plan. He was going to bring me back two or three weeks later, and explain why he did it—and when he did that, it would make me an even bigger star than I already was.

Well, he didn't do what he said he would. After a few weeks, when the ratings were falling off a cliff, Eric Bischoff called me and begged me to come back. And like any loyalist, I came back for more.

Then there was the time Russo had Goldberg spear me

in the ring. They put me on a stretcher and carried me out of the arena, and Russo told me again that he had some great plans. "I'm going to bring you right back," he said. "You'll be hotter than ever."

Again, he didn't call me back. And again, it was Eric Bischoff who finally had to call me to get me to return.

Russo basically used me as a whipping boy. I felt like I was losing more matches than ever. It got to the point where the people went, "Hogan might be old, but *that* guy can't beat him." It got crazy.

By that time, Eric Bischoff had begun fading out of the picture. When Bill Busch took over, Eric had been later reassigned as one of the creative guys, with the under-standing that he and Russo would be fifty-fifty creative partners. But Russo kept jumping on the Jerry Springer bandwagon and trying to outsleaze Vince McMahon, and Eric said that was the wrong way to go.

After four or five run-ins with Russo, Eric decided he didn't want his name on the product anymore, so he stepped or was pushed to the sideline. He kept receiving his weekly payment from Ted Turner, but he had nothing to do with the sleazy kind of wrestling that Russo was try-ing to instill in us.

Little by little, Russo and WCW just ran the product into the ground and out of existence. And for me personally, those two years when he was in charge were hell. The only thing this guy was clear about when it came to the wrestling business was that he wanted me out of it.

Then came the last straw. At *Bash at the Beach 2000*, a

A Slippery Slope

Pay-Per-View event held in Daytona, Florida, I was supposed to wrestle Jeff Jarrett for the WCW world title.

A WCW guy named Johnny Ace came over to my house a few days before the match to tell me what Vince Russo had in mind. He said Russo wanted Jeff Jarrett to beat me one-two-three. And then he wanted Scott Steiner, who was known as Big Poppa Pump, to come into the ring and help Jeff Jarrett beat me up. Hell, they were going to beat me up so bad I would have to be taken out of the arena on a stretcher.

It didn't surprise me. At that point, I was used to having to lose matches and get carried out on a stretcher. So all I said was, "Okay, then what? What are we going to do the next night, on *Monday Nitro*?"

And Johnny Ace, Vince Russo's liaison, said, "After *Bash at the Beach*, Vince doesn't have any more plans for you."

"But I have several months left on my contract," I said. "And he's not going to bring me back? That won't work for me."

Johnny Ace said there was an alternate finish where Jeff Jarrett would win the match but get disqualified somehow. Then I would beat everybody up and look like Superman. And as I was kicking everybody's ass, Jeff Jarrett would sneak out with the title belt.

Vince Russo was trying to appease my ego with that finish. But just like the other scenario, I wouldn't be coming back. So I told Johnny Ace, "Sorry, brother, but that doesn't work for me either."

Obviously, I had to talk to Vince Russo in person. So I went early to *Bash at the Beach* and sat down in a bus with

Russo and Eric Bischoff. And I said, "Look, Vince, I know you want me to leave WCW, but my contract gives me creative control. So here's what I'm going to do. I'm going to beat Jeff Jarrett for the title belt tonight. Then we'll have twenty-four hours to think about our future plans."

I didn't know exactly what I would do on *Monday Nitro*. The important thing was that I wanted to keep my career at WCW and beyond, if it came to that, on a positive note, so I could pick it up again at the same level somewhere else.

It sounded reasonable as far as I was concerned. But Vince Russo didn't think so. He got all pissed off and said, "That's not what I want. I want Jeff Jarrett to win tonight. And if I was trying to screw you, I'd tell Jeff Jarrett to just lay down in the middle of the ring and the hell with it."

I said, "Sure, that'll really work. Jeff Jarrett can just lay down and I can pin him one-two-three and take the belt. But if we do that, we're going to piss off a lot of people who want to see us wrestle."

"No," said Russo, "that's what I want to do. I want Jeff Jarrett to lay down."

I said, "But that's screwing over the fans."

But that's the way Russo had it go down. Jeff Jarrett laid down in the middle of the ring, I put my foot on him, and the referee counted to three. Then they handed me the title belt and all the fans were upset, just as I had predicted.

However, what I didn't expect was that as I was getting ready to leave the building, Vince Russo would go back out to the ring and grab the microphone and defame me.

He started with telling everyone in the arena that there

A Slippery Slope

was no way in hell I could ever beat Jeff Jarrett. (Of course, I've got my own opinion about that. I've never fought him in a real fight but I think I might have been able to beat this two-hundred-thirty-pound guy.)

Then Russo said lots of other things, like the whole match was bull, and that I was a baldheaded piece of crap, and that I would never work for WCW again—which I didn't, even though I had several months left on my contract with WCW. But that wasn't the worst part. He also called me a politician, which suggested that I would take covert and undue advantage of opportunities to manipulate my fellow wrestlers.

Russo put me in serious danger by saying that. The other wrestlers will hurt a guy real bad if they think he's maneuvering behind their backs. They'll get you in the ring and then they'll hurt you.

And Russo wasn't done, because then he said I held back guys like Booker T for the last fourteen years. I took exception to that for a couple of reasons. First off, I had only known Booker T for the last *four* years. But what really pissed me off was the implication that I was a racist. I mean, when you talk about somebody holding back an African-American guy in my business, that gets translated into racism.

And it took its toll on me. I lost salary, merchandise royalty revenue, and my standing and reputation in the wrestling business. But the biggest hit I took was in my own head. After what Vince Russo did and said about me on television, I started second-guessing myself. I started wondering if maybe I wasn't what he said I was and I became increasingly depressed.

For the next couple of years, it seemed nobody remembered that I was the guy who made wrestling king in the eighties and nineties. It seemed nobody remembered that I was the guy who slammed Andre the Giant.

All I heard was "Aren't you the guy who was too old to wrestle and got fired by Vince Russo? And how could you let him say those things about you?"

In the meantime, I have sued WCW for breach of contract and defamation substantially based on this incident with Vince Russo. In the suit, I pointed out that I was supposed to be used in a certain number of Pay-Per-Views a year as the featured wrestler, and WCW didn't do that. And I pointed out that I had creative control, which meant that anything WCW did with me, I had to agree to it. But the interview that Vince Russo gave after my match with Jeff Jarrett was something we never discussed. Adding to it all the outcome of my match with Jarrett was not as we agreed and it violated my WCW contract.

Unfortunately, the lawsuit could only get me the money that was coming to me. It couldn't restore my reputation or repair the enormous emotional damage done to my self-esteem and embarrassment and emotional distress caused to me and my family.

I needed to fix that myself somehow. I needed to lift that dark cloud that was hanging over my head. I just didn't know if I could still do that.

A Slippery Slope

Setting the Record Straight

60 Let me tell you what I think of Booker T.

The guy is a talented wrestler who takes a tremendous amount of pride in what he does. I would trust him in the ring with my life, and that's saying something. For me to trust someone, they have to not only have good timing but be strong enough to throw me the right way and break my fall.

Booker T can do all of that. Plus the guy can talk, which is very important in the wrestling business.

Now, I'll also tell you I think Booker T made a mistake by being in WCW too long. I think he should have left WCW three or four years earlier and gone to New York, instead of waiting and becoming part of an acquisition with a bunch of other wrestlers. I think he would have been a bigger star if he'd have come to WWE on his own instead of as part of the WCW package.

So, contrary to what Vince Russo said in the ring that night at *Bash at the Beach*, I didn't hold Booker T back in any way, shape, or form. The only one who did that was Booker T himself.

Owen Hart

61   Owen Hart came from a family of wrestlers. His father, Stu Hart, ran a wrestling promotion out of Calgary, Alberta, and his brother, Bret, was an accomplished technical wrestler.

Owen was a real good person, a family man who was tough enough to take all the bumps and bruises of the wrestling business and still remain very even-keeled. He wasn't a drinker or a hell-raiser. He was funny, he was sincere, and he was a good friend.

At various times, Bret Hart and I didn't get along. Owen would say, "Terry, I think my brother's overreacting, I'm on your side."

Back then, I said, "We'll keep that between us. I don't want to be the one to drive a wedge between two brothers." But when Bret was having his pissing fits, Owen thought it was ridiculous.

After I left Vince McMahon and joined WCW, Owen was playing a superhero character named the Blue Blazer. He was training, saying his prayers, and drinking his milk, so I wonder who that was supposed to be making fun of.

Meanwhile, his brother, Bret, was trashing me in the Calgary papers. Ever since 1993, he had been calling me a lowlife because of the misunderstanding about who I was going to drop the belt to when I made my exit.

When both of us wound up in WCW, Bret came up to me and said he had overreacted and he was wrong, and I accepted his apology. We became friends after that. And when Bill Goldberg seriously injured him by accidentally kicking him in the head, the only guy Bret would wrestle would be me, because he knew I would be careful not to hurt him.

One night when I was still with WCW, I was watching a World Wrestling Federation Pay-Per-View. Owen was in his Blue Blazer character. He was supposed to be lowered from the rafters, unhook a little early, and stumble into the ring like a goof.

But that's not how it went down.

Either he unhooked way up at the top or a wire broke—

we still don't know. But he fell a long way before he hit the canvas. And then they pulled the camera off the ring and shot the crowd, and the crowd's faces told me something terrible had happened.

They never shot back to the ring, so I didn't know what type of injuries Owen had suffered. I sure as hell didn't want to believe he was dead, but I have to admit that that possibility occurred to me.

Right away, I called Eric Bischoff. I said, "Eric, find Bret. I think something bad has happened."

Eric contacted Bret and told him the news. Bret called and found out, yes, something bad *had* happened.

Vince McMahon had a tough call on his hands as to whether to cancel the show or continue. I can't even imagine what that decision was like. For whatever reason, they kept going on with the show.

It was just a tragedy. I went to Owen's funeral and sat with his dad, Stu Hart, all day long. Vince McMahon and Pat Patterson were there. There was still some heat with me and Vince, but I said hello to him and his family.

At the end of the day I was the last one to leave. I stayed there with Stu and Bret even after the last family member left. I felt a connection with them.

I saw Bret maybe once or twice more after that, and it seemed like we were on good terms. Then all of a sudden I started getting faxes from wrestling fans that Bret was trashing me in the newspaper again, saying I was a no-good son of a bitch. I don't understand it.

The Hollywood Knee

62 The first time I hurt my knee was when I was playing junior high school football. I wasn't even a starter. I was in eighth grade, so I was a sub.

I remember it was late in the day and for some reason I didn't have a pad on my left knee. I was on the line and we were hitting and when I dropped down in the dirt I landed on a rock.

That rock just blew my knee out. The top of it swelled and I couldn't bend it all the way. So from that point on, I just walked around lockstep with this bum knee that never got any better.

Of course, I didn't know anything about knee surgery at the time. Hell, I don't even know if they cut on knees back then. But I never addressed the problem. I just learned to live with it.

When I got into the wrestling business I worked around the stiffness in my knee. That's one reason I adopted the boot in the face and the legdrop as my finish—because it kept me from doing more demanding finishes like a cross body block.

Then came the night I wrestled the Iron Sheik in Madison Square Garden. If you watch the tape, you'll see what happened. Right before I got out of the Camel Clutch and beat him, I hit the ropes and jumped up in the air to drop a knee on his chest. And I always landed on my left knee to protect the guy.

But I hit a board under the canvas that wasn't lined up quite right and my knee felt like it exploded. It felt like I blew it the hell apart. So I won the belt. But when I went back to my hotel room, I told my wife, "You're not gonna believe this but my knee is gone. I blew it out."

She said, "What do you mean?"

"What I mean," I said, "is if I tell Vince McMahon that I blew my knee out he'll take this belt away from me. I won't have the run we talked about."

So we never told Vince what happened.

But I stuck with the finish I'd been using to protect my knee all along—the three big punches, the boot in the face, and the legdrop—and I tried not to pivot or twist any more than I had to. That was the only way I could survive.

I kept my problem a secret all through the years I was wrestling and the year and a half I did *Thunder in Paradise*. But while I was in WCW, the situation got progressively worse.

Every time I wrestled, my knee would get stiff. I couldn't walk up stairs, I couldn't even bend my leg to pull it out of the damn bathtub.

Of course, it always got better after two, three days, so I kept my mouth shut just like I always had. Eventually the swelling would go down, the fluid would move around my leg and drain out from behind my kneecap, and I could walk again.

Then I got to a point where it just wouldn't get better. It had been two whole weeks and I still couldn't bend my leg. I couldn't even push the clutch in on a car, so there was no way I could do anything in a ring.

I finally fessed up and confided in Eric Bischoff. I said, "Brother, my knee is all blown to hell. It's pretty bad."

So he said, "You'll be better for it if you get operated on. We've got this guy who's a specialist."

So I asked around about him. I was told he's the best, he puts everybody back together.

Of course, we had to work my injury into the story line. So we shot an angle where Diamond Dallas Page put a figure four on my leg around the ring post and leaned back, and supposedly that tore my knee apart.

So I ended up having my first knee surgery in 1998, about fourteen years after my knee first started bothering me.

The doctor cut on my knee and cleaned it up, and he videotaped the whole thing. He talked about my knee the whole time it was being scoped. "Yeah," he said, "this is Hulk's knee." He was going back and forth, playing to the camera.

When he was done, I walked around on crutches for a few months and waited for my knee to come around. But it never felt right. I just couldn't seem to get any stability. I'd lean on it maybe twenty pounds' worth and it would want to go out on me.

A year later, I was still having problems with it. It hurt. It was wobbly. I would walk around in the house with a flashlight so I wouldn't make a misstep, because just missing a three-inch step would totally cause me intense, intense pain.

My whole life changed—and not for the better. I didn't like to go to restaurants anymore because if I sat down I couldn't straighten my leg out when I got up. And I could only get up at all when I was leaning on my wife. I wasn't even walking anymore, I was hobbling. And guess what? My hip had started to wear out because I'd been catering to my knee for so many years.

Finally, after about a year of this, my attorney, Henry Holmes, recommended a guy named Dr. Fox in Beverly Hills. Dr. Fox took one look at my knee and said, "You need a total knee replacement."

I said, "Well, Doc, I don't want a total knee replacement. But I'd sure like you to take out that spur you found in the X-ray."

So I let Dr. Fox go in there and clean my knee up a little bit more. He also removed a huge spur from the back of my knee, which was affecting the outside of my hamstring.

And immediately I felt better. The pain was almost gone.

I hung around L.A. for a few more months, walking around on crutches the whole time. I kept seeing Dr. Fox and I kept doing the rehab work, even though I knew more about training than the rehab professional. And then I went home and I figured I had gotten a reprieve from this knee thing.

Right around Christmastime 2001, Vince called and asked me about *WrestleMania*. I was enthusiastic and thought I might be able to pull it off. We started talking about it creatively and we both got real excited. But when we started talking money, Vince backed off. Ultimately, Henry Holmes was unable to make an acceptable deal. It seemed Vince was unwilling to agree on salary or to a long-term deal, because he felt that I was damaged goods because of what happened at WCW.

Meanwhile, I decided to take my boat out. When I came back it was low tide and she got stuck in the mud. In the past when that had happened, I would get off the boat and walk through the mud like a jerk. Then I would climb up on the dock, wash myself off, and ten hours later, when the tide came up in the middle of the night, I would bring my boat in. But I was sick of doing that.

So I looked at the dock and I looked at my boat. She was forty feet long. If I backed up to the windshield and got a running jump, I could probably make it to the dock. So I got all my crap together, my phone and my belly pouch, and backed up as far as I could.

Then I took a couple of quick steps, got up some momentum, and jumped off the boat. I cleared the water,

Hollywood Hulk Hogan

no problem. But when I went to land on the dock, I led with my left leg—the one that had the bad knee—and boom, it exploded!

I thought, "Now I've done it. I've blown my knee out again."

The dock was hot because the sun had been beating on the wood all day. And I couldn't stand up even if my life depended on it. Somehow or another I dragged myself back to the house, told my wife the foolish thing I did, and admitted that it was time for a total knee replacement.

A friend of mine who's a knee specialist, Dr. Alan Hughes, lives down the street from me. I called him up and he took an X-ray. "Yup," he said, "you did it this time."

But he gave me a slim ray of hope. "There's a guy up in Buffalo, New York," he said, "who's been peddling an unorthodox approach to knee surgery for about ten years now. Everyone thinks he's a voodoo doctor but you might want to go see him. His name is Repicci."

So I flew up to Buffalo, New York and had Dr. Repicci take a look at me. As soon as he looked up from the X-ray, he said, "Total knee replacement. You're done."

I said, "Can I *wrestle* with a total knee replacement?"

"Well," he told me, "the problem is you won't have any control when you're going forward down an incline. For instance, if you play golf, you'll always have to back off the green."

I said, "That won't do it. I've got to run down the ramp every night. Listen, Doc, I just want to get back in the ring for one more match. Can you patch me up enough for me to do that?"

I told him about the dark cloud that had been hanging

The Knee

over my head since Vince Russo fired me from WCW. Instead of everybody remembering me as the guy who slammed Andre the Giant, they were saying I was the bald-headed guy who hung around after he was all washed up.

I said, "I've got to fix that, Doc."

So Dr. Repicci looked at my X-rays again. "Well," he said, "your kneecap is out of alignment with the other bones in your leg. If we reshape the kneecap and move it over, that might give you some relief. Let me think about this."

The next time we spoke was on the phone. He said he wasn't eager to work on me because he knew this wasn't the long-term answer—and he was afraid if it didn't work, I'd blame him for it.

I understood that. He didn't want his reputation to be destroyed. He didn't want to be known as the guy who ruined Hulk Hogan's knee.

I said, "Doc, I'll sign anything you want. You've got to help me out."

"Well," he said, "since you've expressed to me that you want to get back in the ring, even though you may destroy your knee in your first match, I'm going to have you sign some papers."

So I signed a waiver saying that I knew what I really needed was a total knee replacement, and that this procedure was a secondary choice motivated strictly by financial gain. Of course, I wouldn't have turned on him anyway, but I signed the waiver to put him at ease.

And even then, he had second thoughts. Repicci's nurse, Polly, told me that after I left Buffalo, Repicci told her he had decided not to cut on me. He said he'd been busting his ass to get some credibility for this new surgical method he had—not taking the kneecap off but moving it over—and if I bitched or complained he was screwed. So as of Thursday, two days before the operation, he had decided he wasn't going through with it.

When I came up to Buffalo on Friday, he was all set to tell me he had changed his mind. But when I saw him, I was saying, "Yeah, man, I can't wait. This is going to be great, brother." I just ran him over with verbiage.

So he said, "Okay, let's do it."

I was there to get fixed, man. I wasn't going to accept anything less.

So Dr. Repicci went ahead and reshaped my kneecap. Then he moved it over so it lined up correctly with the rest of my leg. And after the surgery, we talked.

I asked him, "How did it go?"

He said, "It went perfectly. Couldn't have gone any better. Of course, your kneecap is bone on bone. Your meniscus is gone, your patella tendon's destroyed, and your ACL is halfway gone too. But it seems you have so much muscle around your kneecap that your knee looks stable. By the way, how does your right knee feel, the knee you weren't complaining about?"

I said, "It feels perfect. Why?"

"Because your right knee is actually worse than your left." He happened to have X-rayed it and it was totally trashed.

Dr. Repicci wanted me to stay up there in Buffalo for four days. So I stayed there and so did a friend of mine who had made the trip with me, a radio disc jockey from Tampa who goes by the name Bubba the Love Sponge.

The second day, I got a visit from Dr. Repicci. My knee was swollen, I had stitches and a big scar. There was blood everywhere. It smelled like medicine and stunk like hell, the grossest smell you can imagine. I had so many antibiotics and pain pills and stuff in my blood, it just made Bubba and me want to puke.

Dr. Repicci took a look at the knee and said, "Squat down."

I said, "Brother, I've been walking on crutches, I can't squat."

But he insisted. So I got out of bed and I started to squat. Blood was just going everywhere. But Dr. Repicci didn't want me to stop.

"Go ahead," he said, "go down all the way."

So I put my ass on my calves and then I stood up. "Is that enough?" I asked.

He cleaned the knee up and changed the dressing and told me all the blood I had seen was normal. Then he said he'd be back the next day.

Sure enough, when he came back the next day, he said, "Get out of bed."

Oh jeez, I thought. And I got out of bed.

He took a look at me and said, "Let's see you walk."

So I walked down the hall and back again.

"Okay," Dr. Repicci said, "I'll see you tomorrow."

All night, I wondered what type of torture he had in mind for me next. When he showed up in the morning, he didn't keep me in suspense. "I want you to jog."

I didn't think that was such a good idea. I mean, he had just told me there was nothing but muscle holding my knee together.

"It's okay," he said. "Your leg's good and strong. I want you to jog."

So I tried to jog down the hall. And son of a bitch, I was able to do it.

Dr. Repicci said, "You're fine. You can leave tomorrow."

I couldn't believe it. "What do you mean I can leave tomorrow? I just had a major operation a few days ago."

"You can leave, no problem. And in six weeks, you can wrestle again."

I thought maybe I'd heard him wrong. I said, "Are you kidding me?"

"Not at all," he told me. "You're fine. In fact, if you change your mind and decide not to wrestle and you don't hurt your kneecap, you can probably walk around this way for seven or eight years. But if you wrestle, you're almost definitely going to screw it up and need a total knee replacement."

I didn't care. The important thing was that I was okay to do what I said I wanted to do. I could get into the ring again and wrestle.

So I went home. And six weeks went by, and the knee got better and better.

But I was nervous. I knew that Dr. Repicci had said six weeks, but I was forty-eight years old. I figured somebody my age needed a little more slack. So I gave the knee more time to heal. The truth was I felt good enough to wrestle at

The Knee

the twelve-week mark, but I didn't. I kept waiting to make absolutely sure.

Finally, I did wrestling work for a start-up promotion in Orlando one night. It was around Christmastime, three and a half or four months after the surgery. For the first time in my career, I wore a brace. And not just a brace, but double knee pads under my tights and another knee pad on top of the brace in case I fell on my knee.

No problem. The knee felt great.

And it *still* feels great. In fact, it's the only part of me that doesn't hurt.

On the Block

63

When WCW was on a roll they were making almost a hundred million dollars a year. Then, when WCW took a nosedive, they were losing many millions of dollars a year. So what you had was a damaged brand.

But that didn't mean the company wasn't worth a lot of money. WCW had a ten-year deal to provide prime-time programming for TNT and TBS, two of Turner's cable channels. A prime-time cable deal and a damaged logo was still worth a hundred million bucks on the open market. Hell, you can fix the

damn logo if you've got the two television vehicles.

But all of a sudden, America Online merged with Time Warner. I'd heard the rumor that some bigwig came in and told Ted Turner to move his office down to the end of the hall. Ted moved and his phone quit ringing.

This bigwig, at least this is what I'd heard, looked at what was generating revenue and what was not. Evidently, he saw that he could take Andy Griffith reruns and put them on the tube and generate a point or two, which was a lot of money—or he could put half a million a week into a wrestling show and not turn a profit.

So, duh, what was he going to do? Keep losing money just because he liked wrestling? This bigwig said that wrestling didn't fit into the company's business plan anymore. He was going to take it off the air.

All of a sudden, WCW had lost its TV vehicles. All that

was left was a damaged brand. So all these bids that were coming in from other companies for a hundred million dollars went away. They dried up.

When that happened, I got a phone call from Eric Bischoff asking me if I wanted to buy WCW.

I said, "No. Why?"

"Because," he said, "you could probably get it for about five million bucks."

I said, "Why would I want WCW without TV rights?"

"Well," Eric said, "for the story lines. And with your name attached to it, maybe you could get TV rights somewhere else."

I said, "Hmm. Let me think about this." I didn't want WCW myself, but I thought I knew somebody who might.

Vince McMahon and I had run into each other and talked on several occasions since I left the company. The first time was in that hotel lobby when I was shooting the *Three Ninjas* movie. Then we talked at Owen Hart's funeral. And over the last few years, we had talked on the phone during the holidays—just brief conversations, how are the kids, that kind of thing.

Around Christmastime in 2001, our conversation was different. We talked about me coming back, but we were unable to make a mutually acceptable deal with Henry Holmes.

Still, we were on good terms. So when I heard about a deal I thought could help him, I didn't hesitate to give him a holler.

"Listen," I said, "I think you might have bid eighty or a

hundred million bucks for WCW at one time. You can probably pick it up now for three million bucks, maybe three and a half."

"Oh really," he said. "And why would I want WCW when there aren't any TV rights attached to it?"

"Because I'm the biggest wrestling fan in the world," I said, "and I'm tired of watching Undertaker fight The Rock every week, I feel like I've been watching the same match for the last five years. Please buy WCW for the story lines, if nothing else."

In the end, Vince bought WCW. I think he paid a few million bucks for it. Some wrestlers, like me and Goldberg, didn't come with the deal. But some of the guys did go to WWE, because some contracts *did* roll over, and that gave Vince the guys and story lines he wanted.

And it gave him something else. It gave him the whole WCW wrestling catalog, hundreds and hundreds of hours of wrestling. It was like buying the damn Beatles. You could put it on a twenty-four-hour wrestling channel and make tons of money.

I didn't know the catalog came with WCW or I'd have been all over it. I could have sat at home in my office and watched little tapes all day and made millions of bucks. I guess I blew that one.

64 After WCW was absorbed into WWE, there was really only one wrestling brand around. That created an interesting situation. Even though nobody could knock Vince McMahon and WWE off the top of the hill, anybody who came in and started a wrestling venture of their own would instantly become Number Two.

And Number Two in a competition where there's no Number Three might not be such a bad place to be. Anyway, that was the theory.

In the business world, perception is everything, and people had this perception that Hulk Hogan was a powerful brand name. So a lot of my friends, ex-wrestlers and talent who were just coming up the ladder, started talking to me in the fall of 2001 about putting together a new company. They wanted to call it the XWF—the Xtreme Wrestling Federation.

These friends of mine said they wanted to make their headquarters in Tampa, which I liked because I could stay home with my family and hang out on the beach. They said they wanted to avoid the Jerry Springer tits-and-ass style wrestling, which I liked because I had disagreed with that stuff from the first time I saw it. And they said they had two big backers—a guy from the richest family in Bombay, India and another guy who had become a billionaire in telemarketing.

They wanted to do wrestling the right way. And they didn't even want me to get into the ring. All they wanted me to do was run the company.

My dad had just gotten sick at the time. He was in the hospital and I was visiting him nearly every day, trying to make sure he got better even though he was eighty-eight years old. So when I was given this opportunity to start a new company, it was exciting because it gave me something else to think about.

So right away I began thinking that I would start this new venture in Europe and then maybe come back to the United States and cut a network deal or a Pay-Per-View deal, because if it went to Europe first and it was successful, it would be awesome. Then I called my attorney, Henry Holmes, who also represented DirecTV, and I said, "Henry, I need that DirecTV account."

Henry said that he was involved in making DirecTV's next contract with Vince, but that DirecTV would take a close look at any new venture run by me.

Our backers were telling me they didn't mind spending forty or fifty million bucks. They were talking the talk.

So I set everything up and went into the office for two weeks to write ten hours of TV with wrestlers who didn't even have contracts yet. They were going to work for me out of loyalty until we got a payroll going.

It was starting to look good. Everybody was going to go, "What is this? And Hulk's running it? Who knows what he's going to do."

Finally, it came down to deal time. I had meetings in L.A. and we were approaching the point of no return, so I said, "All right, guys, this is judgment day. I'm getting ready to guarantee delivery of a product and put myself at risk for twenty million dollars. You guys are the billionaires and all you can tell me is how much money you have. Now I need you to tell me if we're in business or if you're just weekend warriors."

All of a sudden, they backpedaled. They said they just wanted to make ten hours of TV for three hundred grand, then see if we had anything.

You do not compete with Vince McMahon if you've only got one bullet in your gun, because if you hit him with one shot you're not going to kill him. You're only going to make him madder.

I told them, "Sorry, I'm the wrong person for this job. I'm not here to pioneer. I'm here to make deals."

So they came up with an offer—two million bucks up front if I would lend my name to the company and give them a hand now and then. Two million wasn't a lot of money for what I was bringing to the table, but it would pay my bills in Tampa and Los Angeles, and we could live without spending the kids' inheritance. And I was the major stockholder in the company, so if I got this thing on its feet I'd be doing real well.

The problem was they brought in a guy named Ludd Denny to run the company. He was a buddy of one of our backers, a big fat guy with hair down to his ass who said he knew a little about the wrestling business.

Ludd Denny told me about the Dalai Lama blessing his family, and how he saw a shooting star when he was a kid . . . all these stories. And he told me about all these other companies he ran. But he never talked about wrestling.

He told me one time, "Wrestling's just another business."

"No," I said. "You don't understand. Wrestling is *not* just another business. Wrestling is completely different from GTE or Microsoft. You don't have a clue what you're dealing with. You'll go in there to set up a deal and if somebody doesn't get paid under the table, you're going to find yourself with a spike up your butt. You won't even know what's happened to you. You gotta swim with the sharks in this business."

Unfortunately, my name got thrown around even before the deal was inked. Universal jumped the gun and put up life-size posters that showed me presenting the XWF all through their theme park.

A couple of my friends were involved in this company— Jimmy Hart and Brian Knobbs—so for my friends' sake, I went on camera and did an interview saying, "Hey, I don't know what I'm going to do yet, but if I do decide to wrestle again this is the place to be."

So I exited gracefully and put them over. And that was my experience with the XWF. They're still trying to make a go of it, but it's an uphill battle.

Hollywood Hulk Hogan

The
Look

Hollywood

Hulk

Hogan

65

Even after you work out for a couple of hours a day, it takes some doing to look like Hollywood Hulk Hogan.

For one thing, you've got to shave your body with a razor. If you wanted to feel silky soft like a young lady, you would have to do it every day. But if you don't mind grossing people out because you feel like sandpaper, you can probably get away with every four or five days.

By now, I've got it down to a science. I can shave my whole body in about fifteen minutes, from my eyes all the way down to my toes. That includes back, armpits, stomach, legs, everything.

Then there's my hair. My natural color used to be blond, but now that I'm older it's starting to get gray around the sideburns. So I just bleach my hair and mustache so it's all the same color.

My beard is a different story. It's three different colors now, black, blond, and gray, about a third of each. I want it all dark so I get the Grecian Formula dark dye and use that every so often.

So it's constant maintenance, brother. It's crazy.

The only thing I don't have to fake is my skin color. My mother's half-Panamanian, so I'm dark to begin with, and my skin gets even darker when I'm out in the sun. So that's at least *one* thing I don't have to work on.

Hulk

Hogan

66 In mid-September of 2001, my father's health started to decline rapidly. The guy was eighty-eight years old and had lived a great life, but he was getting old and old people start to break down.

When my dad was in his seventies, he had five-way bypass surgery and got his hip replaced, and he had survived those problems. But little by little, the quality of his life had gotten worse. Finally, he had a stroke that paralyzed his throat and kept him from swallowing food into his stomach. Instead, it would

go into his lungs, which made him aspirate, which made him get pneumonia. The doctors had to do a tracheotomy and he never recovered from that.

I went to see my father almost every day he was in the hospital from his stroke until his death on December 28, 2001. In one of our many conversations, he said something I'll never forget.

"Terry," he said, "I don't like what that guy Russo did to you. And I don't like the kind of wrestling I see on television these days. Go back and fix it, Terry. Go back and fix wrestling and fix what happened to you."

Then it got to where he couldn't talk because of his tracheotomy. But when he saw Vince McMahon on TV on Monday and Thursday nights, he would perk up and a light would go on in his eyes.

And even though he couldn't say it anymore, I could hear it: *Go back and fix it, Terry. Go back and fix it.*

After my dad passed away, I got a call from Vince. Against the advice of some of his people, who thought I was too old or had too much of an attitude, he asked if I was interested in getting back into the ring.

With my dad's words still rolling around in my head, I said, "Hell, yes I am."

Vince said, "Well, how would you like to work with The Rock at *WrestleMania*?"

I said, "Let's do it."

At that time, Vince didn't know if he wanted me to win or lose.

I said, "I don't have to win. I just have to have a good

match. Let The Rock beat me, let his movie come up, let him make millions of dollars. Let him make all the wrestling world look better. Then we'll see."

But in all fairness, I had to admit to Vince that my knee was hurting. I'd had three surgeries and Dr. Repicci had told me the knee could go on me if I didn't watch out.

Vince told me he didn't need much—just a couple of *Raws*, a couple of *SmackDowns!*, and *WrestleMania*. A total of five events a year. (Of course, it turned out to be a lot more than that, but that's what he thought at the time.)

I thought even my surgically repaired knee could handle that. And I wanted desperately to prove myself and undo what WCW had done to my career. So I was willing to withstand the pain.

Then Vince told me Kevin Nash and Scott Hall were coming back. I said, "Well, would you put the New World Order back together?"

He said, "Yeah, that could work."

Before we were done, I told Vince that I'd help him get a new deal with his DirecTV. I then arranged a meeting in Los Angeles with Vince and Linda McMahon, my and DirecTV's attorney, Henry Holmes, and Michael Thorton, one of the key executives at DirecTV.

In the end, Vince McMahon made the deal with DirecTV at that meeting in Los Angeles, and Hollywood Hulk Hogan was going to wrestle for WWE and on DirecTV.

But getting Vince's approval was different from getting the wrestlers' approval. I didn't know how I would be received by guys like The Rock and Triple H, who had

Hollywood Hulk Hogan

established themselves as main-event wrestlers and Superstars.

Because I was *the* star for a long time, and now I was coming back. I didn't know how they would take that.

Vince told me that I would be accepted more readily if I changed clothes in the same locker room with everybody else. That was no big deal. I had only had a separate dressing room before so Vince and I could talk without being interrupted.

Vince also told me I should pay for my own cars and fly commercial and not expect any special treatment. I didn't have a problem with any of that either.

Still, I didn't know if I was going to get heat from the boys. I didn't know how much they would resent my being there, or if that resentment would eventually turn into trouble.

Kevin Nash and Scott Hall had the same misgivings. We had been at each other's throats back in WCW, but that was water under the bridge. So we took an oath that we would watch each other's backs, especially in the ring. If I heard anybody say anything negative about Hall or Nash, I would let them know, and they would do the same for me.

I mean, we were coming in as a unit. We knew we might not always be that way, and eventually we might end up taking different paths. But for the time being, we were going to stick together.

Then, in February, we got to the Staples Center in L.A. and the guys were magooing us. When you magoo somebody, you're saying one thing but thinking something else. That's what the other wrestlers were doing to us.

They were saying, "It's good to see you," but they didn't really mean it. They were waiting to see what our role was going to be.

For the next couple of weeks, I watched the Stone Cold Steve Austin–Vince McMahon show. Very intense eye contact between them. Like they were saying, "What do you think?" "I don't know, what do *you* think?" Back and forth, real close communications. But I was on double-secret probation so I kept my mouth shut.

The first time the fans saw the nWo on a WWE TV show was at *No Way Out* in Milwaukee on February 17, 2002. Kevin, Scott, and I came out to the ring and said we were

misunderstood. All we wanted was a chance to prove it.

All of a sudden, The Rock showed up to "greet" the new guys. And that's when it started to get weird, brother.

The Rock had been on TV every week. He was a star with a multimillion-dollar movie coming out, getting tons of publicity. And I had come to Milwaukee with nothing but past accolades.

Everybody—including me—expected The Rock to get a lot more cheers than I did. But it seemed like it was 60 percent Rock and 40 percent Hogan. I had barely shown my face and I was getting almost the same reaction he was.

I said to myself, *This could be a problem*.

Then we got to the Allstate Arena in Chicago and it sounded almost like fifty-fifty. It was getting scary, brother.

Chicago is where The Rock asked me if I would wrestle him and I agreed. Then he stuck his hand out and we

shook on it. But when I went to walk away, he pulled back, picked me up, and slammed me down on the canvas.

But Hall and Nash caught up with him and dragged him back into the ring, where we supposedly kicked his ass so bad they had to call an ambulance. Then I got hold of a semi and rammed the ambulance with The Rock inside.

No matter what I did, the fans still loved me. In March, I wrestled Rikishi—who happens to be the nephew of Afa the Wild Samoan—at the University of South Florida, where I went to college.

I told the fans there they made me sick and flipped the bird at them. "I hate you people!" I yelled at them.

Didn't matter. They kept on cheering.

I told them, "The reason I left this place is because it smelled the same way it smells tonight. I'm just here to kick ass, make my money, and leave this town just as fast as I can, because you people stink!"

"YAAAAY!"

I couldn't figure out what I was doing wrong. No matter how mean I was, I couldn't get the fans to boo me.

At the Joe Louis Arena in Detroit, I met up with The Rock again. And this time, the crowd was *definitely* split fifty-fifty. The same thing the next night at the Gund Arena in Cleveland.

Vince McMahon said, "Oh my God." This wasn't the way we had planned it.

It was like back in the AWA, when Verne Gagne had to turn me into a good guy because the fans wouldn't stop cheering for me. Different place, different time, but the same deal.

And *WrestleMania* in Toronto was only a few days away.

Hollywood **Heat**

Hulk Hogan

67

A few days before I saw The Rock in Detroit, I was at a *SmackDown!* in San Antonio, Texas. I had been running hard for a few weeks, and on the plane I started feeling kind of run-down, kind of flushed.

My car was at the airport. But when I went to load my bags into the trunk, I couldn't pick them up. I was so weak that I didn't have the strength to lift my own bags. So finally I said screw it and got a cabdriver to get me home.

When we got to my house, I still couldn't lift my bags. Fortunately, this cabdriver was nice enough to pick them up and walk with me through these gates I have in front of my house. After you get through the gates, there's a cobblestone courtyard. Just before we got halfway across the courtyard I fell down.

I remember the cabdriver saying, "Thank God you got your hands out in front of you or you really could have hurt yourself."

I guess I fell pretty fast, but I was still alert enough to get my hands up. So I stood up with the cabdriver's help and said, "Thanks, brother, I'm just really tired."

The next thing I knew I was waking up in the emergency room. The cabdriver was standing there and he said, "Mr. Hogan, you fainted again. I got you to the emergency room. Are you going to be okay?"

I mumbled something and that was it. The cabdriver took off. Then I found out that I had a 104-degree fever and it was two o'clock in the morning.

Finally, about three hours later, my fever went down to 102 and I tried to get them to release me. I only live two blocks from the hospital, I told them. I guess they finally let me go about five-thirty.

When I got home, I crawled into bed and slept for God knows how long. I guess my wife thought I had gotten in a little late and didn't wake me in the morning. In fact, I didn't get up until four o'clock in the afternoon when my kids got home from school.

I'm just glad that the cabdriver picked me up off the ground the night before, because I fell right by the garage door, and my wife never looks when she backs the car out.

Hollywood Hulk Hogan

She would probably have backed over me at eight o'clock in the morning when she took the kids to school. There would have been a big thump and that would have been it.

But now that I think about it, I would have probably been dead by then anyway, lying outside all night with that type of fever. I was on my last leg and I didn't even know it.

68

By the time I got to Canada, the customs people were kissing my shoes. I could have been carrying a case of machine guns and it wouldn't have been any problem. I was walking through customs and the customs agents were saying, "Beat him!"

I said, "Oh God."

In the days preceding *WrestleMania*, Vince McMahon ran *Axxess*, an event where people paid fifty dollars a ticket to see The Rock's wrecked ambulance and the WWE Hall of Fame featuring the memorabilia of Andre the Giant,

"Classy" Freddie Blassie, and other WWE immortals. They started taking a poll there, asking the fans who they would like to see win the match Sunday night—me or The Rock.

Almost everybody who came through wanted Hulk Hogan to beat The Rock. That *really* got us panicked.

So Vince and I talked Saturday morning and went over our options. One thing we decided was to turn me back into a babyface. "If the fans want to love you," Vince said, "we can't fight it. We've just got to go with it."

We also reopened the question of whether I should win the match or go ahead and lose it as planned. Then we batted around the idea of maybe resurrecting the red and yellow from my good-guy days.

By Saturday afternoon, we had decided everything except what I should wear. nWo black? *Hulkamania* red and yellow? Vince said he wanted to think about it.

Finally, around five o'clock in the afternoon—as I was starting to look forward to a good night's sleep before the match on Sunday—Vince got me on the phone again.

"Monster?" he said.

"What's up, brother?"

"Monster, we need the red and yellow."

Well, the only place I knew of where I could get that stuff on short notice was my basement down in Clearwater, Florida. But I couldn't trust anybody else to find it. It was like King Solomon's mine down there. We would have needed to hire an archaeologist to dig the stuff up.

But Vince was serious about me wearing my old colors,

so I got on a plane late Saturday afternoon and flew back down to Clearwater. As soon as I got home, I went straight to the basement and got a bunch of my red-and-yellow stuff. Then I went back to the airport and hopped back on the plane.

I got back to Toronto Sunday at two-thirty in the morning. I was tired and cranky. But there was still time for me to get a decent night's sleep—a whole four hours, maybe.

Anyway, that's what I was thinking as I walked into my suite in the hotel.

But when I got to my room, I saw that there was somebody in my bed. It turned out to be Chris Sader, one of my biggest fans since he was a little kid. So I went and kicked open the door to the room where my wife was sleeping with my son and daughter and said to her, "What the hell's going on?"

"Well," she said, "I saw Chris down in the lobby and he didn't have enough money for a room. So I felt sorry for him and told him he could sleep here."

I said, "Well, that's just great, because the guy that's going to be sitting in the third row tomorrow night is going to be nice and rested, but the poor bastard in the ring is going to be beat."

But I didn't have the heart to wake Chris up. So I ended up crawling onto the edge of this king-size bed with my wife and my kids. There we were, all in one damn bed, and I was hanging off the side of it going, "Son of a bitch, son of a bitch, all I want to do is go to sleep."

It ended up costing Vince McMahon eighteen grand to send me down to Florida to pick up a red-and-yellow tee shirt, and a couple of pairs of red tights and yellow tights. And it cost me a night's sleep before one of the most important matches in my whole wrestling career.

But here's the kicker. When I called Vince and told him I'd brought the stuff back just like he wanted, he said, "It's okay, we're not going to need it."

I said, "What?"

After Vince had had a chance to think about it, he had decided the time wasn't right after all. When we brought back the red and yellow, he wanted to make a really big deal about it. And as usual, he was right.

By then, it was about three in the afternoon and I went into the arena to watch the guys talk about their matches that night. Almost every wrestler was in the ring or around it, saying I'm going to do this, you're going to do that.

But not me. I was sitting around fifty rows back. There wasn't a chance in hell I was going to get near the ring until it was time for my match.

I had already sat down with The Rock in the locker room a couple of weeks earlier. We came up with the high spots—a few exciting parts of the match. We would go back and forth, nip and tuck, the two-legends thing.

But we didn't talk about every last detail of the match because we wanted it to look spontaneous. We didn't want The Rock anticipating my every move. We wanted him to react naturally.

And when we went out there, the ball would be in my court. The bad guy always leads the match. The heel controls the tempo. And after twenty-four years in the ring, I pride myself on being the best at that.

After a while, the wrestlers cleared out of the ring. Everybody went backstage to play the waiting game. I thought a lot about how much was riding on this one night, this one match—probably the biggest one of my career.

I had something to prove—to the world, to my fans, to myself—and I had endured three knee surgeries to do it. I

couldn't worry about screwing up. I just had to go out there and do what I do best.

All of a sudden, I said that bonehead thing to Vince McMahon about collecting my money and wished I hadn't. Then I heard my music playing and went through the curtain. As I walked down the ramp on the knee Dr. Repicci had cobbled together for me, I heard more than 68,000 people suck every bit of air out of that building, creating a vacuum I thought would pull my damn eyeballs out.

Then they let out a scream that made my bones vibrate. It was a rush, brother, the biggest rush I could ever have imagined. When I got into the ring and I ripped my shirt off, people cheered like crazy. When I flexed my muscles, they went nuts. I said, "Oh my God, this is unbelievable."

A couple of seconds later, The Rock came out—and they booed him, just as we expected. But it was my job as heel to make sure they ended up cheering for him and booing me. That was my job. It was what I was paid to do.

I couldn't let The Rock go down the tubes just as they were releasing *The Scorpion King*. I knew how big this picture was for him. Most wrestlers only get bit parts in movies. The Rock was the first wrestler other than myself to be a featured actor.

And it wasn't just big for *him*. It was big for the whole wrestling business.

Okay, I thought. Let's do it.

To start with, I locked up with The Rock and pushed him down. When he took the big bump, people cheered like crazy. They just went nuts.

Then I beat him down with a clothesline and pounded the hell out of him, and the fans were definitely on my side. That's when I called the first babyface spot.

I said, "All right, now duck my clothesline, bounce off the ropes, and hit me with a bigger clothesline."

He hit me with that flying clothesline and I took a big-ass bump and flipped over, and started crawling up the ropes like he killed me. And the people booed him out of

the building. They were yelling, "Rocky sucks, Rocky sucks!"

At that point, I got scared. It wasn't going to be easy to fix, but I had to do it—and I didn't have a hell of a lot of time. We couldn't walk out of the ring without the people cheering for The Rock.

What I didn't realize was how wrestling-wise The Rock had already become. Most guys would have panicked in that situation. But not him, not a guy whose father and grandfather had been stars in the wrestling business even before I got into it.

The Rock knew how to use his facial expressions and his physical abilities to turn the fans' reaction around. He acted bewildered, off-balance. And little by little, he got the crowd on his side.

All of a sudden, the cries of "Rocky sucks!" started fading away and the fans stopped booing him. They were becoming too enthralled with this clash of titans that was going back and forth across the ring.

About halfway through the match The Rock tackled me. His shoulder rammed into my broken ribs and cracked them all over again. I didn't just feel it, I heard it. It was like a thick tree branch snapping in a hurricane.

I told The Rock that I was hurt, I couldn't breathe. But he wouldn't let me off the hook. He talked me through the rest of the match. "Come on," he said, "stay with me."

As the heel, I was telling him, "Duck the elbow, watch out for the hammer."

And he was saying, "Keep going, don't stop."

So at that point, we were talking to each *other*.

Toward the end, The Rock was supposed to Rock Bottom me three times and then give me the People's Elbow. The first couple of Rock Bottoms tore me apart and I whined like a dog that had gotten hit by a car.

He said, "Can you take another one?"

I said, "No."

The Rock said, "Come on, brother, one more for me."

Even though he was a kid, I respected the hell out of him. I didn't want to let him down. So I said, "Okay, let's do it." Then he Rock Bottomed me one last time. By the time he dropped the People's Elbow on me, I was done. I couldn't have taken anything more.

By the end of the match, we had the fans cheering for both of us. We gave them a match that will go down as the greatest *WrestleMania* moment ever.

Then we put the icing on the cake. Holding my ribs because they were really killing me, I offered my hand to The Rock. When he took it, the noise in the place was deafening. It was so loud it hurt to listen to it.

The handshake was Pat Patterson's idea. I didn't like it when he first suggested it, but once I got out there I said, *Hell yeah, it works.*

All of a sudden, the crowd didn't care anymore who won the match. All they cared about was seeing two icons bonded together for all time, united in mind and spirit. And the story was The Rock might be Mark McGwire, but the baldheaded guy next to him was Babe Ruth.

But it wasn't over. After The Rock left the ring, leaving

me there all by myself, my nWo brothers Kevin Nash and Scott Hall showed up. And they were acting like they were mad because I had broken my vow of loyalty to them.

The whole deal with the nWo was that we were going to be the poison—all three of us—and if we stuck together, there wasn't any one guy who could beat us. We would take Stone Cold out, then we would take The Rock out, and then everybody else, one by one. But when I was offered a match with The Rock at *WrestleMania*, I jumped at it. So according to Nash and Hall, I had let my ego get in my way.

And not only did I not kill The Rock, I shook his hand. That *really* pissed them off. So they jumped me and beat my ass.

But The Rock heard the crowd roar and knew something was up, so he turned around and got back into the ring to help me. Together, we beat Hall and Nash and cemented our friendship, and Hulk Hogan was a good guy again.

Magic can happen when you're out there, brother. Magic. The Rock was perfect. Beyond perfect.

I was crying like a baby. I had done something that everybody said I couldn't do. I had showed everybody who doubted me that I was still the man and I could do this better than anybody. And as I walked up the ramp to leave the arena with this kid who used to hang around the wrestlers' dressing room, I said, "Brother, we knocked that out of the park."

When I came backstage, people were crying and wiping their eyes. There was so much emotion. People were so moved by this passing of the torch.

I was overwhelmed with happiness but also with relief, because it could have gone the other way. I could have slipped on a banana peel out there and those people in the backroom would have said, "Well, we told you he was too old. We told you he's got a bad knee and a bald head and he can't do it anymore."

All that bull I'd been hearing for the last few years, I could have been hearing it for the rest of my life. But I turned it around.

The Rock and I did that.

Kids Who Imitate Wrestlers

69

No matter how many times we warn people not to try the moves we make in the ring, some kids still think they're invincible.

Sure, professional wrestling is entertainment and the ending is predetermined. But there's a lot about it that's real. We don't try to knock each other's teeth out because then we couldn't wrestle the next night, but we still hit each other. We just try to do it in places where we can take it.

One night after I came back to WWE, they told me they were going to swing a chair at me and they were going to "send it." I've been in the wrestling business more than twenty years and I didn't know what that term meant.

Then I got into the ring and they swung a chair at me, all right. But they didn't hit me with the flat of it. They hit me with all the sharp parts coming at my face. Thank God I got both my hands up in time, or I would still be in the hospital—maybe dead.

Now I know what "send it" means. It means no regard for safety whatsoever.

This stuff's dangerous, brother. If you do it at home, you're gonna get hurt. That's the real deal.

What's Old Is New

Hollywood

68 Vince McMahon said he would need me only five days a year. Then I walked out at *Raw* in Chicago and the whole deal changed. *Hulkamania* is back, brother. It's back with a vengeance.

After I wrestled The Rock at *Wrestle-Mania X8*, Vince McMahon said, "We sure stumbled on something."

And I said, "Boy, we sure did."

By the next week, Vince was saying he wanted me to work with Triple H. I said, "Sure, I'll put him over."

Wrestling Triple H was what we had talked about a year earlier. Vince booked the match. Then a week later, he decided he wanted me to beat Triple H and win the belt. I said, "Fine."

The match came up and once again, the fan reaction was tremendous. For the sixth time, I had won the championship—something I never thought would happen.

It's funny. The one guy who didn't believe in Hollywood Hulk Hogan was *me*. And to be sitting here now, bitch-slapped by *Hulkamania* . . . damn, brother, it's strong.

So's my knee, as a matter of fact. I've been wearing a brace on it just as a precaution. If I fall on my knee now it's like falling on a cloud. I should have done this twenty years ago.

The one thing I don't understand is why the fans love me so much. I can't jump off the top rope and drop-kick. I'm pretty damn limited in what I can do, and I always have been. And I sure as hell don't look like Brad Pitt.

Maybe they see some grisly warrior who stood the test of time. I don't know. But whatever it is I've got to roll with it.

Fortunately, I don't have to carry WWE like I did in the old days. Now there are other guys to shoulder the burden.

The Rock, for instance. A gifted wrestler. He's not just one of the best, he may be *the* best. I've been in the ring with a lot of guys, but I haven't found anybody like this guy. I can draw money with this guy for the next ten years.

I pray to God The Rock is the next Arnold Schwarzenegger or Bruce Willis because all the people in Hollywood will say,

"My God, look what this wrestler did. How about that other wrestler? We might be able to make money with him too. And what about all those other wrestlers?"

So the better The Rock does and the bigger his movies are, the greener that grass is going to be for all of us.

Another guy who's going to carry the burden is Triple H. People said he left WCW because of me or because of people like me who have been around the business too long. They said he wanted the young guys to take over.

By the time I got to WWE, Triple H had secured his position as a main event wrestler and become very solid in his work. And with a couple of years of Titan Training, he had become even more solid as a person.

He doesn't care anymore who throws the first punch or who knocks whose tooth out. He doesn't care who wins or loses. He just wants to do what's good for business. So

what a nice surprise it was to meet Triple H again. Triple H the businessman has so much in common with me, I think we could actually become very good friends.

And if we're talking about shouldering the burden, let's not forget about Vince McMahon. One of the things that used to piss me off when I was in WCW was when Eric Bischoff would say, "We're putting McMahon out of busi-

Hollywood Hulk Hogan

ness this week. That's it, he'll never last another week."

I would say, "You have no idea what you're talking about. I know Vince McMahon. He ain't gonna go away. He'll come down here and murder us before he'll let us drive him out of business."

Vince McMahon is a fighter.

It's great now to actually sit in a room with him and get all the heat behind us. To air all of our grievances in a room and say, "All right, you're totally wrong and I'm totally wrong," it's just an extreme pleasure.

Right after I cut ties with the XWF, I was approached by another network about putting a wrestling show together. Their thinking was they could throw a bunch of money up, a couple of hundred million dollars or so, and get into the wrestling business.

Of course, they wanted to start out with a pilot. But wrestling isn't a business where you stick your toe in and test the waters. If you're going to get into the wrestling business, you sell your house and take the money out of your kids' college fund and invest everything you've got. It's either a total, balls-to-the-wall commitment or you don't do it at all.

I learned that from Vince McMahon.

Now that I'm in the twilight of my career, I want to be on his team. I don't want to try to compete against God in heaven or the devil in hell, and I definitely don't want to compete against Vince McMahon in the wrestling business.

Right now, I'm just going to ride this wave with WWE and see how far it takes me. Vince said to me a couple of

weeks ago, "I had Hulk Hogan during the eighties, when we took wrestling to a fever pitch, but I've never had anybody as hot as you are right now." He's never seen anything like this.

This time it's gonna be bigger than the eighties, I guarantee you. Let's hope the world is ready for it, because I am. It's gonna be bigger this time, brother. Remember I said that. Mark it down.

Somewhere along the line, I'll be happy to put this thing to rest.

I mean I could actually walk away from it now if I had

to. I would do it if my wife cussed me out and said, "That's it. You're not Hollywood Hulk Hogan. You're embarrassing me running around like an idiot in your trunks."

If she told me I was done, I'd be done. It would be over.

And it would be okay, because I've done it all. I've proven my point. I've put an exclamation point on the legacy, and laid all the doubts to rest.

I don't have to be in the spotlight anymore. I can be content shaving off my mustache and just being plain Terry Bollea. I can let it go at any time.

But right now it's still of interest to me. It's still fun, cracked ribs and all. It's still a challenge to go out there every night and see if I can get a little bigger reaction than the last time.

I know it'll end someday.

But it won't be today, brother. It won't be *today*.

What's Old Is New